ADVANCE PRAISE FOR
ENGAGEMENT IN SARANAC

"…creates a suspenseful tale of adventure mixed with family deceit…true to the Agency's tradecraft as well as to the local culture of the Adirondacks…a book as lucid as an Adirondack stream with twists, turns, and bumps…an exciting adventure leaving you wanting more and eager for what's next."

—**Charles McManus**, West Chester, PA

"An intense, cinematic spy story exposing human vulnerabilities—personal, social, political, and moral. The novel deftly interweaves insightful, witty analysis with events at roadhouse cafes, woodland trails, and canoe-quiet lakes."

—**William Conger**, Chicago

"A delightful follow-up to Heinz's Six Spies in Saranac. Ev Hastings is back as the charming and lethal (retired?) KGB spy, along with undercover CIA agent Joe Boudreau and his wife, Linda, who sparkles as his adventurous, if deadly, pregnant wife. Captivating local settings in the tri-lakes area of the Adirondacks. Cold War action in the dark Adirondack woods. What more could you ask? *Engagement in Saranac* is a great read!"

—**Chris Angus and Kathy Straka**, Canton, NY

"A (perhaps) former KGB assassin who has joined forces with the CIA (maybe) and a CIA operative who is the New World equivalent of British master spy George Smiley seek to unravel murders and learn who is furnishing US military intelligence to the Soviet Union. A Cold War era story that still resonates today. Side trips into vicious local politics, divorce, child custody, and canoeing. It's all there and all well written."

—**Irvin Slate**, Hot Springs, Arkansas

ENGAGEMENT in SARANAC

ENGAGEMENT in SARANAC

Jack Heinz

Deeds Publishing | Athens

Published by Deeds Publishing in Atlanta, GA
www.deedspublishing.com

Printed in The United States of America

Cover design by Mark Babcock.
Cover art courtesy of William Conger.

ISBN 978-1-950794-81-2

Books are available in quantity for promotional or premium use. For
information, email info@deedspublishing.com.

First Edition, 2022

10 9 8 7 6 5 4 3 2 1

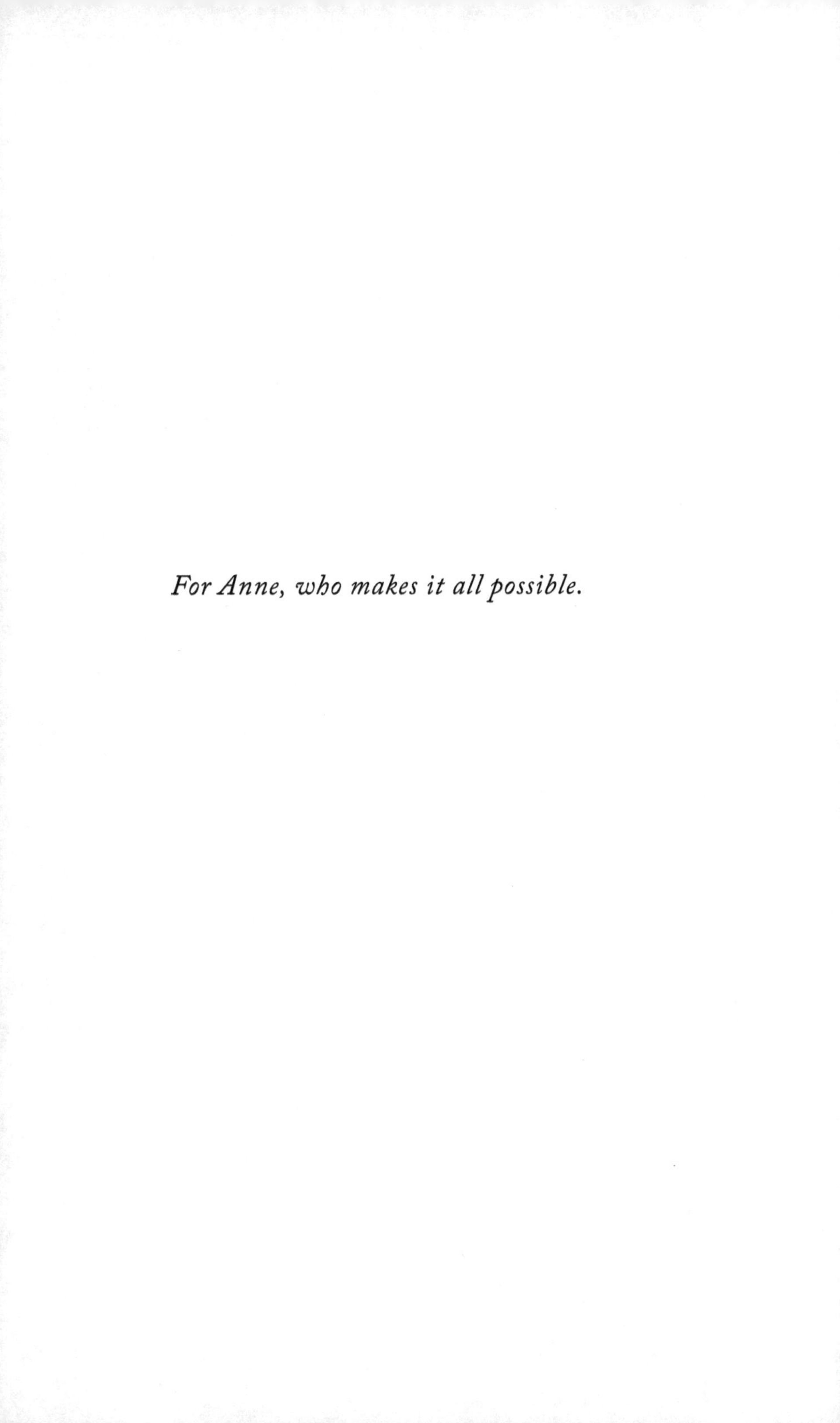
For Anne, who makes it all possible.

"The deficiency of strength may be greatly supplied with art; but the want of art will have but heavy and unwieldy succour from strength."

— Pierce Egan, *Boxiana*, 1830

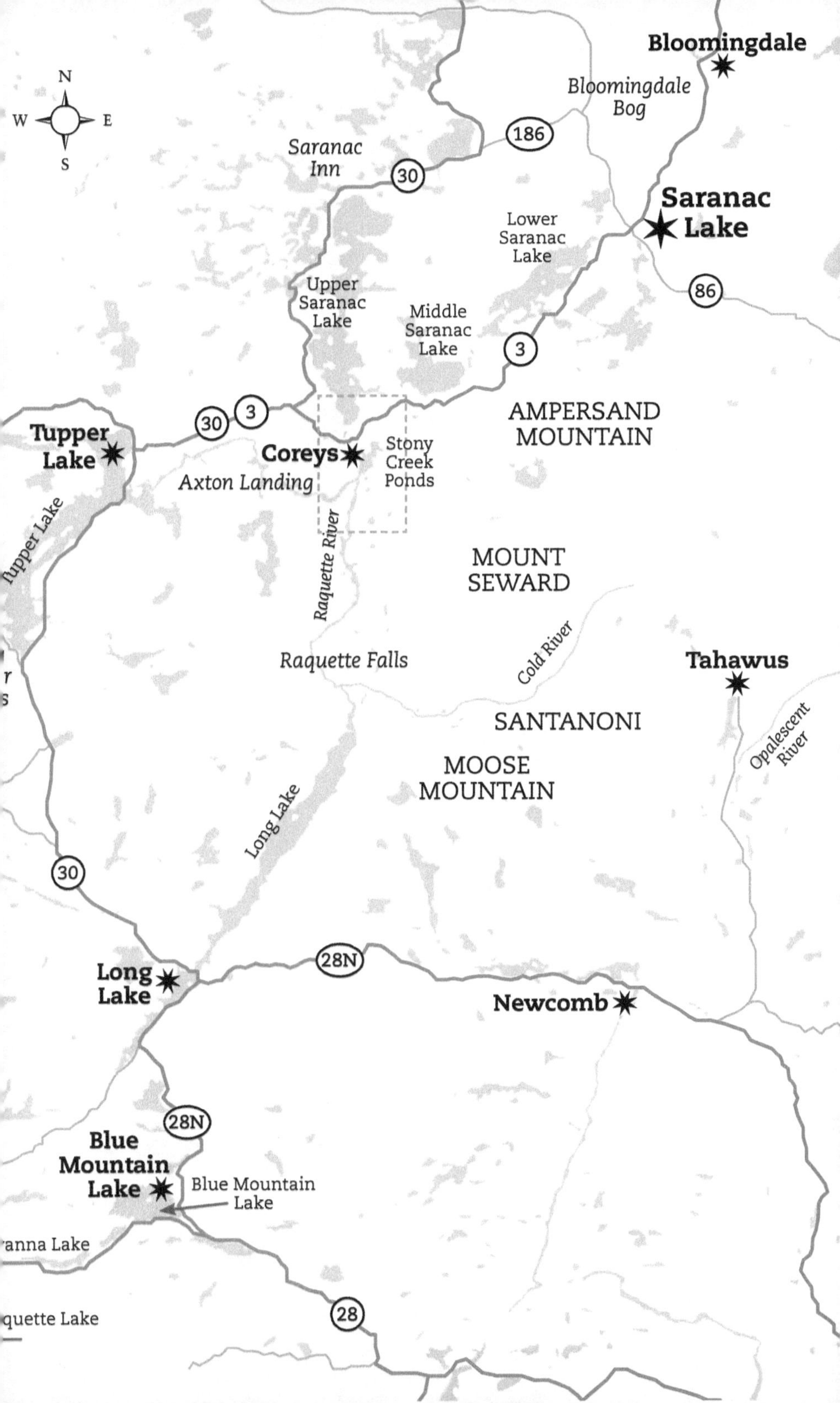

N
W E
S
Bloomingdale
Bloomingdale Bog
186
Saranac Inn
30
Lower Saranac Lake
Saranac Lake
86
Upper Saranac Lake
Middle Saranac Lake
3
30 3
AMPERSAND MOUNTAIN
Tupper Lake
Coreys
Stony Creek Ponds
Axton Landing
Tupper Lake
Raquette River
MOUNT SEWARD
Cold River
Tahawus
r s
Raquette Falls
Opalescent River
SANTANONI
MOOSE MOUNTAIN
Long Lake
30
28N
Long Lake
Newcomb
28N
Blue Mountain Lake
Blue Mountain Lake
anna Lake
28
quette Lake

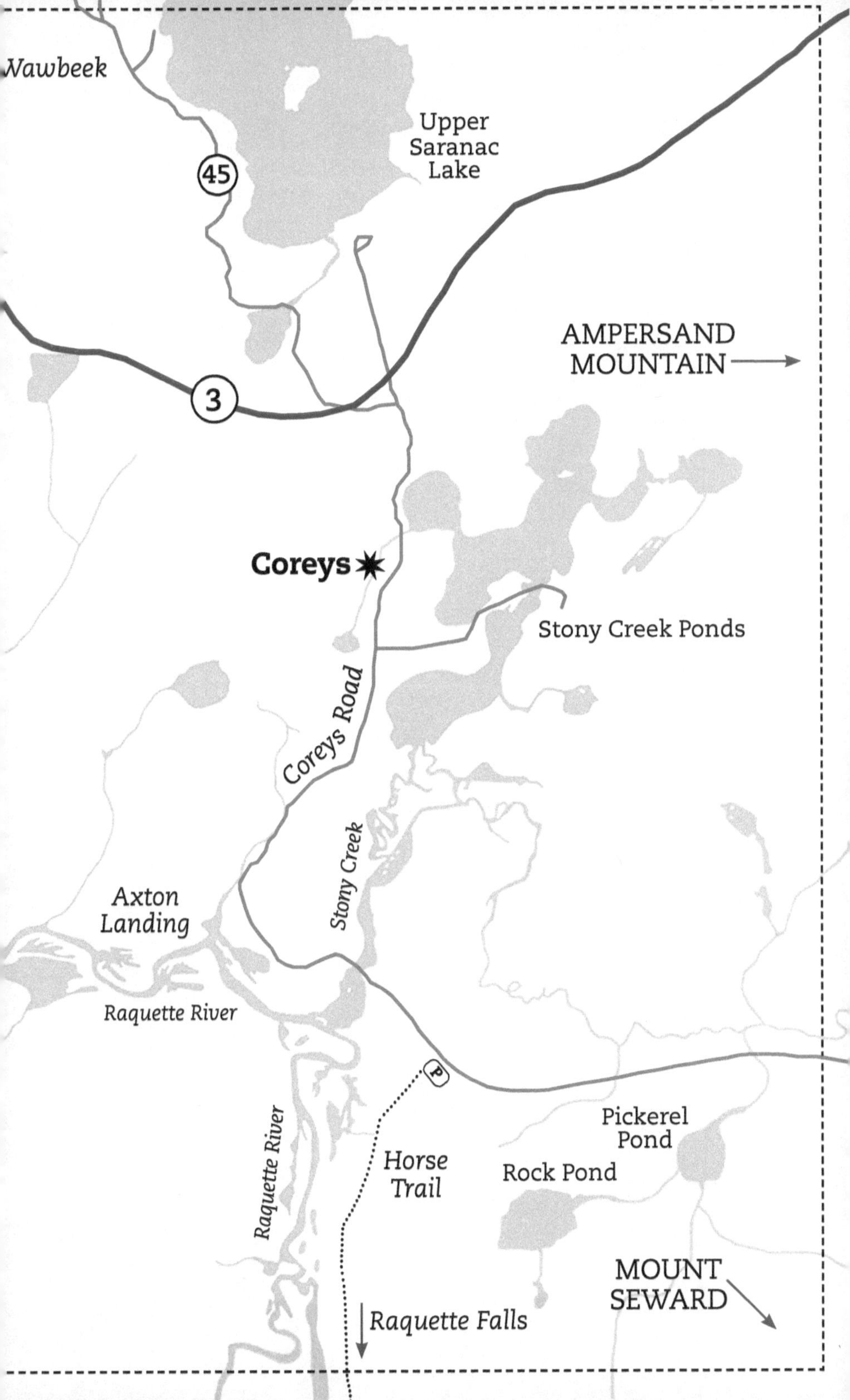

Nawbeek
45
3
Upper Saranac Lake
AMPERSAND MOUNTAIN →
Coreys
Stony Creek Ponds
Coreys Road
Stony Creek
Axton Landing
Raquette River
Raquette River
P
Horse Trail
Pickerel Pond
Rock Pond
MOUNT SEWARD
↓ Raquette Falls

1

When the phone rang I was being harassed by a fly. It was one of those that looks like an ordinary housefly but bites. Hard. The damn things hurt. The swatter was ready in my hand. I missed. As usual.

I mostly did paperwork, which I didn't like. I'd thought about quitting, but that would've been complicated. The problem was that I also had an Air Force commission as a cover job. You can't just walk away from the Air Force when you feel like it. My connections, however, could've managed it.

The phone rang three or four times before I got to it. The fly was enough annoyance without the phone call. How much can a public servant be asked to endure? But I answered. A voice said, "Captain Boudreau, this is Colonel Hatter-Hatton of the 12th Fusiliers."

"Who?"

"Come now, Joseph, you heard me. You know who this is."

"It can't be."

"And yet, you know it is. Meet me at the Bide-a-Wee tonight and you'll be able to confirm the miracle with your eyes." Then he played his trump card. "My appearance has changed a bit, so I'll wear my new keeper's jacket. If you wear the one I bequeathed to you, we could compare them, see which is of better quality, see whether the standards of British tailoring have declined."

"I have the jacket. The bullet hole has been rewoven."

"Yes, it was a pity that I had to deface it, but it made my demise more persuasive."

"I still can't believe it."

"Be at the Bide-a-Wee tonight when the small hand is at eight on your Bulova watch."

"Got it. I will."

And then I got back to the fly.

* * *

The Agency had offered me a bigger job, but we would've had to move to Virginia so I could work at Langley. I turned it down. Linda and I like Saranac, and we have family and friends nearby. Rabbit let me stay on as their man in upstate New York, a job that had never existed before. It was sort of an early pension. Rabbit said I was there in case of emergency. I was never sure what that meant.

They stuck me in a small office at the federal prison in Ray Brook, but I wasn't really hidden. I drove there every day in plain sight. I suppose people who knew me as an Air Force officer wondered what I was doing at the prison, but nobody said anything. They probably didn't care, or they thought it wasn't their business, or they weren't paying attention. I didn't wear my uniform unless I wanted to get a free cup of coffee or it was Memorial Day. The KGB, of course, knew who I worked for.

Saranac Lake, Tupper Lake, and Lake Placid, referred to as the Tri-Lakes, are towns and lakes on the border of the High Peaks region of the Adirondacks. Since most substantial towns here have the name of a lake, we usually omit Lake from the name and just say Saranac, Tupper, and Placid. There's a smaller village named Saranac farther north, up near Dannemora prison, but people here know where we're talking about.

Hastings had appeared in Saranac once before. That was in 1965, in the days when I was courting Linda. He was then working for the KGB, searching for one of their spies who was missing. I found the missing man dead, floating in the Raquette River, and Hastings thought I had killed him. He came after me. If you have ever been pursued by a KGB agent, you'll know that you would rather not. I seriously considered carrying a gun. Later, Hastings decided that I hadn't killed the man, which was right. We cooperated in finding the killer – or, at least, the man I hope was the killer. In either case, Hastings killed him.

The essential point is that Hastings was trained by the British during World War II for missions behind enemy lines. His assignment was to kill important Germans and the people who were collaborating with them. By his account, he also did some free-form sabotage. And then he simply continued to do that work after the war was over, working more recently for the Soviets.

He wasn't at the Bide-a-Wee when I arrived, so I took the table under the framed swatches of tartans. He wanted to be at a table that gave him solid walls on both sides and a clear view of the door. And I knew he disliked tartans. He could sit with his back to them.

As soon as he got there he commented, "This is the right table, young Joseph, a gangster table, not in the open, exposed."

I stood. "I don't think we're in danger. And the new jacket looks bulletproof." He was wearing the replacement for his keeper's jacket.

Hastings said, "You and I know, Joseph, that that has been tested and found untrue."

"Thank you for leaving the old jacket to me. It's very comfortable."

"I assure you that it is more comfortable than this one." Hastings took off his jacket and handed it to me.

I said, "It's stiff." I returned the jacket to him, and he wrestled with it while putting it back on.

He said, "There are two ways to get a tweed jacket to drape naturally across your shoulders, to conform to you. One is to pay a tailor to devote a great many hours to fitting and refitting, cutting and re-cutting. The other is to use it. The tweed will not soften. It never softens, but it can be tamed. This cloth has so much substance that it must be abused. The coat has to be defeated or it will dominate you. You earn the jacket by using it, using it hard."

He looked around the room, warily. "Take care, dear

boy, take care. That's how I have survived." As I anticipated, he took a chair with the swatches of tartans behind him. He was English, not Scottish, and he wasn't having any of the Bonnie Prince Charlie nonsense.

I said, "Speaking of survival, how did you manage that? I saw you bleed out. I saw you die. The light in the tunnel was poor, but I saw you. I held you."

"Yes, and I was touched by that. I truly was. But, quite obviously, I didn't die. I didn't bleed out."

"How'd you manage it?"

"With foresight. I had in my pocket the greatest life-saving equipment known to man. Money. A few thousand dollars, well-placed, can work wonders. It's amazing how efficiently bribing a medical technician or an ambulance driver or an undertaker, or even all of the above, will miraculously restore one to life. I also had the makings of a compress, which I was able to use to staunch the flow of blood from the relatively superficial wound in my leg. Fortunately, there was a great deal of blood on my clothes, lending credibility, but almost all of that came from Riley. I had picked him up and moved him, dragged him into a position where the shootout between us would look more plausible. What you saw was that I appeared to die. And then you left the tunnel and sailed off into the sunset with Linda."

"But your body, the corpse. How was that disposed of?"

"No doubt the undertaker had a spare one lying about. They often do. No one was looking. I was dead. The Soviets didn't want me, the Brits didn't want me, and your fine government was only too glad to be rid of me, so I was just an old soldier permitted to fade away, as General Douglas MacArthur so poetically put it. It was all done very quietly."

"Isn't it dangerous for you to be reappearing now?"

"Yes, of course it is. If the KGB gets wind of it, my life expectancy will be nil. As much as I enjoy your company, I would not be doing this if it were not necessary."

"Not that I'm not glad to see you, but why is it necessary? Why are you here?"

"It's too soon to discuss that now. We'll need more time to develop our project fully, perhaps with visual aids."

I was, of course, very curious, but I knew better than to try to press Hastings on something he didn't want to talk about. So I said, "What've you been doing since I saw you last? Who's your present employer?"

"I've been doing a bit of this and a bit of that. Of course, there's always assassination work available. The demand is pretty constant." He looked thoughtful. "But it was difficult to advertise the availability of my services without making it known that I was alive. Aliases helped, but disguises don't do much to conceal the fact that I'm a man in his late fifties. So, I haven't done many assassinations since I was last here. One or two."

"That's a subject on which I think you could be definite. Which was it, one or two?"

"It's not as easy as that. It's a question of definition. There are subtle differences in how people happen to pass away. But it's true that the result is the same. So, okay, two."

"Are you counting the two KBG men at Lake Clear who somehow got hold of bad mushrooms?"

"No, not counting them, but I hear that the KGB has added them to my tally."

We ordered two more draughts of Guinness. After the waitress was beyond hearing distance, I said, "Doesn't it bother you, or give you pause, to refer to your work as 'assassination'?"

"I don't like euphemisms. I suppose I could say that I do 'eliminations,' or 'removals,' but the first of those would sound like I deal with problems of the bowels, and the second is used for someone who hauls rubbish. Euphemisms are coy, akin to saying that Lady Brett does 'social work among the rich.' It may be amusing, perhaps, but it's coy. Not for me. And I reject the term 'murder.' That sounds unprofessional, ill-considered. I think assassination has more dignity."

"So, if you haven't been doing many assassinations, how have you made a living?"

"I worked in a bookshop, arranging the shelves and responding to customer inquiries. I sold a good many novels by Agatha Christie and Dorothy Sayers, with the occasional *The Thirty-nine Steps* or *The Moonstone*. Mostly Agatha Christie. My accent helped. Sometimes I tried adopting the Rex Harrison manner, but I kept slipping into Robert Morley."

"Who?"

"British actor. Fidgety, pompous. Raised his eyebrows a lot. Had enormous eyebrows. Played Katherine Hepburn's brother in *The African Queen*."

"Haven't seen it."

"Good God, man! Where is your culture? Have you

spent your life under a rock? One does not live by the CIA alone. Get out and about. Go to the cinema."

"Did you like working in a bookstore?"

"It had its moments, but it didn't pay as well as assassination and didn't provide as much stimulation or challenge. There's less problem-solving involved in a bookshop. Of course, neither the shopkeeper nor the customers knew about my professional expertise, but occasionally I made a comment about technique that they found surprising. I had to be careful not to overdo it."

"I can see that that might have been a problem."

We then talked for two more hours and switched from Guinness to coffee, but he still didn't tell me why he was here.

* * *

Rabbit phoned me the next day. His first words were, "Joe, I've received a letter from Ev Hastings!"

Rabbit is, more properly, Charles Maurice Maranville III. When he was in school there was a famous baseball player named Maranville who was called Rabbit, so the school decided that Charles should be Rabbit. Many years later, he still has the name, despite having been a high-priced lawyer in Chicago and, before that, a classmate of Adlai Stevenson at Princeton. The nickname tests his dignity, and he overcompensates. He is now the director of domestic operations at the Agency.

I was surprised by Rabbit's call, of course, and I didn't know how to respond. I didn't want to lie to him, flat out, and say that I hadn't seen Hastings. In addition to being dishonest, that would have been foolish. One way or an-other, Rabbit would certainly learn that Hastings had been in contact with me. I paused and then gave him an evasive reply. I said, "Well, that letter must have been sitting in a mailbag somewhere for a long time."

"The letter is dated and postmarked three days ago."

"Postmarked where?"

"Plattsburgh, NY."

"On the Canadian border, in the northeast corner of the state, on Lake Champlain."

"I know where Plattsburgh is. I looked at a map as soon as I got the letter. But to hell with the postmark! I thought Hastings was dead."

"So did we all. Except Hastings, apparently." I was stalling, and Rabbit knew it. "Is the letter handwritten or typed?"

"Typed, but with a handwritten signature."

"Is it authentic?"

"Our people are working on it — the writing, the paper, the ink, the postmark, all of it. Are you at all interested in what the letter says?"

"Sure."

"It's complaining about you."

"That doesn't sound like Hastings. Do I get to see the letter?"

"Yes, I'm sending it to you by messenger. But first, I want you to level with me. Five years ago, you told me that Hastings had died. Your report was very definite."

"I thought the death was definite. I saw him die. An ambulance came. A mortuary handled the body. But I was wrong. Apparently, some people committed felonies. He's alive."

"You've seen him." It was not a question. "When were you going to tell me about this?"

"Soon. He called me yesterday, but at first I thought it was an imposter. I wanted to confirm with my own eyes, so I met with him last night. The man certainly appears to be Hastings. He knows all the details of what went on when I was working on the TFX matter and pursuing Bill Riley, and when Hastings was…doing whatever it was he was doing."

"Are you sure it's Hastings?"

"I think so. He looks a little different. I think he's had plastic surgery. During the shootout in the mine tunnel, Linda fired a shot that came close to his head, hit the rock wall, and sprayed his face with rock chips. When I saw him in the mine, his face was a bloody mess. Some of the wounds still had pieces of rock in them. The man I met with last night has scars on his face, but they just look like acne scars. He's grown a beard, which may cover some of it. He told me he had bandages covering his face for months, which may have helped conceal his identity. He's not as handsome as he used to be. He's also five years older. But he's already proved that he's a tricky sonofabitch."

"How did he manage to fake his death?"

"He used money. He bribed some public officials and some medical personnel. There should be prosecutions, but not yet. We don't want to announce that he's alive. At least not now. I think he's of more use to us if he stays dead for a while."

"Who have you told about this?"

"No one."

"Not Linda?"

"No."

"Why's Hastings in the Adirondacks, assuming this man is Hastings?"

"Damned if I know. I asked him and he wouldn't tell me. He said he'd explain later. I think he's running from the KGB. He thinks the KGB knows he's alive and that they're after him. He has the details on a lot of KGB operatives. He could do them great damage, and we could sure profit from that. The KGB would invest in trying to prevent it."

"That sounds right. But, as you've already said, he's a tricky sonofabitch. If we get suckered on this, we'll look like prize idiots. We need to be very careful now."

2

I met Hastings for breakfast at the Full Moon. The first thing I said to him was, "Why did you write to Rabbit Maranville?"

"I didn't."

"Now he's got the Agency looking for you."

"I didn't write to him. I'm not that crazy."

"A matter for debate. Somebody calling himself Ev Hastings sure wrote to Rabbit." Our eggs arrived. Then I said, "Who knows you're alive?"

"My wife."

"Only your wife? Would she have told anyone?"

"She knows that she should not, and she's been very discreet under the rather peculiar and difficult circumstances of our long life together, but I suppose it's possible that she told our children."

"How many children?"

"Three."

"Is there any reason why one of them would want to get you in trouble?"

"Who knows? I don't think so, but do we ever know

about our children?" He seemed a little pained. "One of them might have been recruited. Most likely by the KGB." He looked at the front door. "It's a possibility."

"We still need to talk about why you're here. I don't know what I'm supposed to be doing. What's going on?"

He said, "After breakfast we'll take a walk where we can discuss it more freely. The Moon is too crowded. Finish your eggs."

I used my remaining toast to mop up the rest of the two eggs over easy, and then we walked toward Lake Flower. We didn't talk during the two blocks. The bandshell at the lakefront was deserted, and we strolled along the path behind it. The breeze was freshening and there was a chop on the water. It was a day for a sailboat, a heavy one. If you were a good sailor, it would be fun. If not, it would probably be unpleasant. We walked into the wind. Our faces took on color and our words blew away. Because there was no one around, we wouldn't be heard.

Hastings said, "There are problems in the Arctic."

"I'm not surprised. If you look closely enough, you can probably find problems anywhere."

"This is a bit more specific than that. The Pentagon is all abuzz about it."

"They haven't told me."

"Don't feel slighted, dear boy, you're only a captain. No doubt the Joint Chiefs will consult you very soon."

"The Arctic. It's true that it gets cold here in the winter, and we have an Ice Palace then, but we're a hell of a long way from the Arctic. So why the Adirondacks?"

"Camp Drum, dear boy, Camp Drum."

"What about Camp Drum?"

"Training for cold weather operations, crossing the ice, weapons that are reliable at very low temperature. There's a reason why the Olympic biathlon combines cross-country skiing and rifle marksmanship."

Camp Drum was a very large Army base located near the St. Lawrence River, the northern boundary of the United States at that point. Just a few years later it became Fort Drum, but in 1970 it was still Camp Drum. It extends over more than 107,000 acres. When it was expanded in anticipation of World War II, five whole villages were abandoned to make way for the base. In 1941, an Army city was built there with 800 buildings, 240 barracks, 84 mess halls, schools, a hospital, and numerous warehouses and other buildings, all constructed within ten months. It's a big place, with challenging terrain and a harsh climate. Winter temperatures at Drum reach thirty degrees below zero.

I was still puzzled. I said, "But why are *you* here? I'm the CIA's man in the North Country."

"Ah yes. Their man in the North Country. Do you like Graham Greene? Have you read 'Our Man in Havana'? Very amusing" He looked behind us, as if he had heard someone. "Graham and I dined at Rule's from time to time in the old days, to compare notes."

"Before you had a falling out with MI6, no doubt."

"I suppose it was, young Joseph, now that you mention it."

"Still, what does this have to do with Camp Drum?"

"Planning, my friend, planning. Your government is

very enthusiastic about contingency plans. The Pentagon devotes untold sums to the effort—literally untold. Just try to find the budget numbers." He looked behind us again. "It's easy to imagine that the plans might travel, get out. There are so many of them that this or that piece is likely to slip away. There's an abundance, a multitude of them. What is the collective noun for 'contingency plan'? Perhaps 'a panorama of contingency plans'? Or, better, 'an anxiety of contingency plans.'"

"You're having too much fun with this."

"I'm exuberant because I'm glad to be back in the game, Joe, but I'm still vigilant. People are assiduously trying to kill me. In any event, as I was about to say, some of those plans seem to have turned up in Moscow, or so the Joint Chiefs believe. And they also believe that the plans reached Moscow via Camp Drum."

"Since when did you become a messenger for the Pentagon, and why would Camp Drum have the plans?"

"All will be revealed in good time, my boy. Some of the troops that are being trained to execute the plans are based at Drum, and I gather that they are now engaged in testing alternative strategies."

"Does anyone really think the Soviets would try to take Alaska? That's crazy. They'd have to be nuts to try that. And why would the Arctic be worth it?"

"No, of course no serious person thinks that they would try to capture Alaska. It's a bit less direct than that, but nonetheless quite threatening."

"Who sent you here?"

"Your government."

"I can't just take your word for that."

"Of course not. That would be very unwise."

"I'll have to confirm it and seek advice."

"Of course. No doubt you will want to call Rabbit."

"I've already talked to Rabbit. He claimed to be surprised that you are here."

"Oh dear." Hastings stopped and surveyed a full 360 degrees. He was interested in a woman with a baby carriage coming toward us, but he continued. "I suppose there are two possibilities. One is that he was not being straightforward with you—perhaps he was cautious because he wasn't certain about the security of the call. The other possibility is that Rabbit has not been informed. That would be embarrassing for him, the poor man. He is getting a little long in the tooth."

It occurred to me that maybe the Agency didn't regard this as within Rabbit's jurisdiction because they didn't define it as a domestic operation. Maybe they called it international, which it was. But I still didn't know who sent Hastings here. I would need to talk to Rabbit again, immediately. He was my boss. I reported to him. If I was going to be working on this operation, I would continue to report to him until ordered to do otherwise.

We reached the boat launch where the big wooden inboards go in and out, and we inspected a nice Chris Craft moored there. We were done for the day. I wasn't going to get any more information that would be of use, so we went across the road to the Lakeside Deli to get another cup of coffee.

I got a call from Rabbit the next day. He said, "I have

confirmed that Ev Hastings is now a consultant to the US government. A great many sins are committed under the label 'consultant'."

3

Two days later was a Saturday. Since there was nothing scheduled for either Linda or William, she took him to the Full Moon for a mid-morning doughnut. The weather was unseasonably cold, but it was warm in the cafe. They sat at a table in the back of the Moon and shared the weekend edition of the Adirondack Daily Enterprise. Halfway through their doughnuts, a middle-aged man wearing a tweed jacket and a Rex Harrison hat stopped at their table.

He said, "William, you have certainly grown since I saw you last. How old are you?"

William said, "Almost eleven."

Linda, stunned, managed to say, "He's ten." She could think of nothing else to say.

Hastings said, "I can see that you're surprised. Joe hasn't told you that I'm back in town?"

Linda, in a hushed voice, said only, "No."

William knew that his mother was upset. He said, "Who's this man, Mom?"

She hesitated and then said, "I'm not sure. I think he's

someone I thought I would never see again. I can't really believe it."

Hastings smiled in a friendly way but kept his distance.

William stared at him boldly and said, "What's your name?"

Hastings cleared his throat. "Good boy! That's the right question, put directly. A man after my own heart." He put a hand on one of the empty chairs at the table but didn't sit. "As your mother knows, my name is changeable. Sometimes it depends on the day of the week. But the name by which your mother knows me, or she once did, is Ev Hastings. That's good enough. You may call me 'Uncle Ev.'"

Linda said, "William will call you Major Hastings."

He replied, "If you insist on formality, it should be 'Colonel Hastings.' I've been promoted. That is to say, I promoted myself, owing to advancing age."

Linda, having recovered a bit, said, "So Joe knows you're here?"

"Yes, he does. We may have occasion to work together once again."

"Is that what it was, 'working together'?"

He replied, "I like to think of it that way."

She said, "I wasn't sure that I recognized you. I didn't see how it could be true."

"I know I'm not as handsome as I once was, but you are just as lovely as ever, my dear. Joe will be able to explain my presence. I've told him about it."

Linda didn't invite Hastings to join them. She wanted to talk to me first. William must have been puzzled by all this. I didn't discuss it with him until much later.

* * *

I called Rabbit and gave him the news.

"Okay, Chief, here's the latest. I was careful not to tell Linda about Hastings being back, but then he comes over to a table in a restaurant where she's eating with our son, and he announces himself, by name, and he tells her that maybe we're going to work together again."

"What, exactly, did he say?"

"Linda told me he used the words 'work together.'"

"Did he say what you'd be working on?"

"No. And Linda got the impression that it was not a done deal, it was just a possibility."

"It's sure as hell not a done deal so far as I'm concerned! What the hell's going on?"

"Here's what I've learned from questioning him. He says the Pentagon thinks the Soviets are planning an operation in the Arctic, and DoD believes that there's a spy at Camp Drum, the Army's base for cold weather combat."

"What makes them think that?"

"Their sources in Moscow, covert ops, tell them the Soviets have our contingency plans, and the Pentagon thinks those came from Camp Drum, or at least could have come from there."

"So, Army intelligence is looking for a spy. Nothing new in that. How in the hell does Hastings get involved?"

"That part makes sense to me. They know that Hastings worked for the KGB. He has inside information, plenty of it. He knows the KGB's people and the way they work, the top brass. If somebody at Army intel found out that

Hastings is still alive—and there's a lot of ways that could have happened—they'd want to try to recruit him. One of the Army's sources could have run into Hastings and recognized him. Then they decided to use him."

"Why didn't they just kill the sonofabitch so that he would stay dead?"

"Because they're trying to solve the problem at Drum."

"Yes, of course. You're right, but I just don't like the man. I don't know if you've ever been read in on how many of our people Hastings killed over the years. Why would the Army trust him?"

"I don't think they trust him exactly. I think the Army believes that he wants our protection. He claims that the KGB is hunting for him and wants to kill him. That's certainly plausible. Hastings killed, or the KGB believes that he did, several of their agents—including Colonel Kuznetsov, Vasily Rostov, and the two men at Lake Clear. They have good reasons for vengeance. On top of that, he knows too much. The information he has is a threat, and he's clearly unreliable. If CIA had an agent like that, you wouldn't want to have him running around. If KGB knows Hastings is alive, they'd want to eliminate the threat. The best thing he could've done was stay dead. He knows that, but it's hard to do if you're in the open air."

"Do you trust him?"

"No."

"Then how can we work with him? 'The enemy of my enemy is my friend' doesn't always work. You can get nasty surprises if you rely on that."

I said, "Granted, but you still have to make some decisions about how to proceed. Sometimes it's a close call. I think I can work with him by going in with my eyes open and being careful. I know him. I think I understand him, at least partly."

"He's switched sides before."

"Yeah, more than once. And he'd do it again if he thought he needed to and could get away with it. But he's a practical man, and he's been pretty good at calculating the odds, and the odds for him now look a lot better on our side."

"That could change."

"Yes, it could. Somebody close to the situation would need to monitor it."

"That would be you."

"I assumed it would." I paused and considered my words. "There's a peculiar sort of honor in Hastings. If you start with the knowledge that he's a professional assassin, you take that as a given, then his actions make sense. He becomes more understandable and predictable."

"I think you like the man."

"It isn't a question of liking him. It's a matter of understanding him. He's a professional—and I'm a professional. He sees his motivations as being professional motivations. If you accept his premises, that's probably correct. But do I like him? Oh, there's no doubt that he can be charming when he wants to be. But that's irrelevant. That's superficial." I paused again. "I think it's true, however, that at some level, in some ways, I respect him. I respect what he's able to do, his skills, his craft. He's cool under fire."

"Don't be beguiled by him."

"I won't. I've been through this before. I know what I'll be dealing with."

"Good luck! Keep me informed. Keep me fully informed."

* * *

I hadn't seen Hastings for two or three days and he hadn't called me, so I looked for him. None of the hotels in Saranac, Tupper, or Placid had a guest who fit his description, so I tried Long Lake and Blue. No luck. I began to worry that the KGB had caught up with him.

It was a Wednesday. I was at my office at the prison when I got an internal call.

"Captain Boudreau, this is the front gate. There's a man here in handcuffs who says he wants to see you."

"In handcuffs? Is he in custody?"

"No, he's alone. He says he was playing a sex game with a young woman and it got out of control. I don't believe him. Should I call the psych doc?"

"Does he have a British accent?"

"Yes."

"He's not as crazy as he sounds. I hope. Not believing him is a good place to start, Sergeant. Watch him closely. Escort him under armed guard to a secure cell and lock him up. I'll see him there."

"He says he's hungry."

"Feed him in the cell, not before. He's tricky."

"Got it, Captain. Will do. Do you want to talk to him now on the phone?"

"No. Not yet. Just let me know where he is."

I called Rabbit. I asked him whether Hastings had been on assignment somewhere, working for the Agency. Rabbit told me that was not the case. I told him that Hastings had shown up at the prison gate, in handcuffs. Rabbit said, "Oh, for Christ's sake, who's he killed now?"

I assured him that I would try to find out. We agreed to keep quiet until we knew more. A low profile seemed like a good idea. Then I asked for more information about the Army's plans that had been found in Moscow. He was not forthcoming. He had consulted James Jesus Angleton, director of counterintelligence, a famous spy-hunter.

Rabbit said, "Using the 'need to know' principle, Army Intel and J. J. Angleton have determined that all you need to know is what Hastings has already been told—that is, that at least one of our contingency plans for Arctic warfare has turned up in Moscow and that the plan was being executed at Camp Drum. That plan could have leaked out of the Pentagon, of course, but the brass there didn't like it when Angleton suggested that possibility, so you're assigned to investigate and find the bad man at Drum."

"Or maybe woman?"

"Or maybe woman, I suppose, but that seems less likely. There aren't any women in the team working on it at Drum, and I doubt it would be a topic for pillow talk."

"Could I be given the names of the people working on the project? And does the thing have a name?"

Rabbit said, "Sure. It's called 'Project Iceshield' and I'll get you the names of people."

So, I went to the cell to see Hastings. The sergeant had

told me the location, and the guard on the cellblock let me in. When I got there, Hastings was enthusiastically attacking a large plateful of food.

He said, "This is very good meatloaf."

I sat down on a bench in the cell. "You've been without food for too long."

"The fare at the county jail was not to my liking. This is better."

"How long were you there?"

"Two days."

"What got you locked up?"

He said, "I was investigating." I grimaced. He said, "It was all very straightforward. I was doing research at the public library, in their files, on Camp Drum. But they seemed to feel that I had accessed materials without proper permission." I grimaced again.

"Was the material secret?"

"I don't think so. Does the public library have secret material?" He smiled. "But I did pick the lock on a filing cabinet."

"Ah, I see. Did they tell you that they wouldn't let you see the files that were in the cabinet?"

"No, not exactly."

"Well, then, why did you pick the lock?"

"The files I wanted to see were in a room, or a couple of rooms, that they called the archives. That's where they store the ephemera, and you can look at it in those rooms, but only there. You can't take the files out, and you can't sort through them. You have to request one file at a time and sign for it, and you have to wear washable white cotton gloves when you look at it, and you can't have a pen in your possession. You are permitted to make notes in pencil on paper they provide. But there was only one staff person on duty in the archives, and she was busy with customers who were requesting one file at a time. So, I decided to expedite the process."

"You were impatient."

"That is an apt way to describe it, yes. And then there was a misunderstanding with the police officer who was called to the scene. He didn't like my identification. He forcefully asserted the view that Evelyn is a woman's name. And he pronounced it wrong. We had words."

"And fisticuffs?"

"No, certainly not. It was a library! I did, however, protest."

"I'm sure you did."

"I didn't hurt the young man."

"I'm glad to hear it. I hope an official apology coming from DC will solve the problem." I stood and walked to the door of the cell. "Why didn't you just call me? Surely they permitted you one phone call."

"I thought you and the Agency might prefer that I not make public the kind of work you actually do. I thought we should fly under the radar, as it were, and that you should be left out of it, especially since my action would reveal our interest in Camp Drum."

"Yes, that was good. And you seem to have handled it. Handled it in an unorthodox way, I suppose, but you handled it. How did you get away?"

"I was being transported from the jail to the court in

Saranac, for a hearing. The transport was a van, and I was the only passenger. Fortunately, my hands were cuffed in front of me instead of behind my back. A poor practice. No doubt an inexperienced officer."

"Wasn't the van locked?"

"Of course it was. But it seemed to me that an open hearing in court might be counterproductive, so I decided to depart." He paused, trying to make me ask him how he got out. I waited until he gave up. He said, "Have you ever noticed the small nail driven into the side of the heel of my boot?"

"No, I haven't."

"Don't feel bad. Neither did the police. When there's a bit of mud on the boots, you'd have to clean them to see it, and even then, it doesn't look out of place."

"And the nail is a lock pick?"

"Quite an efficient one, yes. It's not big enough to be used as a weapon, but it's very good on the right sort of lock, if you know what you're doing."

"And then you walked out?"

"Not walked, no. Unfortunately, it was necessary for me to make my departure when the van was underway, which required a roll on the ground. I was worried about the cuffs, but actually they may have helped. They prevented me from using my hands or arms to break my fall, which might have resulted in a broken wrist or arm. As it was, my shoulders and hips took the brunt of it. It did result in my becoming a bit dusty and rumpled."

"Can you walk?"

"I can, certainly. How do you think I got here?"

"And you walked on the road, in handcuffs?"

"Not on the road, young Joseph, beside it. In the trees where there was cover."

"And no one bothered you or stopped you?"

"I don't think the handcuffs were obvious. The police didn't want to have to struggle with me to put my overcoat on—they would have had to take the cuffs off, get my arms through the sleeves, and then put the cuffs back on again—and I was not cooperative, so they just draped the coat around my shoulders and buttoned the top two buttons. The coat mostly hid the cuffs. A couple of people on the road looked at me in an interested way, but I stared back at them, sternly. I think my appearance discouraged them. Perhaps a dusty man of stern visage, with torn clothing, did not seem worth the bother. They felt it better to let someone else take care of it."

I changed the subject. "So, while rifling through the library's files on Camp Drum, did you find anything of interest?"

"Perhaps. There were memos indicating that soldiers at Drum were being trained for duty at the Nike missile site near Point Barrow—for both defense duties and technical duties."

"The Nike launch station isn't a secret. It's been in the newspapers."

"Yes, but what hasn't been made public is the extent and nature of the US defenses there, the kinds of weapons at the site and the number of troops. And there were also memos on the Soviet proposal to build a dam and bridge across the Bering Strait, intended to melt the polar ice and warm Siberia."

"So there would be a road across the Strait? That would provide an invasion route."

"Not a very big one. A naval landing would be more efficient, and the vehicles and people on the bridge would be sitting ducks, but your Agency was nonetheless concerned about it."

"If it wasn't a real threat to us, why did the Russians want to do it and why did we care?"

Hastings said, "The Russians wanted to warm Siberia. The USSR has the largest land mass of any country on the globe, but the majority of that land is covered by permafrost. It's uninhabitable. There are enormous amounts of natural resources in Siberia—oil, coal, natural gas, iron, nickel, other minerals—but they can't exploit them efficiently because it's too cold for workers to live there. As the world is now, your country has an enormous strategic advantage, a temperate climate that permits mining, manufacturing, and transportation. Warming Siberia would permit the USSR to compete and perhaps to prevail. With the oil and iron buried there, Russia would be a powerhouse."

"How would the bridge warm Siberia?"

"By diverting ocean currents. The bridge would also be a dam. In fact, it would primarily be a dam, 56 miles long and 200 feet high. At present, a cold Pacific current flows up the east coast of Siberia and goes into the Arctic Ocean. It prevents warmer, saltier water from the Atlantic, the Gulf stream, from flowing into the Arctic. That helps to keep the Arctic frozen. Because saltwater freezes at a lower temperature than freshwater, if the Arctic Ocean became saltier it wouldn't freeze as much of the year as it does now, and the Russians would have shipping lanes to Europe that would be more dependable—a much shorter trip than going through the Suez Canal. The melting of ice and snow would also make the Arctic less reflective. If the Arctic melted, it would absorb more of the warmth from the sun's rays. At present, the snow and ice reflect much of the sunlight."

I said, "Surely the Russians couldn't dam the Strait without our cooperation."

"No, they'd have to use force. There would be a lot riding on it—for both sides." Hastings surveyed the cell. He said, "This is a comfortable place for us to meet. We can speak freely here since none of the other cells on this hall are occupied. Perhaps we should use this as our conference room. The meatloaf is good."

"How long would it take to melt the polar ice?"

"It depends upon how they go about it. The Russians propose to speed up the process by pumping water, a great deal of it, out of the Arctic Ocean and into the Pacific. Since salt water is heavier than fresh, the top layer of water is less salty and it freezes first, so if you remove the top layer of water, the remaining water will be less likely to freeze. That will keep Russia's shipping lanes open and warm Siberia faster. The pumping will also make more room for the warmer Atlantic current to enter."

"What's the legal status of the Arctic Ocean? Who owns it?"

"My research in the public library tells me that the Ocean is international waters, but several of the islands have been claimed by the nations that are adjacent to them. In effect, nations have extended out their boundaries."

Hastings looked into the hallway outside the cell. It was empty. Then he said, "About a decade ago, the United States had another project, top secret, code-named 'Iceworm.' The Army Corps of Engineers tunneled into Greenland's ice. There were hundreds of miles of tunnels with a railroad running through them to permit missiles with nuclear warheads to be moved around constantly so that the Soviets would never know where they were. There was also a dormitory under the ice to house the soldiers stationed there, with all of the comforts of home, and a nuclear reactor to supply the power for all of this. The construction of that was too big a project to conceal, so your government claimed to be building a scientific research station. I doubt that the Soviets were fooled. But that's all gone now."

"What happened?"

"The ice shifted and the tunnels collapsed." Hastings finished the last of his coffee. "It must be wonderful to pay taxes in a country that can afford such a spectacular failure."

"Yes."

"When the tunnels collapsed, your country had to go fight a war in Vietnam just to get rid of the excess wealth. And that venture is not going so well either."

"Thank you. So why have you signed-on?"

"Any port in a storm, as we mariners say, dear boy." He picked up his empty coffee cup and stared into it a moment. "The chaps in the Pentagon have a great many ideas. I wonder what amazing feat they're planning now. The Soviets have a big lead in the production of icebreakers. Project Iceworm may have been your government's response to the Soviet launch of the Lenin, the first nuclear-powered icebreaker. The Russians have continued their advance since. They also have nuclear submarines operating in the Arctic."

"So do we."

"Yes, but your country is behind in that game."

The guard came to pick up the tray on which the meatloaf and mashed potatoes had been delivered. When he left, we left with him. Since Hastings had not been admitted to the prison, he didn't need to be released. Officially, he was never there.

I thought that breaking into the filing cabinet was a strange move, an awkward one, even an amateurish one. I knew Hastings was a free spirit, but his work had usually been careful, methodical. Why did he do it? Did he want to be arrested? Did he want to be identified? If he did, there was more going on here than I had been told. But it was a bold move and he succeeded in getting some useful information. The information was background, mostly, but it was more than Rabbit had given me.

Hastings was still caustic, but he wasn't as jaunty as he had been five years earlier. There was now an undertone of desperation. If you know the KGB is after you, it's hard to be cheerful. He'd always been realistic about assessing the odds, and he had told me when he thought the odds weren't good, but he now seemed less determined to survive. That worried me.

4

I'd met Linda's ex-husband, John, only once, briefly, shortly before Linda and I were married. Their marriage broke up when William was four, before she returned to Saranac. But John is William's father, and he was coming to visit him, probably for the weekend.

As might be expected, Linda's version of the story was that John was a jerk. He seemed to me to be simply an ambitious lawyer, standard model. Nothing much. Not nearly as exciting as a CIA agent. At least I hoped that was Linda's view. At first, William was excited that his mother was marrying an Air Force officer, but then he was disappointed when he found out that I don't fly planes.

I've tried to protect both Linda and William from the more threatening realities of my work, but she's insisted on becoming involved in it. She has a taste for adventure, and she's good at it. I managed to get her into the middle of a real gunfight pretty quickly, even before we were married. I'd tried to keep her out of it, but she would not be persuaded.

William has begun to show interest in what I do with

my time, and that may become a problem. The Agency advises us on how to deal with family, but most of the advice is unrealistic. There's a considerable amount of instability in the marriages of covert agents. Since the instability creates a security risk, the Agency would like to avoid it, but that isn't easy to do.

Linda told me that John was looking for a new job. He was not made a partner in the Binghamton firm where he worked for several years. In effect, it was an "up or out" decision. Linda didn't know whether he was coming to Saranac as a part of the job hunt. She hoped not. She thought that, if he relocated to this area, he might try to get joint custody of William. She was given sole custody at the time of the divorce because the lawyers and the judge liked her better—at least she thought that was the reason for it. Some of the long hours John devoted to work were in fact spent in a motel near his office in the company of an attractive waitress.

I asked her how she felt about that. She said she was sorry about it, she wished it hadn't happened. But it seemed to me that she must have been angry.

She said, "You can't get angry at somebody who steps off the curb into the path of an oncoming truck."

I said, "Is that what happened?"

Linda's reply was quick. "That girl was an oncoming truck if I ever saw one."

I laughed. "Was she big?"

"No, but she was devastating."

I said, "John used poor judgment. Is it okay if I'm glad that he got hit by the truck?"

"I don't think it was about me. He was just busy. A new woman was a new project. He always had to be busy, fulfilling his ambition."

Then Linda changed the subject. She gave me some news. I think she intended to tell John and needed to tell me first. She said William was going to have a brother or sister. That was the way she put it. She was then three months pregnant. I stood and gave her a hug. This was very good news. We had been trying to have a child, and we both consulted doctors for treatment, a somewhat distasteful process. So, either something worked, or nature just took its course. In either case, the pregnancy further emphasized my family responsibilities. I wasn't sure what the relationship was at that time between Linda and John, but I thought it wasn't good. I wondered whether the new child would complicate the custody situation.

* * *

A day or two later, Linda arranged for us to meet with John at the Full Moon for breakfast. Just the two of us — Linda and I didn't think it would be a good idea for William to be present for this meeting. We didn't know how it would go. Linda wanted a breakfast meeting because that made it less likely that there would be alcohol. I argued that one or more of us might want a stiff drink, but I've never been known for my ability as an advocate. Linda said that meetings with alcohol tend to be unpredictable. That's probably right.

John was fifteen minutes late. Linda had told him to

meet us at the Moon at seven thirty and he didn't get there until quarter of eight. She was annoyed. Her normal mode is businesslike, and she'd taken William over to her parents for breakfast. It was a good thing that it was vacation time and neither one of them had school.

John apologized, sort of. He said, "Sorry, I got lost."

This seemed implausible or at least odd because he was staying at the Hotel Saranac, which is on the same street as the Moon, just two blocks down. But we let it go.

As soon as we had ordered breakfast, he said to me, maybe because it was easier to talk to me than to Linda, "How are the airplanes?"

"They're fine. Still flying."

"Are you a pilot?"

"No, I'm a navigator. I plot."

"Plot?"

"Plot courses. Keep track of where we are. Make sure the wind hasn't blown us off course. Make sure we're at the proper altitude to avoid hazards on the ground. Watch out for mountains." That seemed to me to be a pretty fair description of the work I actually do. John didn't pursue it. I think he'd lost interest by that time.

Linda and John made arrangements for him to come by our house to visit William, and it would then be up to William to decide whether he wanted to see more of John. Linda wanted to give William some freedom to make his own choices about that. The conversation between John and Linda was civil, but not warm. The other tables at the Moon were not disturbed.

One of the things Linda and I learned was that John

had an appointment with Mac Denleigh to discuss a possible job at the bank where Denleigh was president. The bank had been paying substantial fees to a local law firm and Denleigh thought inside counsel would be more efficient. He wanted to hire a lawyer to serve as vice president, be an operating officer, and handle routine legal matters. John had the qualifications.

I knew that Linda didn't want John to live in Saranac. I didn't either. The situation was even more awkward because, in addition to being president of the bank, Denleigh was chairman of the school board and Linda was a teacher at the high school. She was going to be wanting maternity leave, and the board chairman would certainly have some influence — for better or worse.

Mac Denleigh didn't like me, with good reason. In fairness to John, I thought I should warn him.

I said, "You might win points if you told Denleigh that you don't get along with Linda's husband."

"Why's that?"

"We have a history."

"Will my connection to you and Linda hurt my job chances?"

"I don't know. I suppose that depends on how Denleigh plays the game."

"The game?"

"Some players are straight shooters; some use loaded dice. If I were you, I'd check the dice. Don't use his."

"What does that mean?"

"If he knows that you were married to Linda, the subject will probably come up. Mac Denleigh is not subtle. It's a small town, John. Everything is connected to everything else."

Reasonably enough, John was concerned. He asked, "Can you tell me more about what the problem is, about why he doesn't like you?"

I said, "Sure. It's not common knowledge, but it's not a secret either. Denleigh gave Linda a hard time about her teaching at the high school. This was before he became chairman of the school board. He complained to the principal. Denleigh was playing super-patriot, silly stuff, trying to get Linda fired. It was also before we were married."

"What did you do?"

"I retaliated. I threatened to damage his reputation. He backed off. End of story. But he was angry."

John said, "Thanks for giving me the heads-up." Then he asked Linda, "Has Denleigh given you any more hassle?"

She said, "No."

I volunteered, "After the business about Linda, Denleigh persuaded a local minister to complain to our congressman about my handling of government business. The complaint reached my boss, but nothing came of it. I reminded Denleigh that he didn't want to screw around with me."

John said, "You sound like a tough guy."

"Sometimes you're forced to do the right thing. It depends on the situation."

John assured us that he had other job possibilities, in other towns. He was exploring options in Albany and Plattsburg. Since the letter to Rabbit that was signed Ev

Hastings but that Hastings hadn't written was mailed in Plattsburg, I wondered whether John might have sent it. I'd have to consider that. But I didn't know how John could have found out about Hastings unless Linda told him. Later, when we got home, I asked her. She was indignant. She said, "Of course not!" and then refused to talk to me — for about two minutes.

The rest of the conversation at the Moon was mostly small talk. We finished eating breakfast and had a second cup of coffee. Neither Linda nor John mentioned William's custody. I think both of them were avoiding the issue.

Linda and I reviewed the conversation later. I told her I was worried that Denleigh might think he could make my life more difficult by bringing John to Saranac.

* * *

Rabbit called. "What's this crap about breaking into a filing cabinet in a library?"

I said, "Good question. I think the answer is that Hastings got impatient with the procedures in the archives department. He's a man of action."

"Jesus! That was nuts."

"It sure attracted more attention than was necessary. But he did pick up a good summary of military activity in the Arctic, both ours and theirs."

"The Pentagon could have given that to him."

"Yeah, but they wouldn't have, not without a hell of a lot of bureaucracy. Someone, somewhere in the chain of command, would have found a reason not to do it."

"Maybe." He made a noise deep in this throat. "Hastings is unprofessional."

"That's the most favorable appraisal of him I've ever heard you make. I think you're softening."

"Don't count on it.... You said that he's a man of action. Action is fine in the right circumstances, a very good thing when it's called for. But a good operative also needs judgment. Action without judgment is often fatal." He cleared his throat again. "You're going to have to keep him under control. If you can't do that, can't get him to behave, to work in a professional manner, then you're going to have to distance yourself from him or get rid of him. One way or another."

"If I go up against Hastings, my odds aren't good. He has a lot more skills, more effective ones. It would be like Joe Louis against Tony Galento. I wouldn't last two rounds."

"I don't like that sort of talk, Joe. If you don't think you can do the job, we'll get someone who can."

"What job?"

Rabbit said, "The necessary job. The job that has to be done. That's what you're there for. I think you can do it."

"I appreciate your confidence."

"Don't make me doubt it."

* * *

Eight minutes later Rabbit called again. When I answered, I said, "This is getting to be a habit."

He said, "There's been a murder at Camp Drum."

"When?"

"Today. Three hours ago. I just heard about it."

"Who?"

"The victim was a major. Army. I don't have a name yet."

"Where at Drum?"

"Outside. Maybe during a training exercise."

"Cold weather combat training?"

"Don't know. We're on it."

"Maybe it was an accident?"

"They don't think so."

"I'll go. I'll take Hastings. He'll help."

"Do you have to?"

"Yeah, I do. His feelings would be hurt. Besides, I need him."

* * *

I called Hastings. When he answered, he said, "Sisters Camp." He was renting a house at Coreys that was owned by the Sisters of Mercy in Tupper Lake. He liked the idea of renting from nuns, and Coreys was an ideal location for him, off the beaten path. The KGB would be less likely to find him there than if he stayed at the hotel in Saranac where he might be seen on the street, and telephone calls at the hotel go through an operator, who can listen-in if she's so inclined. Hastings and I both had radio transmitters, but the transmissions could be picked up by ham radio people and any competent intelligence service, so we used radio only in emergencies.

In the Adirondacks, a summer place is usually called a "camp." The one that Hastings was renting had been built around 1910 as a hunting and fishing refuge. It was modest, much smaller and less grand than the house he rented during our last adventures together, five years before. The Sisters camp was only one story, a succession of four rooms snaking along the top of a hill above the Stony Creek ponds. The rooms followed the contours of the land. There was also a screened porch, eleven feet wide and forty feet long, wrapped around two sides of the house. The porch was usable in summer, but it was too cold when Hastings was there. The house was heated by a cast-iron, pot-bellied, wood-burning stove and a large fireplace. A supply of wood was included in the rental. Many of the camps at Coreys don't have telephones, but the Sisters did. The place had been owned by a dentist who was a good Catholic, and when he died, he left it to the nuns. They used it as a retreat, and they got a bit of income by renting it to people like Hastings—well, perhaps I should revise that. I don't suppose they had many tenants who were much like Hastings, at least I hope not.

Hastings, not entirely to my surprise, received the killing at Camp Drum as good news. This was, after all, his specialty, his line of country. It would be like old times. He was not only comfortable with the prospect of confronting a killer, he was exhilarated by it. Moreover, it was clear that the development also meant to him that I was now on his turf; he was in charge. He told me that he would pack his bag. I didn't ask him how many weapons would be in it.

<h1 style="text-align:center">5</h1>

Before we went to Camp Drum, however, there was a debate about strategy. One possible approach was to go through bureaucratic channels—Rabbit or J. J. Angleton would contact the Pentagon to seek their cooperation. That process would start with the office of the Secretary of the Army, who would refer us to Army Intelligence, who would then send it to their people at Drum. The other way was to fly under the radar. As a good bureaucrat, I preferred the first; Hastings, of course, wanted to do it the quick way. In the end, we used an unwise combination of the two.

This was mostly unavoidable. Unless I locked Hastings up, he was going to move, and Rabbit was already talking to the Pentagon. The military wanted us to stay out of it, which was what they always wanted, but the Agency wasn't going to sit still for that, and it has clout at the White House and the National Security Council. Rabbit and Angleton hemmed and hawed while Hastings and I got on the road.

We drove in my old Dodge, an inconspicuous car. The fastest route from Saranac to Drum is simple. You pick up Route 3 on the west side of town and go west through Tupper Lake, where the road heads north for a bit and then turns west again past Wanakena and Cranberry Lake, and heads toward Drum. You meander in order to get around big lakes. As you drive west, you leave the high peaks behind and enter a landscape of lakes and rivers. Somewhere after Wanakena, you've gone beyond the official boundary of the Adirondacks, but it's still pretty undeveloped. You reach Drum in just over two hours, total.

South of Drum, there are a couple of villages, Natural Bridge and Blanchards Corners, where some of the civilians who work at the base live with their families. Hastings and I chose to head for the Corners instead of the Bridge. It was time for lunch. We stopped in at a cafe called the Golden Olympic. The place was long and narrow, with the kitchen at the back behind a swinging door. There was a Formica counter along one of the long walls and a row of booths along the other, with a narrow aisle between. The counter had stools with no backs, and they were bolted to the floor so that you couldn't rearrange them. The place wasn't set up for community conversations; if you stood in the aisle to talk to someone at the counter or in one of the booths, you got in the way of the waitresses, which wasn't appreciated. But, in spite of the impediments, there were vigorous conversations. People sitting in booths exchanged news and comments with friends perched on the stools.

Hastings ordered a bowl of egg lemon soup, a Greek specialty, and I had an American hamburger. Then we listened. But we didn't hear any talk about the killing at

Drum. Maybe it was already old news. Most of the conversations concerned a primary election scheduled for the following week. There were candidates for the city council and for seats on the school board. A man who was about fifty years old, well-dressed in a sport coat, dress shirt, and tie, seemed to know everyone. I think he was the mayor. In any event, he was definitely a local businessman and a leader of the Republican party. There was talk of the need for real estate development, well-rehearsed talk about a familiar subject.

Hastings and I weren't wearing coats and ties, but we were dressed appropriately. It would have been hard not to be. The people in the Golden Olympic were wearing a wide variety of clothes, ranging from bib overalls to the putative mayor's tie. I had on jeans and a decent sweater; Hastings wore a Burberry raincoat. I hoped the diners didn't know how much it cost. Luckily, it was somewhat beat-up as a result of his rolling exit from the police van.

Hastings stood, drew himself up to full height, and squared his shoulders. It was a military stance. He approached the mayor. "Permit me to introduce myself, sir. I'm Colonel Hatter-Hatton, now retired from Her Majesty's army, Scots Guards. I can see that you are a man of consequence in this community and I'm sure you are well-informed."

Hastings used his Colonel Blimp manner, full blast.

The mayor said, "How may I help you?"

"Captain Boudreau and I have been in the Adirondacks, and we heard that there has been an unnatural death at Camp Drum."

"I believe there was. Accidents happen, unfortunately."

"Unfortunately, yes. How did the accident happen? Was it a training exercise?"

A man who had been sitting in one of the booths walked toward Hastings and the mayor. He said, "What was the nature of your military service, Colonel?"

Hastings turned and faced him. "I served in the late unpleasantness in Europe." He was still Colonel Blimp, but there was now a harder edge.

"In combat?"

"Yes indeed, sir. Behind enemy lines. Special operations." That part was true, and I think the man could see that it was true.

"Intelligence? Or sabotage?"

Hastings relaxed. He smiled. "I'd prefer to call it interference with German aggression. And you, sir?"

"I'm Major Johnson. Second Army. If you'd like to go over to Camp Drum, you could talk to Captain Marcus in public affairs. I'm sure that he'd give you whatever information is available. Where did you hear about it?"

Hastings ignored the question about where we had heard. "A pleasure to meet you, Major, and did you serve in the big show? Ah, silly of me. Silly question. Of course, you're too young for that. You will still have been stateside in the early forties. Still in school, what?"

The man went back to his scrambled eggs.

When we left the restaurant, I said to Hastings, "Well, we didn't learn much from that."

He said, "I think we did. It shows us that there's sensitivity on the matter. If it were a training accident, why would they be so closed-mouth, so protective? I think they're in locked-down mode."

We could have gone to Captain Marcus at Drum's public affairs office next, but what we would get there was predictable, not much more than what the local newspaper had: "Major Henry 'Hank' Bradley, born 1936 in Shaker Heights, Ohio. A single bullet wound. The Army was investigating." So, he was age 34, doing well to be a major. A comer. He probably had some responsibility. The newspaper provided no information on his branch or duties.

We thought we would do better if we arrived at Drum armed with some town talk. We didn't want to become too conspicuous in Blanchard's Corners, so we moved on to Natural Bridge. The Bridge Hotel had a popular bar. The hotel is small, three stories tall, and its rooms are well-filled with military personnel who are at Drum for short-term temporary duty and families parked there while the Army looks for permanent housing. But the bar in the early afternoon serves the needs of serious drinkers, celebrants, and sad cases. It seemed like promising territory.

It wasn't crowded when we stopped in, but there were a few customers. One was a middle-aged woman, well-dressed, drinking vodka and orange soda. She was in the sad-case category. I could see that Hastings was considering trying his Rex Harrison/David Niven/Sean Connery mashup on her, but he concluded that she was too involved in her own troubles to pay attention to Camp Drum. She wanted quiet, and we left her to it. Another of the customers was a priest wearing a clerical collar. At first, I thought he was a Catholic, but it turned out he was an Episcopalian having an after-lunch pick-me-up. He was affable.

Hastings struck up a conversation with him. I was always wary when Hastings charted his own course, and with good reason, but the two men hit it off. The priest had been an Army chaplain in Vietnam, and Hastings again rolled out his clandestine service behind enemy lines in World War II. The priest had a mangled hand as a result of a grenade that was thrown into a command post. He also had some shrapnel that had not yet been removed.

When Hastings heard that story, he said, "Holy Mother of God!"

The priest smiled and said, "Are you a Catholic?"

"I was raised a Catholic, and that proved to be useful in my work, when I had to be a priest for a few days."

The priest raised his eyebrows. "That must have been dangerous."

"Yes, it was. I had to remember the right words, and my Latin was a little rusty. When in doubt I just said, '*Kyrie Eleison.*'" Hastings looked thoughtful. "While I was a priest, I absolved the faithful of some colorful sins. The things those people had done made my life seem tame, a paragon of virtue…It troubles me a bit that my intercession with the Almighty on their behalf might have been less than fully effective."

Fortunately, the priest laughed. He said, "I think the important question is whether the sinners made their own connections to the Almighty, and whether they truly repented. Anyhow, I'm sure you gave them comfort."

He was my kind of priest. I never knew whether to believe Hastings's stories. Many of them may have been true. But I suppose that's beside the point. He knew what he was doing.

Hastings asked the priest, "Do you ever do any work at Camp Drum?"

"I fill in there from time to time to help out."

"Did you know Major Bradley?"

"The man who was killed? No, I didn't. It's a big base, and I only know a few of the soldiers. I know the chaplains."

Hastings said, "Bradley was married, I think." If Hastings knew that, I don't know where he got the information. It wasn't in the newspaper. He was probably bluffing.

The priest replied, "I haven't heard about that, one way or the other."

"Will there be a funeral at Drum?"

"Probably not a funeral. There may be a memorial of some sort. The funeral will be the wife's decision… if he had a wife. If he wasn't married, then his parents would decide it."

"Terrible thing. Terrible. I hope he didn't leave children."

"Yes, it is terrible. But there are live-fire exercises."

Hastings smoothed his mustache. "Is that what it was, a training accident?"

"The Army isn't talking, at least not yet. They're looking into it."

"They'll certainly want to do that. Terrible thing. Your Army, I'm sure, like ours, makes every effort to keep tight control of its weapons, but that must be very difficult. There are so many weapons. I never served in that sort of post. But you, my friend, have done counseling of soldiers. I'm sure you saw cases of animosity, conflict, even rage."

"Yes, of course. Soldiers are human and have emotions, and most soldiers are young, impulsive, many with poor judgment. Command-and-control is a tough job. As I'm sure you know, most weapons are kept unloaded, just for that reason. But this death may well have been an accident."

"That would be better than the alternative. Has there been any talk about the circumstances in which the major was shot, or talk about who may have fired the weapon?"

"I haven't heard any, but I'm not close to it."

"I suppose we'll find out."

"Yes, I'm sure we'll know more in due course."

The priest finished his drink and left after shaking hands all around. There didn't appear to be any other customers in the bar who were coherent enough to be worth our time.

We drove over to Camp Drum and asked for directions to the public affairs office. As we expected, it was located close to the front gate so that reporters and civilian visitors would not get very far into the complex. The office was small, and a sergeant was on the reception desk. Captain Marcus was promptly summoned.

We were in civilian clothes, but I had military ID. God knows what ID Hastings had — a range of choice, as usual, I assume. I introduced myself as Captain Joe Boudreau of the U. S. Air Force, and introduced Hastings as Colonel Hatter-Hatton, retired from the British Army, now working as a consultant.

Marcus was polite. He welcomed us to Drum and said that he was pleased to meet us. But then he handed us their press release, which was essentially the same as the information that had been in the newspaper. I said that we had a few questions.

He replied, quite properly, "Who are you gentlemen representing today?"

I said, "We're here at the request of an agency of the U. S. government." That was sufficiently vague to be mysterious, and also annoying.

Marcus said, "I'll need to see your orders."

Hastings was silent, which showed good judgment. I said, "We don't have orders. We're here more informally."

"I'll need orders."

"We could get them, but we'd like to expedite this."

"Can't do that."

I knew we wouldn't get anywhere without authorization from the Pentagon, but Hastings didn't work that way. As we walked back to our car, he said, "How in the hell do you expect to get anything useful if you just go round asking questions and then accept whatever morsels they choose to give you? You must take the bit in your teeth, dear boy, show some initiative, take a risk, be bold."

I wasn't sure what, if I were bold in this situation, I could do boldly. I had to go find a telephone where I could have a private conversation with Rabbit. He said, "We'll work with the Army. I can get whatever paper they want."

Rabbit enlisted J. J. Angleton, who contacted his counterintelligence colleagues at the Pentagon. They prepared a letter for the signature of the Secretary of the Army requesting that we be given full cooperation in our inquiry into the circumstances of the death. For good measure, the Secretary himself called the commanding general at Drum to express personal interest in the matter. That process took a couple of days, and we went back to Saranac until I received word that the arrangements had been made. The people at Drum, or at least some of them, would know that I was CIA. As I had suggested, Hastings was described as a consultant.

We did another drive to Drum. At our request, we met first with the medical examiner. The framed diplomas on the wall told me that he was a forensic pathologist. He was at least sixty-five years old, maybe seventy, wore civilian clothes but was probably retired military, had thick glasses. He knew who we were before we got there, and he knew what we were interested in.

With almost no preliminaries, I said, "Was it an accident?"

"The bullet didn't come from a mile away."

"How close?"

"Hard to say. Not real close. But I'd estimate not more than 10 yards. The force of it knocked him over, flat on his face."

"He was shot in the back?"

"Yeah."

"Was he shot while he was running away?"

"Could've been. Or he was told to run. Or he was standing waiting to be shot. Hard to say."

"Has the bullet been found?"

"Not yet, but I think it will be. There was a large exit

wound. Large caliber. Probably a .45. They'll be out with metal detectors. Probably are now. But there's other metal in that field."

"Was there an autopsy?"

"No. No need for one. Pretty obvious cause."

"Time of death?"

"He was found at 7:00 a.m. They called me. I got to him just before 8:00. He wasn't moved. I estimated that he'd then been dead at least six hours, possibly ten. So that means he was probably killed sometime between 10:00 pm and 2:00 am the night before."

"Both after dark."

"Yep. Both nighttime."

"And records show it was a dark night."

"Yep. No moon. Cloudy. Dark."

"Thank you, doctor."

"It's what I'm here for."

Then we asked to see the place where he was killed. It was just a big field, open, unremarkable. No buildings. Corn could be grown there. It probably was, once, but there would be a short growing season. Both the shooter and the victim would have been fully visible for more than 100 yards in every direction. That is, they would have been visible if there had been light. No witness had been found.

We also talked to a lieutenant colonel in the Army's Criminal Investigation Division (CID), a part of the MP Corps. He confirmed two important pieces of information that Angleton had already been given by the Pentagon: Major Bradley was assigned to a unit training for cold weather warfare. When training was complete, they would be sent to the Arctic. And he would probably, but not certainly, have had access to the contingency plan that was seen in Moscow.

The CID had interviewed the people Bradley worked with. Hastings and I reviewed the records from all the interviews, and we agreed with the CID conclusion that they hadn't found anything useful. We also agreed on the obvious conclusion. It wasn't an accident. It was murder. The question was why. What was the motive? The why would probably tell us the who. It usually did.

What did we know? The contingency plan had gone to Moscow, and Major Bradley had access to the plan. He could have given it to the Soviets, but why would that get him killed? The Russkies would presumably be grateful. If he was in a position to give them classified documents, they'd want to keep him in place. But maybe he'd outlived his usefulness, maybe they thought he was vulnerable and would expose someone higher in their network of agents, or maybe they thought he was doubling. The Soviets were famously suspicious — and so were we. So maybe the KGB had taken him out. But, if that was what happened, it suggested that another soldier was working for them. Bradley was killed on the base. How easy is it to get access to Drum? How heavily guarded and patrolled?

We were reasonably certain that he wasn't killed by the CIA, the FBI, the US military, or the Blanchard's Corners' police — that is, by someone who didn't like people selling US secrets. And military records established that Bradley was married and, as far as anyone knew, the marriage was happy. He didn't have an ex-wife who hated him. The simple fact that he was killed on the job, not at home, was usually a reliable indicator.

Or maybe he wasn't the spy, but he was onto the person who was. Maybe he was investigating, getting too close, threatening the bad guy.

As we were driving back to Saranac, Hastings said, "It wasn't a professional job. I doubt that it was KGB."

"Why's that?"

"If it were planned, you wouldn't do it that way. The .45 is too big for close work, more difficult to conceal, too loud, unnecessary, too much recoil, less accurate. If you know what you're doing, a .22 will do the work well at close range. And it wasn't an execution shot. If you want results, you don't shoot him in the back. Too many bones to deflect it and miss a vital organ."

"But they killed him with one shot."

"Sure. They blew a big hole in him."

"Probably a military weapon."

"Yes, exactly. Not something the KGB would carry around with them. I think it was a target of opportunity. The shooter was probably someone regularly at the base." Hastings lit a cigarette and rolled the car window down. He said, "If you had the subject out on an open field, under cover of darkness, no one around, why would you have him turn his back? It wasn't planned. Why not a head shot, or the heart? It wasn't professional. Not like KGB."

"Maybe Bradley was running away."

"Yes, maybe he was. If so, he didn't get far."

I said, "Or maybe they told him to run away." The pathologist had suggested that.

"Why would they do that?"

"So it wouldn't look like a professional job."

"You're overthinking this, young Joseph. It has all the marks of an amateur."

I thought there were a number of possibilities. The evidence suggested some of them, but it didn't eliminate many. We would have done better to stay at Drum for a few days, roaming the base, talking to people. But that wasn't the deal Angleton made with the Army.

Investigation, at least in my experience, is mostly a matter of asking questions and watching to see what reaction you get. The questions are usually transparent. It's seldom possible to hide what you're asking about. I don't get many opportunities to use the craft I was taught in spook school—dead letter boxes, codes, inconspicuous shadowing, conspicuous shadowing, invisible ink. Someday I hope to use that stuff, just to liven things up. The purpose of it all, of course, is to gather information, and then, once you have the info, figure out how to put it all together. Linda helps. She's smart, and she's a good observer, maybe better than I am. She sees things.

6

Soon after Hastings and I returned from Drum, John called to arrange a meeting with Linda. He came to our house at a time when William was in school. None of us wanted William to hear the conversation. I was there, but I was in the next room.

Their voices got louder as they talked, and I heard them clearly. It is our house, and she is my wife, so I thought it was okay to listen.

Linda said, "You've been completely absent from William's life for the last five years, and now that he's getting old enough to throw a baseball properly you show up here and play catch with him and want to be his buddy—or, even worse, his father. Joe's been his father for the last five years, more than you ever were, and Joe has done a very good job of it. The judge gave me custody of William."

"The decree could be changed."

Linda said, "Just go trotting back to Sue, John. Perfect name for a lawyer's wife. Tell her we don't need her nail salon here."

John was cool. "Nonsense. The world always needs another nail salon."

At that point, I intervened. John seemed to be keeping his temper better than Linda. I didn't want that—it wasn't my picture of how it should go.

I entered the living room and said, "Hold on there! You don't need to get into it again. You two are already divorced. Linda's married to me now. If she's going to fight with anyone, it should be me."

John said, "Mind your own business, Joe. Linda can take care of herself."

"I know she can. The question is, can you?"

He didn't take that well. He inflated his chest, but nothing came of it except a long, slow exhalation. The air and the bluster had to go somewhere.

He put his coat on and then said, "Mac Denleigh says you work for the CIA."

"I'm an Air Force officer."

"Yeah, but the work you do is CIA work. He tells me there was a shooting and men were killed."

"Where does he get this stuff?"

"He says he has friends in Washington."

"I don't doubt that he has friends in Washington, and he's as full of bullshit as they are. You should contact the CIA about this. I'll bet they'd have a good laugh out of it."

"If your spy crap endangers William or Linda, I'll go into court and get custody of the boy."

"No, you won't."

"I'll open the whole thing up."

"Phooey! You're all talk, John. Go get your nails done."

That last remark was a low blow, and it was also unwise. As it turned out, Linda and I needed John's help.

Fortunately, the quarrel didn't escalate further. He's bigger than I am. He's also a tennis player, so he's probably in pretty good shape. But so am I. It would have been a tussle, not the sort of thing that should go on in a civilized household. But I wasn't going to let him push us around.

John had been offered a good job at the bank. He was going to be the general counsel and a vice-president. He didn't especially like Mac Denleigh, which was reasonable, but it was a good offer. He saw himself moving to Saranac, and he wanted to spend more time with William. I didn't have persuasive arguments against either of those things. Still don't. Linda's view of it was that he'd been irresponsible, absent, and now he was just blowing into town and upsetting our lives, maybe because he wanted to upset them. On other days, she said that John didn't care about us, we were irrelevant. He'd failed in his job at the law firm, and now our lives were just collateral damage.

Linda and I talked about it. I said, "Well, John is William's father. There's no way around it, no undoing it."

"John's a jerk."

There was a piece of paper on the table and I started folding it. It was Air Force stationery that I could use for semi-official letters when I was playing that role, mostly responses to invitations to speak at Flag Day ceremonies, school classes, or Rotary clubs. Important correspondence. I mostly used the stationery for paper airplanes.

After a couple of folds, I said, "William will probably figure out that John is a jerk."

Linda said, "I want William to think of you as his father, not John. You're a better man."

I folded the paper again. "If you don't let William and John spend time together, William isn't going to thank you for that."

She said, "You need to spend more time with William. You worry about Hastings more than you think about me and William."

The piece of stationery became an airplane. "Right now, I do. The job requires it."

"Yeah, Hastings is your job and I'm your wife and William is your son. Are you going to make the same mistake that John made?"

I flew the airplane. It sailed across the room smoothly. A good airplane. I said, "It's even possible that I feel sorry for Hastings now. He has a target pasted on him. But Hastings didn't bring John here. He doesn't have anything to do with the John problem."

Linda didn't like the airplane. I had ignored most of what she said because I didn't want to prolong the argument. That may have been a mistake. One of the life lessons I've learned is that you have to forgive yourself for mistakes, or at least most of them. I've had reason to learn that. I've also learned, however, that your wife doesn't necessarily forgive you.

* * *

John started work at the bank, and Linda and I braced our-selves for a long struggle with him on custody issues and possibly William's education. John liked private schools. We didn't. Linda and I were both products of Saranac's town schools and proud of it.

By this time, the teachers and administrators at the high school knew that Linda was pregnant, and someone had passed the word to Mac Denleigh in his role as chair-man of the school board. Linda wanted to continue teach-ing as long as possible, and, so far as we could determine, the school didn't have an established policy on teaching while pregnant. The principal was okay with it. Besides, Linda is a good teacher and the school needed her. But Denleigh is a man of principle, and the principle was that having a pregnant teacher at the school would be unseem-ly, or disruptive, or some such. The exact harm was never made clear. Maybe Denleigh thought that a visibly preg-nant teacher would remind the students of sex, as if they weren't already obsessed with it. Lust can be a disruptive force—I'll give him that.

In any event, Denleigh assigned John the task of re-searching the law on pregnant teachers, making the case for excluding those teachers from the school. He was also supposed to look for school districts that had excluded them and could be used as precedents. It obviously wasn't bank work, but Denleigh ran the bank, and he could do what he pleased. I'm not sure why he chose to give this assignment to John. He knew, of course, that John and Linda had divorced, and he may have assumed that John felt animosity toward Linda and would be happy to cause trouble for her. Denleigh certainly would have liked to cause trouble for me because of our history of antagonism. Or perhaps he simply valued John's lawyerly skills and powers of advocacy.

Denleigh wanted to impose a mandatory, unpaid "leave of absence," in effect a suspension. John, however, had too much decency for that. Linda was mad at him, but John was, after all, a guy that Linda had chosen to marry—just like me. They may have quarreled, but it was pretty clear to me that he still loved her. Of course, that worried me some. At some level, John wanted to please Linda, to court her. I would have to be careful. Denleigh had misjudged John and I didn't want to make that mistake.

In addition to feeling affection for Linda and not wanting to make life difficult for her, I think John wanted William to have a happy, supportive home. John wasn't going to disrupt that.

Linda and John arranged another meeting at our house, again scheduled at a time when William would be at school. I was in the room with them this time, but I mostly kept quiet. The three of us sat at the kitchen table.

John said, "I talked to Denleigh. The man is a sonofabitch."

Linda said, "What's his problem?"

"According to him, the problem is, in his words, 'the spectacle of a pregnant woman walking around the school in full view of the students.' He says that would be awful."

"So now I'm a spectacle. I don't think I've ever been a spectacle before. Or not that anybody noticed." She was calm, mostly. Then she continued. "In the United States, pregnant women are permitted to appear in public. This is an advanced country, enlightened. Are there still places where they practice confinement?" She got up from the table and paced the room. "So, what does he propose to do about it?"

John fiddled with his coffee cup. "I don't know. Certainly he'll put pressure on the principal. Maybe he'll try to get the school board to adopt a rule banning pregnant teachers."

"Fire me?"

"I don't think he could get away with that. Motherhood is generally respected."

Linda pressed him. "Are you going to help?"

"Sure."

"Help him, or help me?"

"Oh, for Chrissake. Don't be crazy."

John could see that she was working up a head of steam. He knew her. I could see it too.

He said, "I'll help you. But, for what it's worth, I think Denleigh believes what he's saying. He's old school, a traditionalist from another era. He's capable of believing things that you and I would find bizarre. It's possible that he's sincere and not simply being a troublemaker. But what the hell! I'd rather think of him as a troublemaker."

I said, "You'll lose your job."

John pushed his coffee cup away. "Screw it. He doesn't pay worth a damn anyway."

Linda said, "That's the spirit! We'll pin his ass to the wall."

John said, "I'd settle for just having you to be able to teach."

I was liking him better.

Then William came in the door, unexpectedly. Linda said, "You're home early."

William took off his backpack and jacket. "Teachers' meeting. School ended at two today."

Linda again, "I wish they'd let us know when they're going to do this."

William opened his backpack and took out a piece of paper. "They gave us a note yesterday that I was supposed to take home. I brought it home but then I forgot to give it to you. Sorry."

Then William saw John and said, "Hello, Daddy." They both smiled.

It hit me in the gut. I was wounded but I tried to hide it. I probably didn't succeed. My attitude toward John had been improving, but now it wasn't. I knew it wasn't his fault. But I realized then that Mac Denleigh had done me a very big favor. By alienating John, pushing him away, Denleigh made it more difficult for John to connect with William. The only job available in Saranac that was worthy of John's skills, and the only one in his price range, was the one at the bank. Without that job, John would have to go elsewhere. I felt guilty about thinking like that, but I thought it, nonetheless. John was William's father, and it was understandable that he would want to act like it. They would have a natural affinity. Both would feel that they should live up to the father-and-son ideal. But there was a limit to my guilt feelings. After all, I couldn't really do anything to change the situation. Denleigh had chosen to interfere with Linda's job, and John had chosen to defend her. John wasn't going to reverse that position. And I sure as hell wasn't going to ask him to.

7

From the intersection of the Coreys and Stony Creek roads, if you proceed about fifty yards south, there's an undeveloped path to a small pond that probably has a name that I don't know. Every scrap of water in the Adirondacks seems to have some sort of name on some sort of map. The names change. The Stony Creek Ponds were once the Spectacle Ponds. I suppose Stony Creek sounded more outdoorsy, more adventuresome.

The path and the pond are entirely surrounded by New York State land, a small part of the Adirondack Park. Vehicles of the 4-wheel drive variety can handle the path, but it would be a rough ride in an ordinary car. It's a beautiful place to walk, and Hastings decided to do that. A small, modest house on the Coreys Road has a driveway that's a convenient entrance to the path. An elderly couple, the Boxalls, own the house and they enjoy sitting on their front porch observing the passersby. Passersby are valued because there are so few of them.

Hastings later gave me a detailed account of what turned out to be an eventful walk. While walking, he considered the letter Rabbit received, the one that purported to be signed by Hastings but that he hadn't written. We didn't know whether the letter was connected with the murder at Drum, but we thought it might be. Because we had examined the killing at Camp Drum as fully as was possible with the limited resources available to us, he thought the letter to Rabbit might be a more productive entry into the problem. Hastings was also concerned about the KGB's pursuit of him, and he hoped the letter might tip the KGB's hand, but their intention was clear. They wanted to kill him. They had reason to.

Hastings had seen the letter. I showed it to him. He said the signature looked like his but wasn't. Whoever wrote it was smart enough to keep the letter short—it didn't say much, didn't rattle on with blather or particulars that might reveal authorship, but it told Rabbit two things: that Hastings was alive and that he was in Saranac. So, the author had to be someone who knew those things, and very few people knew either of them. That narrowed it down.

One of the people who knew, of course, was Captain Joe Boudreau, but the letter was mailed from Plattsburg before Hastings contacted me. Hastings said I could be trusted and that was why he had come to me. I hoped he really believed it. He might have thought, however, that Rabbit would be happy to get rid of him. But he knew Rabbit wouldn't act on that so long as we were working together. The other people who knew were his wife and children. In the days when he did jobs for the KGB, his communication with his family was handled by a cut-out—that is, by a third party whose identity was well-protected.

Now that he was freelancing, he no longer had access to that service, so he had devised his own system for use in the event of an emergency. I knew that his family was living somewhere in England under an assumed name, but I didn't know where and I didn't know the name. I asked him, but he said (as I had expected), "Need to know, dear boy, need to know. The fewer the better." I didn't need to know. Some member of his family could have let the information slip, of course — the old "loose lips sink ships." So, he considered his family.

His wife, Grace, was nearly his age. On the surface, at least, she was a conventional English housewife. Perhaps she actually was that; he never really told me, but she certainly knew about his work. She had to. They had been married for twenty-six years and they had four children, two boys and two girls. Their oldest child was a boy, Montgomery, known as Monty, recently turned age twenty. The next two were the girls, ages nineteen and sixteen. The other boy, the youngest, was just twelve. Any one of them could have let information slip, and once the information was out in the world it could have migrated. The KGB was efficient and had diverse sources. Hastings thought his family was the place to start unravelling it.

Grace was very unlikely to be the problem. She had been with him for a long time, through good years and bad, and she knew the game. She wouldn't make a mistake. Monty was the most problematic. He was the most aggressive of the children and the oldest, the most likely to be restless. If the KGB wanted to recruit a member of the Hastings family, and if their agents had good information, they would target Monty. The girls, Alice and Margaret, were firmly under the watchful supervision of their mother, and they tended to be compliant and relatively passive. But they were interested in boys, and that could be a problem. The youngest child, Clive, was still largely unformed.

This assessment of the family stimulated further thoughts. Hastings is not the most introspective of men, but as he walked, he evaluated his relationships with his wife and children. He recognized, of course, that his peculiar occupation imposed considerable stress. The family had to move frequently, they couldn't really have close friendships with others, he was away much of the time, and they could never be sure he would return. None of them had asked for that life, they had not volunteered for it. They were trapped by the nature of his work.

Grace had made more of a choice, but she hadn't really known what she was getting into, he thought. There was even a real risk that they could be in physical danger. The family might be attacked as a way of putting pressure on him. Indeed, they were more vulnerable than he was because he had been trained for his work and he was feared. But professional spies don't like to target family because reprisals are almost always possible. If there was enough pressure in a tight situation, however, that preference might be set aside.

He told me that a taste for adventure had shaped the choice of dangerous work; it was a young man's decision. Now, three decades later, he recognized the price he had paid. I think he told me some of this as a warning. I don't know how much of it he actually thought while he was walking and how much he just made up to tell me because it seemed to him that I needed to hear it. He said, "You should think seriously, Joe."

As he continued walking toward the pond, Hastings heard a gunshot and saw sparks and rock chips fly from a big granite boulder about ten yards farther down the road. Instinctively, he dove to the ground and took cover behind a large log. A second shot hit the log. He didn't see anyone for him to shoot at, but he fired his large Webley in the general direction of the sound of the gunshots. He waited. There were no further shots. Apparently, the shooter had retired, or perhaps had been wounded or killed. Hastings looked but found no body or blood.

When he got back to the Sisters camp, where there was a telephone, he called me. I drove to Coreys immediately. The two of us walked over to the path to look for footprints or shell casings, and the Boxalls were still sitting out on their front porch. I persuaded Hastings to let me ask the questions. I wasn't sure what the Boxalls would make of him. He was still carrying the Webley, his daytime gun. He wore it in a shoulder holster, covered by the tweed jacket that he favored both winter and summer, but you could tell he was carrying if you knew what to look for. The Webley required a large holster. After six, he carried a Beretta, which was smaller and easier to conceal.

I introduced myself to the Boxalls. They knew my uncles. I asked them whether they had heard the gunshots.

Mr. Boxall replied, "Sure did. I thought it was probably someone shooting squirrels."

"Did you see anyone coming out from the path?"

He said, "I saw that fella there." And he pointed at Hastings.

I asked, "Anyone else?"

"There was a younger man."

"How young?"

"Oh, I don't know. Maybe 20. Maybe older, maybe younger. He had a car. I asked him, 'Did you hear shots?' He said, 'Saw a fox. Not to worry.' He musta missed it because he wasn't carrying a fox."

I asked, "How tall was he?"

"Oh, about the same as you."

"What color was his hair?"

"Didn't see his hair. He was wearing a hat."

"Was there anything special or different about him?"

"I think he was a Limey."

Mr. Boxall had been in the Army during World War II. He was one of the foot soldiers stationed in England during the buildup of troops for the invasion of Europe—what eventually became the Normandy invasion. He didn't like his time in England.

He said, "I don't like the way they talk. The Limeys." Then again, "I think he was a Limey." And he looked closely at Hastings. Hastings didn't recall having met Boxall, but news traveled in the Coreys settlement. There had probably been curiosity and talk about their new neighbor.

I said, "What kind of car did he have?"

"Ford Fairlane. Gray."

"Did you see the license plate?"

"Nope." Mr. Boxall had nothing further to say.

It was starting to rain, so Hastings and I walked back to the Sisters camp.

He said, "Could have been Monty. Damn!"

I said, "It wasn't much of a description. Not much to go on."

"Right age. Right height. British accent. Narrows the odds considerably. Could be Monty."

I said, "Whoever it was had a car, probably a rental if it was a hit-man here sort-term. The Agency can easily search car rentals, but it would certainly be under a false name. Is there enough probability that it was Monty that it would be worth searching the rentals?"

"Unfortunately, I think it's probable."

"What name would he use?"

"Try the name Ibbetson. He'll probably have papers and a credit card in that name."

"Ibbetson?"

"Yeah. That's the name the family is using in England. Of course, the KGB could have given him other papers."

I needed a phone on a hardened line, one constantly monitored for taps. I had to call Rabbit to report the shooting and request a search of car rentals, but since I would have to give Rabbit the Ibbetson name, the call couldn't be made on an open line without endangering the Hastings family in England. The only hardened lines I knew of north of the Air Force base at Rome were at Camp Drum and at my office at the federal prison.

I drove to my office and called Langley. I told Rabbit about the shooting and asked him to order a search of car rentals under the Ibbetson name within a 300-mile radius of Saranac Lake. Rabbit said, "Is this a Camp Drum problem?"

"I don't know. Might be."

"If I'm going to spend CIA money on it, it had better be a Camp Drum problem."

"In that case, I'm pretty sure it's a Camp Drum problem."

"I'm not going to help defend Hastings against his former employers at the KGB."

"Well, if the KGB is trying to get military secrets from Camp Drum and they know we were there investigating the murder, it would make sense that they would come after Hastings to take him out of the game. He's a significant player, a threat to them, and they know it."

"Okay, Joe, we'll run the rental car records. But don't ask for too much."

"The name is Ibbetson." I spelled it.

"Got it. Don't involve the local police. We don't want to start a panic with people thinking that there are KGB agents in town shooting at people. Moreover, State will be concerned about relations with the Soviet Union. I'll have to consult State."

I said, "Hastings and I won't contact the police. I don't think the Boxalls will either, but they could."

8

I received word at my office the next day that an Ibbetson had registered at the North Pines Motel in Bloomingdale, a few miles from Saranac. I tried to call Hastings at the Sisters camp, but he didn't answer. I looked for him and found him at the Full Moon having a cup of coffee and a bagel, which he insisted on calling a "tough scone." By the time we got to Bloomingdale, about a half hour later, the Ibbetson guest was gone. He had checked out that morning, five hours earlier. The motel owner's description of the guest fit Monty, and the man had driven a Ford Fairlane, gray.

I said I was in the Air Force, but didn't show ID. The motel man said, "He wasn't American."

I said, "Oh? Maybe a Canadian?"

The man said, "Farther away than that."

I didn't need to ask more questions because they had the license plate. The motel notes licenses to help them chase down deadbeats. It was a Florida car and Langley traced the plate number to Thrifty Rent-A-Car.

Several hours later, the Agency's fabulous sources told

us that the car had been returned to Thrifty's office in Plattsburgh at about the time that we were at the motel in Bloomingdale. Monty was half a day ahead of us. And now we didn't know what sort of car he was driving.

* * *

I went to my house and found Hastings there, sitting in his car, waiting for me. Linda and William were at their schools. I invited Hastings in, and we sat in the living room instead of at our usual places in the kitchen. I even gave him the comfortable chair, for which he thanked me politely. His manner was subdued, not typical Hastings. I could tell that he had been drinking, but I offered him a bottle of Guinness. He accepted it, and then didn't touch it.

My dog friend, Mac, said hello to me and then went over to greet Hastings. Mac likes visitors, usually, but he seemed skeptical about Hastings, a little stand-offish. He sensed something wrong.

Mac is William's best friend and the constant companion of all three of us. When we got him as a puppy, we were told that he was part boxer and part German short-haired pointer. He doesn't look like either. He has some boxer markings — white feet, a white chest, a white stripe down his nose — but he doesn't have the body or the coat of a boxer and he has the face of a cairn terrier. He's about forty pounds with long legs and long hair that has never been groomed, grey and brown (what some people call brindle). He doesn't bark – he can, but he chooses not to. He chases his tail when he thinks we need amusement, but he could see that this was not an occasion for exuberance. He's smarter than most of the people I know.

Hastings said, "Someone observed long ago that, if it were possible to die simply by wishing to be dead, there would be many fewer people. Humans would perhaps be extinct. So, you see, I'm a very lucky man. All that's necessary for me to end my life is to relax slightly. If I stopped looking over my shoulder, stopped insisting on the restaurant table where my back is to the wall and I have a clear view of the door, I would shortly exit this morass of misery."

He paused. Then he said, "Maybe I deserve to die."

"You mean because of the people you've killed?"

"No, not because of them. They had to die in order to serve the purposes of one nation or another, so the nations decreed that the deaths were just, proper."

"Then what's the sin that should cost you your life? What have you done that you're unable to forgive?"

"My family's pain. I've caused them an unconscionable amount of pain. That can't be forgiven, certainly not by me." Mac stretched and fidgeted. Hastings continued, "Some children are ruined by mistreatment, by being beaten or put to work in a mine. But far more of them are ruined because they were ignored. I don't mean criminal neglect as the law defines it. They are fed. I mean not talking to them, not listening, not paying attention, not giving them love. People need love, Joe. They need it as much as they need food and water. That's why dogs are so popular. Dogs have a talent for giving love. They have more sense than I do."

He was drunk. That was clear, but it was also clear that having Monty shoot at him had been a nasty shock.

I said, "I think you're a more complicated creature. Drink your Guinness. 'Guinness is good for you.'" That was an advertising slogan.

Mac had been lying next to my chair, but he got up, walked over to Hastings, and sat next to him. Hastings put out his hand. Mac licked it.

I said, "Mac knew you were talking about him. He thought you should do so more respectfully, but he forgave you."

Hastings said, "I'm sorry, Mac."

I said, "How do you suggest we look for Monty? I suppose we should try to talk to him, but that'd be dangerous. He's already shot at you once."

"The boy's my son. And we can't be certain that he's the man who shot at me. I didn't see him, and the descriptions we have are half-assed. There are a lot of six-foot British lads with sandy hair."

"'The car rental? The Ibbetson name?"

"The boy's my son. I owe him something."

"Would your wife be in contact with him?"

"I'm not sure. It's possible. But I think it's more likely that he just went off without telling her, possibly with the help of the KGB. If she thought he was intending to kill me, I'm sure she'd have done all she could to stop him. Despite my eccentricities, she loves me."

"Okay. I'll take your word for it. Can you contact her?"

"With difficulty, yes. I would have to go through a cut-out. There are procedures, authentication codes, codes to be sure I'm not being held captive. It would take some time."

"I don't think we have much time. If Monty was the

shooter, he's already made a move. He won't wait for our troops to arrive. He'll move again, soon. He knows you've been alerted now and that we'll be looking for him. That's why he got rid of the rental car."

"Agreed."

I said, "Does he know about me?"

"If he's working on his own, which I doubt, he probably wouldn't know. If the KGB briefed him, then he'll know. If he's working for them, he'll have been fully briefed and they certainly know. I think we have to assume that he knows about you."

"That means he might be hunting me too, seeking to neutralize me, 'take me off the board,' as the boys at the Agency say when they're feeling lighthearted. I would be easier to find."

"Yes."

"But he seemed to know where to find you at Coreys."

Hastings said, "That also suggests KGB. The shooter, whoever he was, was well-informed."

Mac stretched. I held out my hand. He came to me, and I scratched behind his ears. I said, "How do you go about contacting your wife?"

"It'll be complicated. I have to start the process by contacting Cecil Murphy in Madagascar. Not an easy thing to do. The Malagasy Republic is French territory and inhospitable. Cecil, pronounced Sess-ill, not See-cill, has one arm and one leg and is the most lethal man I have ever known. Murphy, of course, is an Irish surname. Whatever else Cecil may be, he is certainly not Irish. It's complicated."

When Hastings claimed to know people like this guy,

I never knew what to make of it. I couldn't be sure about how much of it I should believe, if any. There was no reason for him to invent the man, except maybe that it suited his fancy to do so.

I said, "Why don't you just use my Aunt Mary in Des Moines as your contact? It would be simpler."

"Perhaps next time, dear boy."

When he started dear boy-ing me, there was reason to watch out.

He added, "I'll work on it."

As Hastings left, he said, "Goodbye, Mac."

Mac wagged his tail.

* * *

That night, after dinner, the telephone rang. The phone was in the bedroom and Linda answered it.

I was in the living room, and she came to get me. "Joe, Rabbit is on the phone."

This was highly unusual. It had been years since Rabbit called me at home in the evening. I sometimes worked at night, but Rabbit didn't.

As soon as I got on, he said, "There's been another killing at Camp Drum."

I said, "Another soldier?"

"Yes."

"What unit?"

"Same unit as the major."

"Cold weather combat?"

"Yes."

79

"What rank was the victim?"

"The report I have is that he was a senior non-com, something like a master sergeant. His name was Rafferty."

"Would he have had access to the contingency plan?"

"That's YTBD, as we say here in Virginia. Yet to be determined."

I said, "Hastings's son, Monty, is still at large. We don't know where he is. The two of us have assumed that he's the man who shot at Hastings, and we thought he was motivated by family conflict, by father-son conflict. But maybe not."

"Yes, maybe not." There was static on the line. He may have put the phone down. Then he said, "Army CID is all over it, of course."

* * *

The next day, Hastings came to my office at the federal prison. He had to be escorted in from the front gate.

He didn't speak until the escort left and I closed the door. He said, "I had a surprise visit. Monty came to the Sisters camp and knocked. I went to the door, armed, and his hands were up. He had a pistol in his belt, but it stayed in his belt."

"What did he want?"

"To talk. Mostly to tell me what a sonofabitch I am. I didn't argue the point."

"Did he want you to kill him?"

"Perhaps. But he should know I wouldn't do that — except to defend someone else."

"Was he the person who shot at you?"

"On the trail at Coreys, yes. He did... He didn't say he was sorry. But he seemed to realize that it was a dumb move, or maybe only that it was dumb to miss. He wasn't clear about it. He's confused. Maybe on drugs. I don't see enough of drugs to be sure about the symptoms. Professionals don't use drugs. If they do, they don't live long."

"Who's he working for?"

"KGB, as I suspected. They recruited him with the ideological bullshit. He claims to believe the full Communist Party line about the nobility of the proletariat and the essential corruption of Western capitalism. He talked about England's atrocities in India. It's impossible to rebut that. What England did was almost as bad as what your countrymen did to the American Indians. He also said that I had killed a lot of people. Again, I wasn't in a position to argue. But his real complaint is that I wasn't a good father—essentially, I was an absent one with an occupation that caused trouble—but he said I was a role model. He said he's a soldier, following the family tradition."

"What does he want you to do?"

"Die, I think. He says that he's been assigned by the KGB to kill me, and he intends to carry out the assignment."

"Does he expect you to just sit still and let that happen?"

"I don't know. I think a part of him would like that because it would be safer for him. He'd continue living. But there's another part of him, I think, that would feel guilt. He's confused. He turned his back on me as he left the house and walked away."

"You could have shot him."

"Yes, easily. Maybe I should have. I could have disabled him, knee-capped him.'"

"Why didn't you?"

"I was stunned by the whole thing. And I didn't want to hurt him. He's my son."

"Did he do the killings at Camp Drum?"

"I asked him about that. He claims that he doesn't know anything about Camp Drum, had never heard of the place, had never been there. I believe him. He seemed genuinely surprised by my question. He said his only assignment is to dispose of me, as revenge for my misdeeds, or 'treachery' as the KGB put it."

"How are you doing on making contact with your wife?"

"I'm still dealing with Cecil Murphy. I haven't managed to get to England yet. The family is well-insulated … I think I probably believe Monty's story now, or at least the essentials of it, but I'd still like to get her perspective on it."

9

I told Linda everything about Hastings and Monty and Camp Drum. She's smart, and I find it helpful to talk things through with her. She asks good questions. Rabbit doesn't like having Linda so involved, but I run the show here in Saranac. Her participation in my work had some negative consequences, however.

I arrived home and found William waiting for me. He said, "Mom's upset. Maybe you can help."

I told him I would try. I found her in the bedroom, lying flat on the bed, crying. Mac was next to her, comforting her. I said, "What's wrong?"

It soon became clear that it wasn't sad crying. It was angry crying.

"Who do you care more about, William and me, or Hastings? You spend all your time worrying about him."

"Well, Hastings is in trouble right now. Somebody took a shot at him." She already knew that.

She said, "A young man trying to kill his father is a terrible thing, but why is it the business of the United States government? Hastings is not even an American and neither is his son, so why should the CIA be involved?"

"Hastings is helping us, so maybe we should be helping him. That's the way things work."

She said, "When we were looking for Bill Reilly, you got shot and it was Hastings who did it."

She was talking about a case from five years before. It was a long, complicated mess, the one where Hastings faked his own death.

I said, "Hastings shot the flashlight out of my hand. The wound wasn't much. He knows what he's doing. He's a professional."

"Yeah, he's a professional assassin. He knows how to kill people, but he sure doesn't know how to stay out of trouble. For all you know, he could still be working for the KGB." Linda got up off the bed and walked over to the window. She looked out. "How in the hell did you manage to get yourself involved with Ev Hastings again? Didn't you learn your lesson the last time?"

"Hastings showed up here, uninvited. Certainly uninvited by me. So far as I can tell, also uninvited by Rabbit. But he's definitely here, and the KGB appears to be after him. Somebody's shooting at him, and somebody wrote a letter to Rabbit signed with Hastings's name. I don't think he wrote it. The KGB is our enemy, no doubt about that. And CIA has responsibility for investigating and resisting operations of the KGB. It's my job. And Hastings didn't endanger you and me five years ago, we did. We put ourselves in harm's way in that mine tunnel. He didn't invite us there. In fact, he tried to keep us out of it. And he persuaded the KGB that I wasn't the person who killed Colonel Kuznetsov. If he hadn't done that, they would have sent a hit squad after me. So I owe him... owe him a lot."

Linda wasn't having it. "Hastings worked for the KGB. I don't know what he did to his son to make the boy so angry, but I think the facts suggest that Hastings can't be trusted. I also think he's a little nuts. You shouldn't be involved in that. I want you to stay alive." She cried more then. Mac was concerned. And William was hearing too much of this. That wasn't healthy. Linda knew that, or she certainly should have.

I said, "William, would you please take Mac for a walk?"

He said, "How many blocks?"

"Oh, I think about a dozen."

William had a hard time persuading Mac to leave. But, after Mac had registered his objection, the two of them went out, with Mac looking back at me reproachfully. I liked to think that Mac didn't fully understand the situation, but maybe he did.

When William and Mac had gone, I said to her, "Linda, I'm surprised at you. Don't you think you're being selfish? It's Hastings's life—and Monty's life, too—weighed against your being able to spend more time with me or get more of my attention. How about common humanity as a reason for me to help Hastings?"

"I'm worried, Joe. I don't want you being shot at. It's not selfish for me to want you to be alive and William to have a father."

"I won't be shot at. Nobody wants to kill me, and I'll be careful. He's not still working for the KGB. I'm sure of that. He's having trouble with his son—who is just a boy, inexperienced, not very dangerous."

That last remark wasn't entirely honest. Monty was dangerous because he was inexperienced. He was unpredictable.

She said, "What does Rabbit think about this?"

"Rabbit knows I'm working with Hastings. And he knows Monty shot at Hastings. And he thinks Hastings can help us with the Camp Drum problem."

"I'm going to call Rabbit."

"No, you are not." I said that calmly, I hope. But I certainly didn't feel calm.

She said, "I've met Rabbit. He knows I was with you at the end of Bill Reilly."

"Yes, that's true, and he had some concerns about it. You're not a CIA agent. You're just married to one. Don't interfere with my job. If you intervene, Rabbit isn't going to like it."

"You're my husband. I have a right to be concerned about you."

"Let me handle it. If you get me fired from the CIA, I'll be very unhappy. And if I'm unemployed, that won't be good for any of us."

"Damn you, Joe. Damn you. I don't want you killed. I love you."

"I love you too, Linda. We can love each other while we do our jobs and live our lives. My job really isn't all that dangerous. The truth is that most of the time it's pretty dull. All I do is talk to people and collect information and then send that to Langley. But once in a while there's some action, a challenge. I welcome that. You know that. It may even have been one of the things you liked about me. I hope it still is. But you can love me while you teach history, and I can love you while I investigate. If the KGB is here now, that's something I'm supposed to investigate."

"You can investigate, but no shooting."

"Okay, but then no shooting at the high school either." I tried to smile. "I don't even carry a gun."

Linda said, "The high school doesn't permit guns, but who knows what's in the backpacks." She kissed me. "I love you."

"I love you too." I smoothed her hair. "William and Mac will be back soon. We don't have time to make love. Let's go to Donnelly's for soft ice cream, the next best thing."

She said, "Wrong time of year. Donnelly's is closed now."

"Also Mountain Mist and Skyline?"

"I'm afraid so."

"Too bad. But I still love you." Saranac is better equipped for relaxation in the summer. Lovemaking, however, goes on year-round. I gave up on the ice cream, but not on the rest of it. "While we're waiting for William and Mac, maybe we should behave like grownups and think about what we know about what's going on."

"That would be a nice change. Businesslike."

"Right! Here goes: First, we know that there were two killings at Camp Drum, both of them obviously murders. One of the victims was a major and the other was a senior non-commissioned officer, both of them from the same unit, troops training for duty in cold-weather combat, principally Alaska. Since access to the base is reasonably secure, the probability is that the killings were done by someone who works at Drum, possibly another soldier, but a sophisticated organization like the KGB could have penetrated from outside the base."

"That's a start. What else have you got?"

"We also know, or think we know, that there's at least one KGB agent operating here. Someone took a shot at Hastings, and his son, Monty, claims to have fired the shot, but we don't know whether that was related to the Camp Drum killings or whether it's a different, separate problem. Monty may or may not be here on a KGB assignment. He may be motivated by family animosities and resentments. We don't, so far, have anything that connects Monty to Camp Drum."

"How could you get that?"

"The first thing we should do is talk to people at hotels, motels, and restaurants near Drum to find out whether Monty was seen there. It would help if I had a photo of him. Hastings doesn't have one with him. If Monty was seen near Drum, that would be helpful, but if he wasn't seen it won't mean much."

"He might not have been noticed. Why would people remember him?"

"His accent would be the biggest problem for him, but otherwise he could probably look like just another soldier."

Linda said, "Why would the KGB send a man here?"

"Well, I think there are at least two possible reasons. They certainly have reason for revenge. Hastings killed several of their men. Or they may be trying to get secret information from Drum. Those two motivations could be unrelated, or they may be connected. Maybe the KGB is only after Hastings and not involved in the killings at Drum."

"If the KGB isn't behind the killings at Camp Drum, then what's going on there?"

"I don't know. Good question. We do know that the Russians have ambitions in Alaska, and both killings were in the cold weather unit, which suggests that KGB has reason to be operating at Drum." I was reluctant to mention Hastings again, but I thought he was relevant. "Hastings is convinced that Monty's been recruited by KGB, but I don't know whether that's right. That may just be Monty's ambition. Even if he is KGB, we don't know whether his assignment is Camp Drum or the killing of his father or both of those. Until we have something that ties Monty to Drum, I think we have to regard the two lines of inquiry as unconnected."

"Do you think the KGB killed those men because the men had discovered the spying, so they were killed to shut them up?"

"That's certainly a possibility. But it's also a possibility that the officers who were killed were the people who stole the contingency plans and gave them to the Russians. Then they were no longer of use. They would have been killed for the same reason—to shut them up. But we have no evidence whatsoever supporting either one of those theories. We're now looking at the bank accounts and the financial transactions of the men who were killed, but we need to tread carefully because we don't want to hurt their families."

"Would the KBG recruit a man's son to kill the father? Wouldn't that be unprofessional? Wouldn't KGB worry that the boy would be conflicted, would have qualms, and might back out?"

"Yeah, they'd think of that, but the KGB doesn't have much to lose on the deal. If Monty kills Hastings, then its mission has been accomplished. They get what they wanted. And if Monty doesn't get the job done, KGB hasn't lost. They haven't spent much money and they'll just assign someone else, probably a more experienced agent, to go after Hastings."

Linda said, "Where are William and Mac? They should be back by now. One of us should get in the car and drive around looking for them."

"Don't worry. Mac will take good care of William." And he did. The two of them arrived home while I was still looking for my car keys.

I asked William, "How was your walk?"

"It was fine. Mac had fun chasing a squirrel. He knows he can never catch one unless he gets it cornered, which is hard to do outdoors, but he gets to run."

"That's okay so long as you're not near streets."

"We were in the park."

I said, "Okay."

Linda said, "Don't you have homework?"

"Yeah, of course I do."

"Now would be a good time to get it done."

William went into his room. Mac went with him. Our business was boring.

* * *

The next day, Hastings was sitting at my kitchen table, all business. There was something he didn't want to discuss at the Full Moon. "I talked to my wife, Martha. It wasn't easy. She's well but worried, worried primarily for the other children. The call was arranged by Cecil Murphy, and it worked, but we had a bad connection. Nonetheless, I was grateful."

There was a jar of unsalted peanuts on the table. I tossed a peanut in Mac's direction. He jumped into the air and took it on the wing. Deftly done.

I said, "Is Monty working for the KGB?"

"Here's what she told me: Monty was seduced by an attractive woman in her mid-twenties, perhaps 25 or 26. He's twenty. She's called Alice and uses the last name Henderson, but Martha says she's not a native English-speaker. Her English is very good, but she has a slight accent, close to a German accent but not quite. Martha says Alice was at our house often, and Martha saw more than enough of her. Monty's been enjoying Alice's favors."

"Is Alice KGB?"

"Martha thinks she is, probably, but isn't sure. Monty and Alice are both Marxists, of course. I'm not sure whether that's a seriously considered view or a matter of convenience. Martha doesn't know whether Monty is working for the KGB, but she thinks he's directed or controlled by the KGB, probably through Alice."

"Alice is telling Monty what to do?"

"That's what Martha thinks."

"Where's Alice now? Is she in England?"

"Martha doesn't know."

"Did Alice travel with Monty?"

"Same answer."

"So Alice could be here."

"Could be."

"Well, that gives us two people to look for, not just one."

Hastings went to the sink, got a large glass of water, and poured it into Mac's bowl. I thanked him.

He said, "I told Martha that Monty is using the Ibbetson name. She says Alice knows him by that name. Since we have to assume that both of them are working for the KGB, Martha and I agreed that the family has to change its name and move once again. But that's very disruptive and expensive, and of course it's especially hard on the children…I'm worried about my family, Joe." His voice was choked. "If the KGB realizes how much I care about the family, they'll attack it. And that affects how I should handle Monty, what I should say to him…. Bad things happen in our lives, Joe. The most difficult part is to learn how to accept it."

Mac took a big drink of water. Hastings nodded at him and smiled. Mac, always the therapist, knew what to do.

I said, "What name will your family use?

"I was thinking of Cipriani."

"You wouldn't make a very good Italian."

"You forget my fondness for spaghetti with butter and oil, not red sauce, accompanied by Montepulciano."

"Why Cipriani?"

"I've always liked Harry's Bar in Venice. It's owned by the Ciprianis."

"Good reason. Not sound from a tradecraft standpoint, but good. Do your children look Italian?"

"No. That way, no one will think Cipriani was chosen as an alias. It has to be their real name."

"A stroke of genius."

"I'll work on a family history. I think we probably came from somewhere in the Alps."

10

As it turned out, we didn't have to look for Monty's friend, Alice.

Hastings was at the Sisters camp, reading Pierce Egan's *Boxiana*. He was pacing the floor of the main room, probably practicing moves that might counter a left jab, and he was visible through windows that faced Stony Creek Road. Bullets came through the windows. Three windows, three bullets. Hastings hit the floor. The Webley was near the door, across the room. He crawled. There was a hasp on the front door that could be locked with a padlock, but it was daytime. The door wasn't locked.

Hastings waited a prudent interval and then speared a fedora on a walking stick and raised the hat to window level, as if someone inside was looking out. Low tech solutions are often best, Hastings says. Nothing happened. There was no reaction from outside. If the people shooting knew who they were shooting at, who the target was, they were unlikely to try entering the house. Hastings had a reputation. He knew that. Having taken their shots, the shooters were likely to run.

Stony Creek Road is a private way, unpaved. It's maintained by the residents. On the day of the shooting, Ken Gilder, owner of Camp Divorce (whimsically named to commemorate an important family event) was filling potholes with crushed stone when he noted a woman in a car. The use of the road is reserved for residents and their guests, and he was certain that she was neither—"There was something about her," he said. Asked to describe her, he said, "Pretty." How old? "Too young for me." He laughed in appreciation of his wit. When more description was requested, he had none to offer, not even when he was asked by neighbors concerned about bullet holes in the Sisters camp.

Two of the Sisters, having been contacted by residents, came to offer solace and to inspect the damage. Hastings assured them that he would repair the damage and that he was unharmed. One of the Sisters asked him to promise it wouldn't happen again. He said, "Don't worry, Sister, the people who did this are unlikely to live long enough to do it again."

She said, "Oh dear."

He said, "Pray for them."

* * *

Hastings and I considered how we might go about searching for the shooter or shooters. I said, "What have we got to go on? Gilder didn't see a gun in the car. No gun anywhere. He can't describe the woman except to say that she's good-looking. No hair color, no skin color, no information on how she was dressed. He says she was driving a car. What make? He doesn't know. What color? Maybe gray, or maybe tan. He says she was young—whatever Gilder thinks of as young. That might be anyone under fifty. The woman could be just some poor tourist who got lost, someone who was sightseeing at the Stony Creek Ponds."

"Don't bet on it."

I said, "The fact is, we don't know who she was, and we don't have enough information to be able to find her."

"When I find Alice, I'll have a conversation with her about whether she was the shooter. I have the description my wife gave me. I'm going to look for Alice."

"She'll probably be with Monty."

"If she is, I'll have the conversation with both of them."

"You should let me help."

"They're kids. Kids playing with fire. They aren't KGB's first team. The first team would not have missed. So where's the first team? At Camp Drum? But the Camp Drum work doesn't look like the first team either. Is the first team here? Or yet to come?"

I said, "Maybe those were warning shots, intended to miss."

"When someone comes to your house and shoots at you through the windows, you ordinarily conclude that they're serious. But the kids had the good sense to shoot from cover. They don't have the ability to confront me, and they know that. It was sensible to shoot from a concealed location. You don't get extra points for doing the job with more risk. The point is to get it done. They didn't do that. They were amateurs. Their location, which I calculate was in the woods on the other side of the road, was too far away to give them a clear view of me inside the house and they didn't have a good angle. Amateurs. I'm going to look for Alice."

"Before you go looking for her, there's something that's been bothering me ever since you arrived here."

"What?"

"Why didn't Rabbit know you're alive?"

"What?"

"When Rabbit received the anonymous letter telling him you were in Saranac, he was surprised, or he pretended to be. But if he really didn't know you were alive, does that mean there's some US intelligence operation Rabbit doesn't know about? Someone in US intelligence, maybe at the CIA or maybe at military intelligence, knew about the contingency plan showing up in Moscow and then recruited you to work on it. But first they'd have to know that you were alive, and Rabbit apparently didn't."

"I couldn't hide perfectly forever. I was going to be recognized sooner or later."

"Okay, so word got back to US intelligence, but why wasn't Rabbit told that you'd been identified, and recruited? Some operation is going on either at the CIA or in military intelligence that's independent of Rabbit. Why's Rabbit being left out of the loop?"

"Do people like him? Do they mistrust him?"

"Rabbit isn't the professional military's kind of guy. He went to the Lab School at the University of Chicago and then to Princeton and Northwestern Law School. Then he followed his father and his grandfather into the family law firm. His grandfather was the president of the Chicago Bar Association in the nineteenth century. Rabbit was a corporate lawyer. He belonged to a lot of clubs."

"How did he end up at the CIA?"

"He belonged to a lot of clubs."

"You mean he was connected."

"Yes, he sure was. Is. "

"So… why's he now out of the loop?"

I tried to answer that. "As I said, he's not a military guy. He had a desk job in Naval Intelligence during the big war, received a direct commission as a lieutenant commander, with no military training—took the Ivy League way in. And his WASP style rubs some people the wrong way. I doubt that he's a favorite of Curt LeMay."

"Government decisions shouldn't get made based on such things." He laughed.

"Decisions in government and everywhere else."

Hastings said, "I think you need to call Rabbit and discuss this. Ask him why, if someone in US intelligence knew I was alive, he wasn't told. If the KGB is here, this is a domestic operation. Camp Drum is in your territory. If someone recruited me to work on the leak from Camp Drum without telling Rabbit about it, that sounds like an intentional insult, a bypass. I think he'll welcome your concern."

"Yeah, he'd like that I picked up on it, and it's a question or an issue that he'll certainly be thinking about. But if he was just kept out of the loop because someone doesn't like him, or because of petty quarrels over turf among the CIA, military intelligence, and the FBI—that is, people wanting to take credit—then Rabbit can deal with that.

Angleton and J. Edgar Hoover are both prima donnas, or worse, but Rabbit can handle it. He's done it before. But, if he was kept out of it because there's some big, super-secret operation going on that they're keeping a very tight lid on, then my involvement would not be welcome. It's possible that you've already told me more than I'm supposed to know … I would be pissing in somebody's porridge, as my old daddy used to say."

"Your father never said any such thing … Even if you do know more than they want you to, it's probably better to disclose that so the brass is aware of it."

He was right, so I called Rabbit. His reaction was quick. As soon as I raised the question about why he wasn't aware that Hastings was alive and had been recruited, Rabbit shut the conversation down.

He said, "I'll have to talk to Louise about it."

When I heard that, I knew it was something he didn't want to talk about on the telephone. His wife's name is Helen, and I didn't know of any Louise. The call was probably being recorded. But I was sure I'd be contacted by him sometime soon.

Rabbit knows my habits. When I stopped by the Full Moon the next day for my morning coffee, the owner told me that a man had called and left a message for "Captain Boudreau." The message was that I should call a particular number in Alabama. That was all. When I called the number, it was answered by a recorded message: "Joe, I think it's time for me to make another trip to your area. I'm going to contact our old friend there." It was a primitive communication technique, but inexpensive and effective, and it required no authorization from anyone and wasn't done on monitored lines.

When I was working on the Bill Reilly case five years before, I met Rabbit at the Adirondack home of a retired general, Caleb Ironwood, known as "Iron Pants" (probably not to his face). He had an old house, the sort of place known in the Adirondacks as a "camp," on Raquette Lake, about an hour and a half south of Saranac. Ironwood had some obscure, semi-secret connection to the CIA, and he was an old friend of Rabbit.

* * *

This part of the story is based on what Linda told me. When she could find the time, given high school teaching and William, she went to a gym for strength training. Her obstetrician told her that the exercise would do no harm and might even be good for the baby. The name of the gym is "Firm All Over," but Linda always called it "Promises, Promises."

She was doing the bench press with free weights, and there was a nice-looking woman, maybe ten or a dozen years younger than Linda, using the bench next to her. Linda had never seen the woman before, but that wasn't unusual. Saranac attracts tourists, and some of them buy short-term memberships in the gym.

Linda was watching the woman out of the corner of her eye, and she could see that the woman was doing a similar workout. Each of them was curious to see how much weight was on the other's bar. But Linda wasn't competing—she had two ten-pound weights on a forty-five-pound bar. Just enough. If the muscles became over-developed, she thought that might interfere with her tennis strokes.

The younger woman monitored Linda's technique, and she now did this more openly. Their eyes met and Linda smiled. The bar had knurled markings, equidistant from the center as a guide for placing your hands. After a few minutes and several lifts, the woman stood, turned toward Linda's bench, and watched. Linda stopped lifting. The young woman said, "May I give you some advice?" Her manner was polite.

Linda said, "Of course."

"It will give you a better exercise if you spread your hands farther apart. You have your hands positioned inside your shoulders. If you place your hands on the bar so that your arms are just outside your shoulders, you will find that the lift is more difficult, but you will develop more than just your triceps. You might want to try it with less weight, perhaps just the bar."

Linda noted that the woman had a British accent, but one with something a little bit off. Linda isn't an expert on accents. I had, of course, told Linda about Monty's girl-friend, Alice, so the woman's accent was of particular interest.

Linda said, "Thank you. I'll try it." She stood to remove some weight from the bar. Then she said, "Are you visiting here?"

"Yes, I'll only be here for a week or two, I think. It's lovely here, but a bit chilly."

"If you think this is chilly, you should wait until January

and February. Then you could see the Ice Palace and the Winter Carnival."

"I know the winter Olympics were held here once."

"Yes, at Lake Placid. Only a few miles away. In 1933."

"Before I was born."

Linda was pleased to be able to say, "Me too." She didn't add, "just barely." Then Linda said, "Are you from England?"

"Yes, I live in Dorset. Do you know the area?"

"No, I've never been to England."

"A pity. Dorset is very different from the Adirondacks, but also quite beautiful. And popular with tourists. It's in southwestern England, on the southern coast."

"It sounds lovely."

"Yes, you should visit." The woman sat on her bench and placed her hands on her bar. She said, "I'm at Lyme Regis. There's a recent novel, 'The French Lieutenant's Woman,' set in Lyme Regis."

"I'm afraid I don't find the time to read novels."

"You're right, of course. Our time should be better spent."

Linda wasn't sure what to make of this, so she changed the subject: "Are you traveling on your own?"

"No, my boyfriend is with me. And some of our friends may join us soon, some people who work for the same company."

"That sounds like fun."

"Yes. I'm sure we'll have a jolly time. Going about to see the Adirondacks."

"Do you enjoy traveling?"

"Oh, yes. It has its rewards."

"Are you from England originally?"

"No, I was born in Switzerland but sent to England for my education, and I liked it so much that I stayed."

"Switzerland! Do you ski?"

"Yes, of course. And we hope to be able to do some skiing here. Are you a native of the Adirondacks and do you ski?" The woman stood and removed the weights from her bar.

Linda said, "Yes to both, born and raised. And anyone with that heritage should ski, both cross-country and downhill."

The woman said, "Perhaps I'll see you on the slopes," and she picked up her gym bag and headed toward the back door.

Linda wanted to follow her, but that was hard to do. She didn't want to be obvious about jumping up and rushing out the door after her. Linda tried to be casual and not move too quickly. Luckily, she had her car keys in her pocket.

A large parking lot behind the gym extends the length of the entire block. There's probably room for fifty or sixty cars. Linda got out the back door just in time to see the woman get into a blue pickup truck near the middle of the block. She was surprised that the visitor was driving a truck, probably a rental.

Linda isn't trained in tailing, but she knows the basic point—don't be seen. She got to her car as the pickup was leaving the lot. The street runs along the Saranac River, and Linda saw the pickup turn north. If the woman was heading out of town, there were basically two options: Route

3 toward Bloomingdale and eventually Plattsburgh; and Route 86 toward Gabriels, Paul Smiths, and eventually Malone. Linda bet on Route 86, which is smaller and less traveled. It was the right choice. She saw the pickup far ahead opposite Lake Colby and the new hospital. Linda hung back so that she would not be visible. That worked until they got past Gabriels. The road is pretty much a long straight stretch, but there are hills, ups and downs that prevent seeing the road far ahead. Somewhere between Gabriels and Paul Smiths, Linda lost her. The pickup must have turned off onto a side road when Linda didn't have her in sight. The woman could have intended that. Or not.

At this point, of course, Linda still didn't know who the woman was. She was suspicious, but that was all. The gym, however, required new members to show identification, so Linda drove back there and talked to the manager, Pierre, whom she had known since their school days. He looked at the records and found that the woman had signed in as 'Alice Henderson.' Langley later determined that the same woman had earlier used the name 'Alina Novak.' And she was not born in Switzerland, although she may have lived there for a time. She might (or might not) have had a residence in Lyme Regis, but she was definitely a Russian, definitely KGB, and almost certainly a daughter of Colonel Pavel Kuznetsov, the KGB officer I found five years before at Axton Landing, where he was floating in the Raquette River with a bullet hole in his forehead.

This all left us with some serious questions. Was it an accident that Alice/Alina had the bench next to Linda at the gym? Just a coincidence? Probably not. But what was the purpose? Did the KGB intend that she be identified? Was the encounter meant to intimidate us? Was it telling us that they knew who Linda was and where they could find her and that they could reach her at any time? Whether or not they intended to intimidate us, it had that effect, to some extent at least. I discussed it with Linda. She is very brave, but we were both concerned about William's safety.

Of course, we still didn't know where Alice and Monty were. Alice's presence at the gym said that they were not exactly hiding. She was out and about, plainly visible in Saranac driving a blue pickup truck. We at least knew that much. And Linda got a good look at the truck. She said it was not a light blue or Navy blue—it was between the two, "royal blue or maybe Yale blue." That was useful information.

Alice, at least, was not operating at Camp Drum, not at present. Did they have more interest in Hastings than in Camp Drum? Were they interested in Drum at all? But it was possible that Monty was at Drum while Alice was covering Saranac, watching us. They could also have been servicing an agent at Drum, which is not a full-time job. The fact that Alice drove as far north as Gabriels suggested that they were not holed-up in Saranac. But Alice may have known that Linda was following her. There were a lot of "buts".

I reported to Hastings that Alice went to the gym, presumably to make contact with Linda, and that the contact was in fact made but Linda didn't give her any information. We weren't sure, however, that Alice went to the gym in order to see Linda. Alice was physically fit and strong, according to Linda, so maybe the gym was just part of her usual routine. I thought we had to assume that the encounter was not accidental. Did the KGB do it just to worry us?

* * *

Hastings was eager to find Monty. It occurred to me that, when your son shoots at you, that's a significant event in your life. You'd certainly want to deal with it, one way or another. Ordinarily, I thought, you'd try to resolve the problem, to come to a more satisfactory understanding with the boy, to heal the breach, at least to the extent that he'd stop shooting at you. But I didn't know how professional assassins dealt with such things. Hastings was still looking for Monty, and we assumed that Monty was still looking for Hastings.

Of course, I also reported to Rabbit. I had a duty to give him the facts, so I did, but I knew Rabbit wouldn't like it. He'd told me in the past that he didn't want Linda involved in my work. Part of that had to do with formal or legal rules—she wasn't an employee of the CIA, and she didn't have any official status. But I think another part of it was that Rabbit was uncomfortable with women, almost mistrustful of them. He was from an older generation when the norms were different, and he may also have had a seriously bad experience with a woman, an experience in which he felt hurt. I don't really know more about that part of it.

As I've said, Rabbit was a corporate lawyer in Chicago before he was recruited by the Agency, and he went to Princeton. You might expect the director of domestic operations at the CIA to be a buttoned-up bureaucrat. If you did, you'd be correct. But the odd thing about him is that he plays jazz piano, often and seriously, and he hangs out with Eddie Condon, Wild Bill Davison, Pee Wee Russell, Jimmy McPartland, and also Marian. He's a complicated guy. You never know what to expect from Rabbit.

I called him. After I reported Linda's encounter with Alice, Rabbit said, "Look, you're a nice guy, Joe, I like you, and you mean well, but you're sometimes insubordinate. Good agents are often strong-willed, and some of them bend the rules. When they do, we have to box their ears to keep them in line. Do you want me to box your ears, Joe? I know how to do it. And let's not have any more of that crap about your wife running errands for us. She doesn't work for the Agency, is that clear? We didn't hire the two of you as a team."

It was a good thing that this was on the telephone. It would have been harder to take in person. I replied, "I didn't ask Linda to go to the gym looking for Alice, or whatever her name is. We didn't know that the woman would be at the gym. Alice just showed up, appeared. She may well have been looking for Linda, probably was, but I can't control or prevent that. I'd like to. I would if I could. I think it puts Linda in danger. But the cold fact is that having the other side target Linda may help us find them. They may come out of hiding. At present, we don't know where they are, and that isn't healthy. But I'll be damned if I'll use Linda as a lure. That won't happen."

He didn't argue with me. I think he saw that what I said made sense.

Linda was eager to help me, but I argued that we owed it to William and our unborn child that she not be in danger. We agreed that she'd simply go about her normal routine, live her life as she had before she ran into Alice at the gym. And be careful.

11

One of the things about my job is that, when there's trouble—like the murders at Camp Drum or the KGB shooting at Hastings—other events and problems in my life don't stop, don't get out of the way so I can concentrate on the new trouble. I suppose that's true of most jobs. At about this time, or shortly thereafter, Linda was told by one of her waitress friends that Mac the banker (not Mac the dog) was organizing a move in the school board to require pregnant students and teachers to take a "leave of absence"– they would not be allowed to attend the school or to work there. Waitresses hear a lot of conversations. Linda started asking other people about it. She found that the teachers at the high school hadn't heard anything. But a reporter who covers local news for the *Adirondack Daily Enterprise* is a friend of Linda's and she's well-connected. She'd heard rumors but didn't know anything definite. She said she would look into it.

The reporter talked to Mac Denleigh about the rumors. He wasn't eager to have a newspaper story about it, so he tried to butter her up, but he didn't know how to go about it. In the end, she interviewed him, and the newspaper published part of the interview. He said that it was "harmful for pregnancies to be seen in the building."

The reporter asked why.

"High school students are obsessed with sex, and a visibly pregnant woman is a constant reminder of sex. The students giggle about it."

The reporter said, "We permit pregnant women to be on the public streets."

Linda was ready to dismember Denleigh. I told her that I would go see him and have another pleasant conversation, but she wanted me to stay out of it. I think she was afraid I'd punch him in the nose. I wouldn't have… unless he hit me first. But I might have provoked him.

So she called John, her ex-husband. He was then working as the house counsel for a small company in Ballston Spa, down near Albany. I had mixed feelings about getting John involved. On the one hand, he's a lawyer, a fairly skillful one I think, and I believe he still has Linda's best interests at heart. And William is his son. On the other hand, I wanted him out of our lives. His affection for Linda is stronger than is comfortable.

John readily agreed to help Linda, as I expected. He came to Saranac and talked to his lawyer friends here, including the one who was working for Mac Denleigh. One of the lawyers, I'm not sure which one, gave him a copy of the draft of the proposed rule that was being circulated among members of the school board.

There were five board members, all but one of them men. Women did not then have a prominent role in Saranac politics. The lone woman was Lucy Zabals, a sixty-year-old retired librarian and the mother of six children. She and her husband were devout Catholics, and both were known to have conservative political views. In conversations with Linda and me, John speculated about the effect of Lucy's religious faith on her attitude toward the proposed rule. He wasn't sure which way it would cut.

Sometimes the proposal was called a rule and sometimes a policy. The draft said, "No student who is visibly pregnant may attend the school or otherwise be present in the school buildings. Any such student will take a mandatory leave of absence until after the child has been delivered or the pregnancy has otherwise terminated, and until the mother has recovered sufficiently to return to classes. No teacher or other employee of the school district who is visibly pregnant shall be present in the school buildings. Any such teacher or other employee will take a mandatory leave of absence for the duration of the pregnancy."

I don't know whether this was written by Denleigh or by his lawyer, a man named Fred Greathouse. Whoever drafted it, it reflected Denleigh's idea that the appearance of pregnant women does the harm. In his view, simply looking at them would cause trouble.

I thought Greathouse was a peculiar name. One old Saranac Laker told me that it was originally a German name, something like "Groshaus," that got translated into Greathouse during World War One. But another local historian told me the name was American Indian. According to this account, the first thing seen when some ancestor of Fred's was born—seen by the mother or father or the elder responsible for naming—was a big house. Logically enough, this became Greathouse. Someone else said that the name was first "Big House," but was changed because that was what the penitentiary was called in Jimmy Cagney and Edward G. Robinson movies. In any case, the name did not fit the man. To me, the name suggested a substantial structure, expansive and solid, perhaps made of stone. But the man was slight. He was tall enough, but rail-thin and shaky.

John went to call on lawyer Greathouse. They argued. Instead of focusing on the broader question of whether the rule was a good idea or good public policy, a question on which Denleigh was never going to agree with us, John was smart and took a more legalistic approach. He focused on the draft.

He said, "What does 'visibly' mean?"

"It means you can see it. Common language, easily understood."

John pursued it. "Visible to whom? To a doctor, to a woman who has been pregnant, to a young child? Does it mean a slight baby bump, or does it mean when the woman looks like she's carrying a basketball? At the fifth month, one person might think a woman was pregnant while another might think that she had just gained some weight. When does the woman have to stop working? Are there going to be objective standards in the rule? Will you specify an increase of four inches in the waist measurement? Is that the standard? Will all the women at the school need to have their waists measured periodically? That would get you into real trouble. It would be fun to watch."

Greathouse was willing to consider changes. "If the word 'visibly' bothers you, we could just get rid of it. We can simply prohibit pregnant women from working as teachers or being students. Everybody knows what pregnant means, so that gives notice of what the rule requires."

John had anticipated that move. "Yeah, they may know what pregnant means, but they may not know when they are. In the early stages of pregnancy, many or most women won't know they're pregnant. That's true for weeks or even months. That's why we have pregnancy tests. If you drop 'visibly' and just say pregnant, you're going to put women in violation of this rule as soon as they walk through the school door, when they don't even know they're pregnant."

"They will certainly know that they've been sexually active."

"So now you want to prohibit all sexual intercourse, even by married teachers? That's pretty radical. And not good for the birthrate."

Greathouse tried talking tough. "Take us to court. I think you'll find that local school boards have a great deal of discretion in setting the rules for how education is to be conducted within their districts."

"Maybe a great deal, but not unlimited."

* * *

It was midafternoon by the time I got to Raquette Lake. The water was close to freezing and there were a few patches of thin ice, but boats were still running. Rabbit was already at General Ironwood's, and he joined the general in the skiff that came to pick me up from the dock near the general store. There was a strong chop on the lake. We had to zig and zag to avoid some ice, but Ironwood was a skillful pilot. He was old, but strong, setting pole straight, and he knew what he was doing.

The Ironwood camp is a two-story frame house built just before the first world war. It sits at the end of the point formed by the Marion River flowing into the lake. The Marion flows in and the Raquette River flows out. The camp was the ideal place for a confidential meeting because no one could get near without being seen. There wasn't casual traffic going by.

It was too cold to sit on the porch. There were uphol-stered chairs in the living room, but the general suggested that we sit at the dining table. I suppose it was more busi-nesslike. During my previous visit, five years before, Mrs. Ironwood had made lunch for us, but she wasn't there this time. She had stayed in Syracuse. I didn't know whether her absence was significant, but I wondered. The general made coffee. He was wearing a plaid wool shirt, which was out of the same book as his trim gray mustache, but Rabbit was making no effort to blend in. He was dressed in his standard business suit and tie, his corporate lawyer uni-form. I assume that was for my benefit. He was, however, playing with his pipe, which made me feel a bit better.

Ironwood and Rabbit had known each other a long time. They worked together at OSS during World War II, back when the general was a major and Rabbit was a lieutenant commander. Ironwood was the right person to talk to. Before he retired from the Army, he worked in intelligence, and he was connected in the relevant places. His daughter was currently working for the Director of Central Intelligence, Richard Helms. She monitored student organizations in the peace and draft resistance movements—the Students for a Democratic Society (SDS), the Student Nonviolent Coordinating Committee (SNCC), the Weathermen, and so on. The explosion of a bomb factory in Greenwich Village in March, the US invasion of Cambodia in April, and the killing by National Guard troops of student protesters at Kent State University in May kept her office busy.

As soon as we were settled, I started the conversation by reporting the shots through the windows of the Sisters camp. That was probably a mistake. I think I would have done better if I had started with the question of why Rabbit hadn't been told that Hastings was being sent to Saranac, but I avoided that because I thought it implied criticism of Rabbit. It might suggest he wasn't trusted, and I didn't want to embarrass him in front of his friend. It would have been painful. But his reaction to my report of the attack on Hastings wasn't good.

He said, "I want you to stop worrying about Hastings and start worrying about Camp Drum. We've had two Americans killed and our military plans are going to Moscow! We know the KGB is here. Get your priorities right. I'm sure the KGB cares more about Drum and our secrets than they do about Hastings. He's a professional assassin, for Christ's sake. He can take care of himself."

"His life is at stake, sir."

"Professional assassins gamble their lives."

"His family is also in danger."

"And that's another part of the bargain that assassins make."

"You don't like the job he does."

"No, I don't."

"Maybe you work for the wrong agency, sir."

"I've been in my job many years, Joe. You haven't. I'm comfortable with the job I do. If you can't get your priorities straight, you should be in another line of work."

"That's a decision for you to make, sir."

General Ironwood stood and faced both of us. "Gentlemen, gentlemen. You've only just arrived. We'll work this out. I know you enough to be sure that you are both well-intentioned and trying to do the right thing. We'll solve this. You are good public servants. Let's start with that clearly established. But tell me why you're so tense."

I looked at Rabbit and he looked at me. Then Rabbit started to talk.

"Caleb, this is a sensitive matter. Sensitive both professionally and personally. I'd like to be able to tell you what's going on, but I'm not sure that I know. I don't really understand it. Essentially, the problem is I haven't been given information that clearly should have come to me. The question is, why? I'm the director of domestic operations. Ev Hastings was sent to the Adirondacks by someone, not by me, to work on a serious security problem at Camp Drum — or, at least, maybe at Camp Drum. A contingency plan for Arctic warfare went to Moscow, possibly from Drum or possibly from the Pentagon. Then later there were killings at Drum, two soldiers murdered. A serious problem. Army CID is all over it, of course, and the FBI is also investigating, but if Hastings is going to be sent into Joe's territory, we should at least be informed. This is a domestic operation. So why was I not consulted, or at least briefed? I've thought about it. Am I in disfavor? If so, why? I'm old; I've been in the job a long time; are they trying to ease me out? Do they want me to retire, to quit? Do they think my judgment is poor? Surely they have no doubt about my loyalty after so many years."

Ironwood's reply pursued a narrow ground, probably the safer course. He said, "How many people know that you don't like Ev Hastings?"

"It isn't a question of liking or not liking him. I've only met the man once, briefly, through Joe. But Joe's right. I don't approve of Hastings. I don't like professional assassins. I don't think it's the right way for us to do our job."

Ironwood looked at his own hands. I wondered whether he had ever strangled anyone. He said, "Yes, we disapprove of assassins, right up to the point at which we need one."

Rabbit made that same noise deep in his throat. In any event, it pretty clearly signaled disapproval.

Then Ironwood said, "I think I know what's going on. You've been, Rabbit, just one victim in a much broader struggle. The problem is Nixon, Henry Kissinger, and General Alexander Haig. I've talked to Beverly about it."

Beverly is the daughter working for Richard Helms.

Ironwood said, "I suspect that the Soviets find Nixon as difficult to figure out as we do. He's slippery. I think they believe that the Vietnam War has sobered us. We now have an active, even strident, anti-war movement. Nixon won the presidency because Hubert Humphrey was too closely tied to Lyndon Johnson, who was badly burned by his willingness to listen to the Joint Chiefs, the Bundy brothers, and so on. Nixon probably won't be eager to follow that path. General Westmoreland is not in favor at the White House right now. Nixon sometimes talks like a hawk and sometimes doesn't. One of the things the Russians would certainly like to know is whether the United States is willing to get into a shooting war in order to prevent Russian moves in the Arctic Ocean and the Bering Strait. This is a question of political will. The American public and American politicians don't have much enthusiasm for more wars. The morale of our military is at a low ebb and public confidence in our military power is at a low ebb. The Soviets probably calculate that we don't want to fight, but it would be costly for them to miscalculate."

Rabbit lighted his pipe.

Ironwood continued, "Nixon doesn't like the CIA. He says it's staffed by 'liberals', not his favorite people. He doesn't trust the Agency. He's bringing intelligence planning and policy into the White House under the National Security Council, directed by Dr. Kissinger. Kissinger is a Harvard theoretician. He doesn't know how to make trains run—run at all, much less on time. Under LBJ, Dick Helms briefed the president, the intelligence briefings. Now, Kissinger briefs the president."

Rabbit asked, "What are they afraid of?"

"Liberals. Liberal policies. 'Weakness.' A professional assassin would suit their tastes."

I said, "They should be reassured by the hiring of Hastings."

Ironwood replied, "Yes, but the Agency didn't hire him, Army Intelligence did." Ironwood knew the story. "Hastings is on the US government payroll because he was identified by a military attaché at our embassy in Poland. The embassy officer saw him in Warsaw and recognized him. He remembered Hastings from an operation in the late fifties and early sixties, when Hastings was on the other side, working for the KGB. The officer reported to counterintelligence in the Pentagon that he spotted Hastings and he was told he was imagining things. Hastings was dead. The officer said, 'No he isn't.' It developed from there. I strongly suspect that the military attaché in Poland was, in fact, another assassin—it was a case of one of ours seeing one of theirs. They recognize one another."

Ironwood posed a question. "What's at stake in the contingency plan that's now in Moscow's hands?" His questions were designed to focus the discussion. He'd done this before.

Rabbit could have answered that, but he looked at me. So, I took the question. "Missile defense. And maybe missile offense. The DEW line is becoming obsolete, and it needs defending. White Alice also needs defense."

The DEW line is a system of radar installations designed to detect incoming missiles, missiles coming in over the Pole or the Arctic Ocean. DEW stands for "distant early warning". White Alice is the military communications network in Alaska. It provides communication to remote locations.

I went on with my comment. "There's also advocacy for building a mobile missile launch system in Alaska—essentially missiles on a railroad so that they can be moved around constantly, like the railroad we had under the Greenland ice shield before the tunnels collapsed. Expensive stuff."

Ironwood said, "Yes, the Air Force is good at spending money." Rabbit smiled. Since I don't spend much time with the Air Force, I didn't take offense.

Ironwood refilled our coffee cups. It's not often that I've had a general bring me coffee. He said, "Of course all of these particular issues arise in a broader political context. Joe, you're supposed to be an Air Force officer. To maintain your cover, you'd better know what a MIRVed missile is. Do you?"

"I always hated tests. Can I be excused if I have a stomach ache?" General Ironwood smiled, sort of. "Okay, MIRV stands for multiple independent re-entry vehicle, a missile with multiple warheads that are separately targeted."

Rabbit said, "Hell, even I knew that."

Ironwood continued the lesson. "Well, if you know that, do you also know the difference of opinion between the Army and the CIA?"

I said, "No doubt there are many differences of opinion."

Ironwood replied, "No doubt. The relevant one concerns the new Soviet missile, the SS-9. NATO calls it 'SCARP.' The CIA analysts think the missile is not MIRVed; DoD intel says that it is. Kissinger likes the more threatening estimate. It would mean more defense, a bigger military.

Mel Laird says that the Agency is exceeding its authority and opposing administration policy."

Melvin Laird, a former Republican congressman from Wisconsin, was the Secretary of Defense.

I said, "What are the biggest points of contention?"

"The Soviet ICBMs is certainly one of them. Another is Chile. The White House doesn't like socialists — our government generally doesn't like socialists. The Agency did everything it possibly could to defeat Allende in the presidential election, but he won, despite our best efforts, so now that he's been elected, we are making a big push to get the Chilean military to remove him with a coup. The CIA, especially Helms, is less enthusiastic about this than Kissinger and Nixon are."

Rabbit wanted to get back to the main point, the thing that was bothering him. He said, "Why's the Army going it alone on Camp Drum, without informing us?"

Ironwood lit a cigarette. He said, "Ellen wouldn't let me do this if she were here. But she isn't." He paced the room. It's not a large room and he circled it twice. "The Army has egg on its face. It wants to try to solve its own problems. They've lost a contingency plan, gone to Moscow. That's a black mark on their security record. And now they've had two killings at Camp Drum. At best, that reflects on command and control. They're in crisis mode. The reputation of the Army within the government is suffering. The White House is watching. Mel Laird is unhappy. Helms is in trouble. So, Rabbit, I don't think you should feel that being kept out of the loop reflects on you, personally. Your domestic operations division is just collateral damage in a much bigger battle between the Pentagon and the CIA—and the White House, the FBI, the National Security Council, and so on. It's interagency warfare. It isn't good for the nation, and it's particularly bad right now, but it's happened before. There are too many goddamn empire builders. Everybody watching out for their careers. Ignore them, as much as possible. Just do your work, as you think it should be done." General Ironwood stood and walked toward the door. He paused. "That being said, don't expect to be thanked for it. The administration may not want integrity. You should give it to them whether they want it or not. It's the right thing to do, in the long run, but you may pay a price for it."

12

I met Hastings at the Full Moon for breakfast. He was wearing the keeper's jacket, as he often did, but today there was a variation. Since the keeper's jacket doesn't have a breast pocket, his colorful paisley handkerchief was now rolled and tied around his neck. I said, "If you come in here next time wearing that damn handkerchief around your head like a hippie, I'm walking out. Why don't you just hang a sign on you saying, 'I'm not from here.'"

"You are a wonderfully charming fellow, young Joseph, but you are sorely lacking in panache. I think the reason you seldom wear your Air Force uniform is that you feel the sky-blue color is too flamboyant."

"I was taught that spies are supposed to be inconspicuous."

"I use a different strategy. My attire is designed to make people turn their heads and look away in embarrassment." He sat at the table. As usual, he chose the chair facing the door. He said, "I find that, when a man is as lethal as I am, he need not advertise his masculinity. That requirement is nicely taken care of."

I said, "You've had a complicated life."

"It didn't seem complicated at the time. I knew what the tasks were, and I carried them out. Sometimes the work was difficult, but that was the challenge." He toyed with his omelet.

I said, " Do you ever have qualms about the killings?"

"Oh my, yes." Hastings appeared thoughtful. He paused. "Of course I do. Indeed, 'qualms' understates the case. I suffer terribly. The guilt raises my blood pressure, produces excess stomach acid, and has even given me nervous dysphasia." He looked up. "And the worst part of it is that it spoils my aim." Then he paused again. "When I get that question, I usually put on a small show of emotion. But I'll give you the compliment of candor. The answer is no. The first time or two, there was a spot of bother, but I got over it long ago. Does that shock you?"

"It does, a bit."

"One should not persist in an occupation for which one is unsuited. Nervous surgeons should go into infectious disease."

"Please don't give me the line about needing to cut out the cancer."

"Touché. But that is the way I feel about it. In my line of work, guilt is counterproductive. Guilt causes hesitation, and that can be fatal." He paused. "Guilt is unlikely to persist. The assassin who suffers from guilt will have a short life. When I blew up German factories, Joe, civilian workers in those plants were killed. Some of those civilians, many of them, were there against their will. Most of them weren't German—many were Poles,

Czechs, Slavs, many of them were Jews. But I blew up the factories and those men were killed. The governments of Britain and Russia gave me medals for that. The men who died—most of them—were innocent. They bore you or me no ill will. The people I've killed more recently deserved it much more than those unfortunate laborers. I did the job I was assigned, was ordered to do. The bombardiers in high-altitude bombing do it all the time. Do we want them to be broken men? Is that what we pray for them?"

I said, "I think you have more regret than you're willing to talk about. It isn't natural to be so content when you look back on your life."

"I'm not looking back." He applied butter and orange marmalade to a slice of whole wheat toast. "Speaking of the future, is Linda going to be able to keep her teaching job while she's pregnant?"

"I'm not sure. John's here now, and he's been working on it."

Hastings said, "That's too bad."

"No. He's been helpful. I think he's a good lawyer."

"Keep him in his place."

I said, "Linda doesn't make the same mistake twice."

"She's smart, but that hasn't made other smart people immune to romantic errors. She's also a good shot, as I recall." He finished his omelet, wiped his mouth with the paper napkin, put the napkin on his plate, and pushed the plate to one side. This was all done emphatically. "Speaking of the same mistake twice, there have now been two killings at Camp Drum. How are you doing on curbing that crime wave? Have you taken repressive measures?" Hastings stood and stretched.

I said, "I thought you were working on that with me."

"Yes, indeed, of course I am. We will get that sorted. There's also the small matter of my son shooting at me. And his girlfriend also. I haven't noticed much progress on that front either." He put a ten-dollar bill on the table, put two ones on top of it, and turned toward the door.

I said, "Where are you going?"

"To Camp Drum. Are you coming? Tempus fugit."

So once again we drove to Drum. We left Saranac at about ten and we arrived there before noon. As we neared Drum, we were stopped, along with all of the other traffic on Route 3, by guards wearing orange vests. They stopped us to permit emergency vehicles to pass—an ambulance, several police cars, and a tow truck. We thought there'd been a serious road accident and we didn't inquire about it. When we got to Drum, we found out what had happened.

Near the eastern edge of the military reservation, which is the extensive property occupied by the base, there's a good-sized lake and a small village, both called Lake Bonaparte. Early that morning a car had driven off a pier and into the lake. A body was found in it. By the time we reached Drum, the authorities had identified the man in the car as yet another soldier who served in the unit training for cold weather combat.

Hastings and I made our way to CID as quickly as possible. That took some talking. There was nobody there who knew us. We had to explain several times who we were and why we were there. I wasn't in uniform and being a junior officer in the Air Force wouldn't have done me much good anyway. The CID didn't greet us with enthusiasm.

And the reception by the medical examiner wasn't warm either. As soon as he saw us, he said, "It's the happiness boys again."

I said, "The happiness boys?"

"Yeah. When a violent death happens around here, who shows up? A fake Air Force officer and a character recycled by the J. Arthur Rank Studios."

Hastings laughed and said, "I'm pleased to find an American who knows about J. Arthur Rank, but I think of myself as more the Cary Grant type—he's a Brit too you know."

The doctor said, "So is Boris Karloff."

I said, "Doctor, could we do some professional work, please? I haven't had lunch."

"Certainly, Captain, what would you like to know?" The medical examiner had retired from the Army as a colonel and he enjoyed calling me a captain, a rank for which I was becoming a little old, but he knew who I worked for.

I said, "I'd like to know who's doing all of the killings at Camp Drum, but I don't suppose you can tell me that."

"Sorry. Not my line of work."

"How about the second death, the non-commissioned officer, was he killed in the same way as the major?"

"Yes. Shot from behind with a weapon of large caliber."

"The same gun used to kill the major?"

"The bullet from the first killing was never found. There are too many pieces of metal in that field. They couldn't do a ballistics match, but the nature of the injuries to the two victims would not be inconsistent with the same weapon having been used in both killings."

Hastings said, "The same killer." It wasn't a question.

The doctor said, "In the United States, we find it difficult to determine, by examining the wound, who pulled the trigger. Perhaps you do it better." He didn't smile.

But Hastings did.

I asked, "What about today's death? The body found in the car that went off the pier?"

"That body just came in a short time ago. The autopsy is not yet complete."

"Was the decedent shot?"

"No."

"Did he die before or after he went into the water?"

"After. There was water in the lungs."

"Can you tell whether the victim was conscious when he went into the water?"

"No. Can't tell. But he was breathing."

"Were there injuries to the body?"

"He was hit on the top of his head and his nose was broken."

"Did someone hit him? Or were those injuries the result of the car crash and the plunge off the pier?"

The doctor said, "I can't tell. So far as I can see, it could have been either."

"Might another examiner have a different opinion?"

"Possibly, but I doubt it."

"Could we see the body?"

"I don't know why not." He stood. "We won't have to walk far." He went across the room to a door in the wall near where Hastings and I were standing. He opened the door into a small examining room. A body covered by a sheet was lying on a table. There were surgical instruments on a trolley beside it.

The doctor pulled back the top of the sheet. He said, "There are some incisions farther down." We saw a young man, white, probably in his mid-twenties, not especially muscular, and only a little battered. The doctor pointed to the skull and said, "Note here," and then at the nose, "and here."

Hastings and I could see the injuries. I said, "May we see the hands?"

"Sure." He exposed the hands on both sides. "Look but don't touch." Then he examined both hands. "I don't find injuries. They aren't broken, and there are no recent wounds or abrasions. Unremarkable."

So far as Hastings and I could see, that was correct. I asked, "How long had the body been in the water?"

"We can't be precise about that—at least I can't—but I'd estimate that it was about three to six hours. Since he was pulled out of the water at about 8:30, that would mean that he went in sometime between 2:30 and 5:30 a.m., when it was dark."

"Did you find alcohol or drugs?"

"I don't have a report on the blood. The tech hasn't done that yet, but there was nothing obvious. I saw that he hadn't had breakfast."

That reminded me that I hadn't had lunch, plus suggesting a sharp pain in the stomach. We thanked him, courteously, and left.

* * *

Hastings and I talked to many people at Drum, people at the top of the chain of command and people at the bottom. We learned that the man in the car was Alan Cross, a private, age 23, from Poplar Bluff, Missouri. He had a spotty military record with various incidents of misbehavior. I asked Langley to look for more history.

The most important information we turned up concerned Cross's relationship with the two men who were shot. I say, "We turned up," but CID had examined the same records, which indicated that Cross complained about both Major Bradley and Sergeant Rafferty, as well as other officers, commissioned and non-commissioned, and the officers, in turn, gave him bad conduct ratings, mostly for insubordination. Almost all of this action took place within the cold weather combat unit, where all three of them served. One witness said that the major and the sergeant "chewed out" Cross and Cross was angry. I asked, "Angry enough to shoot them?"

He said, "You never think that's going to happen."

* * *

Hastings's wife had sent him, by indirect means, a photograph of their son, Monty, and Hastings showed it to several soldiers and asked them whether they had seen him around. Two soldiers, interviewed at different times and places, said they thought they recognized him, but neither was certain about it. Neither was sure where or when he'd been seen. That was not much help. Monty might have been at Camp Drum, presumably making contact with someone, or maybe not.

In my experience, eyewitness accounts produce uncertainty. Written records or numbers are often more productive, but records weren't going to tell us whether Monty had been in the vicinity of Drum. He could have made trips there and returned to Saranac Lake the same day. Even if he stayed in a motel near Drum, we didn't know what name he used. He might have been meeting with a soldier or soldiers at Drum, and we had no way of knowing with certainty whether he had.

Then we received a report that another top-secret document had been found in Moscow. It dealt, as the earlier one had, with plans for the defense of our missile bases in Alaska. There was certainly a spy, and the spy was almost certainly involved with Alaska defense. At what level, we didn't know. The Soviet asset would have to be someone with access to the plans, but that could be either at Drum or at the Pentagon, and the person didn't necessarily need to be a ranking officer. Anyone with access to the right filing cabinet could get hold of the plans. The papers were filed in "hardened" or reinforced filing cabinets, referred to as "safes," locked with built-in mechanisms, not padlocks. But perhaps the combination wasn't necessary. In Pentagon offices and at Drum, the safes were commonly left unlocked during the day, in normal business hours. It was a nuisance to be unlocking and then locking them again every time someone needed a file.

We made inquiries. We found, in the personnel records,

that Cross had worked for a time in an office that had the relevant files.

This complicated matters. There were various possible motives for the killing of Cross—too many of them. One theory, relatively straightforward, was that the deaths—all three of them, we thought—were connected to the secret plans found in Moscow. It was certainly a suspicious circumstance that the violent deaths were all within the cold weather unit, the troops responsible for executing the stolen plans. There were various possible motives, however, some of which pointed in different directions. Cross might have felt that the investigation was closing in on him. Suicide was a possibility. Maybe Bradley and Rafferty suspected Cross of working for the Soviets, and he killed them in an attempt to prevent being caught. It was even possible that all three of the dead men had been working for the Soviets and that there was then a falling-out among thieves. Perhaps Cross feared that Bradley and Rafferty would sell him out—would throw him under the wheels of the on-coming investigation. Or perhaps it was all about money, about who was going to get the biggest share of what the Soviets were paying.

Or, perhaps the KGB, maybe Monty and/or Alice, killed all three of them—the major and the sergeant because they were getting close to catching Cross, and then Cross because he was no longer useful. When caught, he would have incentive to expose the KGB agents and use that as a negotiating chip with the FBI and the Department of Justice. He was a loose end.

I said to Hastings, "How the hell do we sort all this out? It's just a morass of speculation and supposition."

He said, "Not entirely. We know the sequence of the deaths. Cross was the last to die. He could have killed Bradley and Rafferty, but they could not have killed him. The sequence also suggests that, if the KGB did the work, Cross was more valuable to them than Bradley and Rafferty—in fact, the latter two may have been acting in opposition to the Soviets. I think it's likely that Cross was the spy, and the major and the sergeant were in his way, in one way or another. Some of these possibilities or theories are more likely than others. For example, if Monty or Alice were operating on the base, they would've been spotted immediately. So, the KGB wouldn't have used them for that. They're too different from the American soldiers. They're almost as strange as I am. Indeed, for the KGB to have killed all three or even one of the soldiers without being observed is relatively unlikely unless they used a professional assassin employed on the base, probably employed as a janitor, a cook, a secretary, or a carpenter, for example. In other words, not Cross. Cross wasn't a professional assassin. But I don't think any of the killings were done by a professional. They have the marks of an amateur. I've said that from the beginning—too messy, too sloppy. Awkward."

In any event, it seemed likely that the deaths were related to the stolen documents. If both things happened in the same place at the same time, that was probably not mere coincidence. Hastings and I agreed on that. Cross's conflicts with Bradley and Rafferty over relatively minor disciplinary matters hardly seemed sufficient to motivate the killing of two men.

After lunch, Hastings and I drove to Lake Bonaparte to look at the site where Cross died. We saw that the road leading to the pier was made of river stone, rocks the size of pecans and some the size of walnuts with the husks still on. No tires could leave identifiable tracks on those stones, and many vehicles had driven the path. When word got around that a car had gone off the end of the pier, spectators came to see it.

We also saw, however, that the pier was higher than the road—there was a small rise in the road just at the entrance to the pier. I don't call it a hill because it isn't big enough, but it's definitely an incline. A car could certainly drive onto the pier, especially if it was already traveling at five or ten miles per hour when it reached the rise, but one person would not have been able to push a car onto the pier from the road. Two strong men might've managed it. A car stopped on the pier could, we supposed, be restarted, and then driven off. There was a small wooden fence at the end, and Cross's car had broken through it. It would not have taken much to break it. I thought that one man could have pushed a driverless car through the fence and off the end, especially if the car was rolling well before it hit the fence. Hastings wasn't so sure. We both thought, however, that it probably would have been impossible for a person to drive the car up the small rise, onto the pier, and then off the end, jumping or rolling out of the car at the last minute and leaving an unconscious Cross in the driver's seat. That athletic feat would have taxed a stuntman.

It certainly would have been possible for a car or a truck to push Cross's car up the rise, onto the pier, and off the end of it. If Cross was unconscious when his car went off the pier, the job was most likely accomplished by using another vehicle to push the car.

Hastings said, "Why would you hit someone on the head, hard, knock him unconscious, and then push his car off the pier? Why not just finish him off on dry land?"

I said, "Maybe the killer was trying to make it look like a suicide instead of murder."

Hastings waved a hand in the air. "Unprofessional."

I told Army CID that I wanted to see Cross's car. They told me it was in the custody of the State Police, pending investigation. I've been referring to it as Cross's car. Using the vehicle identification number, the police were able to identify it as stolen. If possession is what counts in the law, then perhaps it was his car, but it was stolen. The car had been taken eight months earlier from a canoe repair shop in Victory Village, New York, west of Syracuse. But there was no evidence that Cross stole the car. He probably bought it on the black market.

The car was being held at a State storage yard in Malone, a city straight north of Saranac, near the St. Lawrence. I went there, but Hastings stayed in Saranac and poked around looking for Monty and/or Alice. Maybe he hoped that they would shoot at him.

I told the State Police what I was looking for, which was evidence that another vehicle had pushed Cross's car off the pier. The officer who guided me through the yard to the car was named Flambeau. We talked about our common heritage, and I told him that I had floated on the river in Wisconsin that bears his name, but the subject didn't occupy us long. We turned to commenting on the State's collection of cars. But the great predominance of Fords and Chevys limited the opportunities for comment. Fortunately, we soon came to the car that went off the pier with Alan Cross in it (note that I carefully avoid saying "the car Cross was driving"). It was a Ford, light gray, seven years old.

Officer Flambeau and I both saw, immediately, that there were scratches on the rear bumper. Flambeau, who knew more about these things than I, said he thought the scratches might possibly be matched to particular kinds of cars or trucks—not to a single vehicle, but to a type—for example, to light trucks that have bolts through their bumpers at particular places. The most promising observation, however, was that there was red paint on the bumper and on the panel just above the bumper. Flambeau said it was possible that the paint could have come from the grille of a truck that had been used to push the car. We scraped off a sample. If the red paint could identify the manufacturer of the truck, even perhaps the model, we would then know what to look for. There might be such a truck at Camp Drum or in the immediate vicinity. Most optimistically, we could try to match the location of the paint on the Cross car to the place where paint was missing on the suspect vehicle. The police were excited. So was I.

13

While I was in Malone, letters to the editor started appearing in the *Adirondack Daily Enterprise*. One citizen, who happened to be a member of the board of directors of Mac Denleigh's bank, expressed concern about "pregnancy in the public schools," which, he said, was associated with the decline in teenage morals, a crisis in which rock music also played some ill-defined role. The complaint did not distinguish students from faculty, married women from single, or adults from sixteen-year-olds. The problem, it asserted, was aggravated by the presence in the schools of "pregnant people." Another letter, however, pointed out that the only people who could be pregnant were women, and then wondered whether this might be discriminatory. It was signed by one of Linda's waitressing buddies, but I suspect John had a hand in drafting it.

The reporter who covered local news for the *Enterprise*, Ellie Castwell, wrote stories about the issue. She summarized the proposal that was being considered by the school board and she quoted advocates for the contending points of view. The Reverend Vince Becker, who ministered to a fundamentalist Protestant congregation that included Mac Denleigh at least some of the time, said that sexual relations outside of marriage were a sin and that our schools should do all within their power to discourage such conduct. Then Linda was quoted as saying that she and I were, in fact, married. She offered to show our marriage license. Reverend Becker responded, noting Linda had been "previously married." I wasn't sure what the relevance of that was. I was bracing myself for a claim that her divorce from John was invalid. Kids at school started teasing William about this. William punched one of them. We had to apologize for that.

One of the choice bits was that Harold Hildebrand wrote a letter proclaiming the opinion that sexual relations were "a gift from God." Reverend Becker was disinclined to dispute that view, which enjoyed widespread endorsement, but he said God intended that His gifts be enjoyed only for the purpose of procreation, not for mere transient pleasure. Several people responded that procreation was exactly what the Denleigh proposal was directed against. The newspaper loved it. People looked forward to the next day's paper to see what would come next. This might all have been fun if it had not been so damned personal and if our family's livelihood had not depended on the outcome.

* * *

I got back from Malone in the late afternoon. A short time later, after Linda and William came home from their schools, John came by. He wanted to talk strategy. William was eager to listen, but Linda said he was a blabbermouth. We sent him upstairs to do his homework. He grumbled.

The three of us settled in the living room. John said, "We need to plan a campaign."

Linda grimaced, "What sort of campaign?"

"A campaign to mobilize public opinion," he said.

I said, "How do we do that?" I had some ideas, but I wanted to hear what he would say.

"First we need to decide what our assets are. Don't worry, I don't mean money. I mean assets like people who'll speak up for us, people who have influence, and interest groups or organizations that'll support our position, like churches, unions, and clubs. Organized labor, the Rotary Club, the Chamber of Commerce, and so on. We also need to anticipate our liabilities. Who'll be against us, and which of them will be mobilized?"

Linda said, "On our side, of course, there's the teachers. I know that a lot of them will back us, probably most of them. But religion may interfere in it."

John agreed. "Yeah, that makes sense. What about the union? Will the teachers' union take a stand?"

"There isn't an official teachers' union here, not one that's certified as the bargaining agent. But there's a local chapter of the national union. I'm not a member. I wasn't sure that belonging to it was a good career move. Maybe I should join."

John said, "I'll meet with the head of the local union. You might want to join it first." He stood and did arm exercises as if he was warming up to get ready to pitch. Maybe he was.

I said, "What about the PTA?"

"The PTA here is gun-shy. To avoid splits, they seldom take a stand on anything, except maybe cookie sales," Linda said.

John sat down again. "Couldn't hurt to talk to them. In a friendly way, of course. Pick one of their leaders who's still of child-bearing age."

Linda said, "That would be one of their female leaders, I presume."

John smiled. "Are there any males?"

"Now we remember why we got divorced," Linda said, not in a good-humored way.

John said, "What arguments have we got going for us? As an old lawyer once told me, 'When all else fails, try arguing the merits.'"

Linda said, "How about freedom? In this country people generally like freedom."

I asked, "What kind of freedom?"

John answered, "What the school board rule would do is banish pregnant women, keep them out of public places like the school. That would deprive women of employment opportunities. They won't be paid during the mandatory 'leave of absence.' It would also deprive female students of their education, putting them at a great and continuing disadvantage."

Linda said, "What about arguing that the rule would promote abortion? If a girl wanted to stay in school and complete her education, or a teacher wanted to retain her job and be paid, her pregnancy would have to be terminated. I should tell you, John, that Lucy Zabals, the only woman on the school board, is a very good Catholic."

I said, "That's a great idea, Linda."

John was cautious. "Abortion is a very hot issue, and very divisive. We might not want to get involved with that. It's been called the third rail of politics. Maybe we shouldn't touch it."

Linda said, "I think there are a lot of third rails in politics."

I said, "Maybe we could handle this by not talking about it publicly. Maybe we could just discuss it with Lucy Zabals, or maybe with the priest at her church."

We agreed to try that.

John said, "Who are the other members of the board? What do we know about them?"

Linda said, "I know Ellie Castwell, the reporter who covers local politics for the *Enterprise*. We have an open-meetings law, and Ellie goes to the board meetings. She knows more about the members than any of us do. Could we talk with her?"

John said, "She might be concerned about the appearance of it. Reporters are generally supposed to be impartial. But they aren't always."

Linda replied, "We couldn't ask her to become a member of our team, but she's a feminist and I can't imagine that she would like the proposed rule."

I said, "If all she was doing was giving us public information, maybe she'd be comfortable. That's what reporters do, after all."

John said, "Sounds like a good way to characterize it. It's worth a try."

We did that. Linda made the contact and Ellie agreed to meet with us. I think she regarded us as potential sources of information, so cultivating us was not a bad move for her. And she wanted to be helpful. We all agreed, however, that it would be better to conduct our conversation in private rather than at a public place. We met at our house at seven pm. I ordered pizza.

Ellie knew what the agenda was, and she came prepared. She got right down to business. "There are five members of the board. Denleigh is the chairman, and you already know all you want to know about him. Linda and Joe, you've crossed swords with him before."

We nodded.

Ellie continued, "He's the only member of the board who's not a life-long resident of this area. All the others are natives of Saranac or the immediate vicinity. Linda told me that you also know a bit about Lucy Zabals. Lucy is a nice lady, salt of the earth type. She has several grown children. She's a serious Catholic. This is her second term on the board, five years per term. She was re-elected two years ago, so she's got about three more years until the next election, more or less. She's conservative politically, a Nixon Republican, not a Rockefeller Republican."

John interrupted. "When is Mac Denleigh up for re-election?"

"He's near the end of his term. He'll be up for election again next March if he chooses to run. He has a little more than four months remaining."

"Will he want to run?"

"I have no idea." Then she continued with the briefing. "Earl Flori is the longest-serving member. He's been on the board forever. He must be seventy, at least, but he's still working. Local barber… has his own shop. Owns the building. He's a good listener. Big family. Not political, so far as I know. Doesn't talk much in the meetings. As I said, he's a listener. He's about to retire. This will be his last term, I'm sure." She ate some pizza. "Next in seniority is Wesley Rasmussen, a businessman. Rasmussen Hardware has been in Saranac Lake a long time. His father had the business before him. Wesley must be about fifty. I could look it up. He's in his first term. Don't know whether he'll run again. We don't hold our local elections on the same schedule as presidential and gubernatorial elections. The powers that be didn't want our elections to get overwhelmed by national politics. They also didn't want the big turnout. School candidates don't run with a party label. I don't know Rasmussen's politics, but I'll bet he didn't vote for Hubert Humphrey."

John asked, "Is he a buddy of Mac Denleigh?"

"Don't know." She paused, then she continued. "The final member of the board is Donald McKim. A Scot, a Presbyterian. He sells insurance—business insurance as well as life insurance and home policies. It's a successful business, apparently. He's forty years old, and an avid golfer. Probably knows Denleigh from the country club. McKim's wife is a silversmith. Does nice work. She contributes to Planned Parenthood; may even be a Democrat. If he's one too, he's probably the only one on the board. But I don't know about him. It may be a mixed marriage.... That's the whole story. Are there any questions?"

John said, "Who's the principal at the high school?"

Linda answered, "Rusty Hesseldenz. His given name is Russell, but he goes by 'Rusty.' I think he took Rusty because it makes him sound like a regular guy, one of the boys, maybe a baseball player. But he's about as strait-laced as they come. Rigid, unbending. What you need to do to get him on our side is persuade him about what the Good Book requires."

Ellie Castwell said, "Yeah, maybe so, but I know him. He and I are a little older than you, Linda. I grew up with him. I think the Good Book is just his public face. His job contract is up for renewal next year. He wants the contract renewed, and you can bet he wants a raise. I don't think he'll cross Denleigh."

John said, "He'll back a winner. That's my bet." He paused, "Is he a member of the board?"

Ellie said, "He's an *ex officio* member. He participates in all of their meetings."

John stood. It was his lecture mode. Or oral argument mode. "He's called an *ex officio* member. It's not clear what that term means, except it means that he's there because of his office, his job. In this case, it probably means that as a matter of practice or convenience he comes to the board's meetings. In the discussions at those meetings, he talks." He turned to Ellie. "How are the meetings conducted?"

She said, "Well, they're informal. Things are decided by consensus. It's hard to find anyone who remembers the last time a vote was taken."

John sharpened his question. "Does the principal have a vote? I think the answer is that he doesn't, not as a matter of law. He isn't an elected member of the board. He's an employee of the board. it would be an unusual arrangement if an employee got to vote on the terms of his employment. But whether the law will determine the outcome is another matter."

I said, "Some of the board members may defer to him. It doesn't much matter whether he has a vote if they just do what he wants."

Ellie said, "I don't think he has that much influence. He's not exactly a powerhouse." She picked up her plate. "I'll just finish my slice of pizza and then leave. I don't want to take part in your discussion about what to do with this information. I will say, however, that the rule would not be good for women. Most of our teachers are women, and only women get pregnant. Enough said."

Ellie Castwell is about five feet tall, weighs maybe a hundred pounds, and is tough as shoe leather. She's good company. People like talking to her, which helps her do her job. We thanked her for the information, and she departed.

* * *

We started our lobbying with Donald McKim because John thought he could speak McKim's language. John said that a businessman who sold commercial insurance would be much like the people he worked for, both in his old job and in his new one. John plays golf with his clients, and he talked golf with McKim to warm him up. But McKim's wife had read the *Enterprise* stories on the pregnancy issue, and she had berated him about it. His vote was an easy sell. McKim said, "Laurel would kill me if I voted for that rule. Don't worry about me." We had one vote in the bag.

Then we moved on to Earl Flori. Because he's a military veteran, I wore my uniform, the class A dress uniform, when I went to see him. That made me uncomfortable. It's more formal than my usual clothes, I'm not accustomed to it, and I felt like a phony, using the uniform for our personal benefit. But I'm happy accepting an easy pass from traffic cops. What the hell. We may as well accept what we are offered. In any case, I don't think the uniform helped. As Ellie Castwell had told us, Flori is a listener. He didn't have much to say. He heard me out, politely, but was noncommittal. Then a customer came in and wanted a haircut. We were talking at his shop. It was probably a mistake to talk there, but that was where he offered to see me. End of conversation. I didn't know where he stood.

We tried Lucy Zabals next. John had done McKim, I took Flori, and Linda approached Lucy, one mother to another. But Linda reported that the meeting was difficult. Lucy was Old School. She didn't hold with promiscuity, and Mac Denleigh had done a good job of painting a picture of rampant hedonism at the high school. Lucy was genuinely concerned about the moral fiber of today's youth, but she was sympathetic to teachers like Linda who wanted to have children. Lucy is all in favor of children. At the end of their conversation, Lucy said she thought it might be helpful for her to talk with Father Barolet, the priest at the church she attended.

Linda, John, and I discussed the Lucy problem. We concluded that, since John is a professional advocate, he should make the case to the priest. To prepare, John put together a position paper, an outline for his argument. It built on the letters to the *Enterprise* that called the proposed rule "an attack on procreation." John argued that the Denleigh proposal "incentivized abortion"—to stay in school or keep their jobs, women would need to end their pregnancies.

Mac Denleigh spoke to a Catholic women's group and argued that the proposed rule would benefit the unborn child by removing the mother from school or from her employment so that she could devote full attention to the welfare of "the life within her." He didn't get an enthusiastic reception from the women. One of them worried that the exclusion of pregnant girls from school would deprive unborn children of the nutrition provided by school lunches. Other women agreed with her. Malnutrition, they said, does not produce healthy babies.

Father Barolet heard many arguments, from many parishioners, but he was eventually persuaded that discriminating against pregnant women would endanger innocent life. Abstinence was fine, he thought, but he knew that the flesh is weak. He heard confessions. When innocent life existed, it had to be protected. In the end, Lucy Zabals heeded the wise counsel of Father Barolet. She announced her opposition to the rule. We had a least two votes.

But at that point, before we had an opportunity to talk to Wesley Rasmussen, Ellie Castwell discovered that Denleigh had been buying votes. Rasmussen received a loan from the bank so that he could expand his hardware business and Flori's granddaughter was hired by the bank as a teller. The *Enterprise* quoted John as saying that these facts created the appearance that shareholders in the bank were financing Denleigh's political activities—only "the appearance," mind you.

I asked Ellie, "How did you find out about that?"

She said, "Confidential informants. Secrets." Then she laughed. "No, not really. The Flori girl is in the lobby of the bank, big as life, handling deposits and withdrawals. And the hardware store is going to get bigger. That's going to be pretty obvious too—there's no way to hide it. Reporting isn't rocket science."

I thought but did not say, "Sounds a lot like my work." In investigations, what you need to know is often in plain sight, if you know what to look for. It isn't always obvious. This time it was.

If Flori and Rasmussen voted with Denleigh, those votes plus his own gave him a majority of the board. It probably would not be a popular decision, but he would prevail, 3 to 2. Of course, we weren't certain that Flori and Rasmussen would support the rule. It would look bad if they did, and that might hurt their businesses, but a deal is a deal. Maybe the votes were bought and paid for.

We went back to the drawing board.

John said he could file for an injunction to try to prevent the board from adopting the rule. He also said that he didn't think it would work because the board had not yet even voted on the rule, much less put it into effect, and courts don't ordinarily block government bodies from doing things they haven't yet decided to do. John said he'd have to argue that the injunction was necessary because "irreparable harm" would be done if the board adopted the rule and there was then delay while the various parties litigated the validity of the rule. That would be a hard sell, he said. Even if the court didn't grant the injunction, however, the filing of the motion would slow Denleigh down, get him some more bad publicity, and cost him money for lawyers' fees. If he tried to pay those fees from school board funds, that would give us another issue.

I asked John, "What's the law on this?"

He said, "The law is what the judge says it is."

I replied, "Oh. *Alia iacta est*."

"What?"

"Latin. I was an altar boy. The die is cast—it's a gamble."

John said, "You have me at a disadvantage. I was never an acolyte."

In the motion for the injunction, John also attacked the legality of the rule. The written filing said: "The proposed rule is void for vagueness. If enforced, it would deprive citizens of their right to notice of what the law requires. What does 'visibly pregnant' mean? As our courts have said, it would be necessary for people 'to guess as to its meaning and speculate as to its application.' Moreover, it is overbroad. It reaches and restricts constitutionally protected conduct, including public education and access to employment opportunity free from discrimination on the basis of sex."

Denleigh's lawyer, Greathouse, argued that it was

'speculative' whether the board would adopt the rule, and that the court would be able to consider the legality of the rule if and when it had been adopted. At the hearing, John replied that prompt action was necessary due to exigent circumstances.

The judge said, "What sort of circumstances were those, counsel?"

"Exigent circumstances, your honor."

"Where did you learn that word?"

"I believe I learned it in law school, your honor."

"That figures. Law school has ruined many a good man." The judge was amused.

John said, "But only a very few women."

"True, true." The judge looked at his papers, "The women were ruined by the men who went to law school.... Spell those exigencies out, if you would, please."

"Certainly, your honor. Teachers such as my client, Mrs. Boudreau, are already considering their options. If they want to have children, they may have to seek other employment. If they want to continue teaching, they'll have to move to another town. Or if they can't afford to lose money due to the mandatory leave without pay, they may have to have an abortion. That is an inhumane choice, and it is a choice that may need to be made very quickly. An abortion done at a later stage of the pregnancy may be dangerous to the health of the mother, or the termination may be prevented because it's then too late for it to be legal. For the students, suspension from school is ordinarily a punishment. So, in effect, the girl is being punished for becoming pregnant. Maybe that's what the proponents of this rule want. But then, a moral code would be imposed on pain of punishment—the deprivation of education. I think the court needs to act now, to prevent the harm before it occurs, before the irreparable harm has been done."

The judge leaned back in his chair, looked at the ceiling, and then addressed Denleigh's lawyer. "Mr. Greathouse, if I were you, I'd advise my client to consider this carefully. Tell them not to rush into it. It may be that the proposed rule is a bad idea. It might even be illegal, at least as drafted. But that remains to be determined. An injunction at this point, however, would be premature. The school board hasn't adopted the rule. If it does, then Mrs. Boudreau and her friends can come running into this court asking for an immediate order putting a hold on any action pursuant to the rule. Nothing would happen, nothing would be enforced, until the court has heard and considered full argument on this matter, fully briefed, with full citations of applicable law. Just so there will be no mistake about it, counsel, that means research. Am I understood?"

Both lawyers said yes.

The judge said, "The motion for an injunction is denied."

Back at our house, John said, "If I were Greathouse, I'd get the message. The judge pretty clearly doesn't like the proposed rule. When he said that the injunction was denied, he didn't say 'for now,' but he might as well have. We didn't win, but I think we're ahead on points." John was pumped up. He was feeling good about himself.

I had to leave then to go back to my office. Linda told me later that, after I'd gone, John tried to kiss her on the lips. He also grabbed her around the waist, lower than was welcome. She slapped him, hard.

Mac saw and heard it. He was upset, and this triggered a reaction that was predictable but always surprising. When he's feeling especially good or especially nervous, he chases his tail. He doesn't do this halfway, he goes all out. The more he gets into it, the faster he goes. He plants one leg straight and pushes off, and then plants the opposite leg and pushes, moving him in a circle. He pivots. After he gets warmed up, he does this very fast until he is spinning like a somewhat wobbly top. You hear the force of his straight legs hitting the floor. It's spectacular. If Linda and I laugh or applaud, it clearly pleases him. He now sometimes does it, I think, just to entertain us or get applause. But he also spins to break tension, to relieve stress. This was one of those times. Linda said it was hard to tell which impressed John more, her slap or Mac's spin.

Linda and I agreed that we wouldn't tell John I knew about this. Confronting him would have made it difficult, or maybe impossible, to continue to work with him. We needed his legal services.

When I got home, I could see Mac was upset. He doesn't speak, but he comes close to it. It's a good thing I wasn't there when it happened. John would no longer have been our lawyer. Or he would have been a lawyer without teeth.

14

As I've said, the car that went off the pier into Lake Bonaparte had been stolen several months before from a canoe-building shop west of Syracuse. The shop is owned by Jack McGrievey. I thought we needed to talk to him, especially about the red paint on the rear of the car. I wanted to know whether the paint had come from a vehicle that pushed Cross off the pier, probably a pickup truck, or whether it was on the car before it was stolen. The paint wasn't fresh.

McGrievey wasn't available by telephone. When I first tried to call him, he was on a road trip to Chicago to get a new head for his snare drum, a head made of real animal skin, not plastic. Chicago was the place to get it. McGrievey plays in a jazz band that specializes in 1930s standards, especially those that were in the repertoire of the Boswell sisters and the musicians they sang with.

After he got back from Chicago, McGrievey was always working in his shop when I tried to reach him. His wife was very polite and pleasant, and was happy to take messages, but the shop didn't have a phone and I didn't think messages would work. I decided that I needed to drive there. The shop is about two hours beyond Camp Drum, so I could combine trips to the two places.

The State Police, Army CID, and the FBI had already started looking for a red pickup truck or van. Local police in Watertown, Ogdensburg, Sacketts Harbor, and even as far south as Syracuse were alerted to be on the lookout for a vehicle that fit the description. It could have been farther north, in Canada, but that would have been more complicated. The paint color was described as "cardinal red." The bulletin didn't specify whether this referred to the bird, the clergyman, or the baseball team. The vehicle would have some missing paint on the front.

Then the Agency's lab, to which I sent the paint scraped from the Cross car, notified me that it was not paint used for autos or trucks. It was house paint of a rather common type. That was a puzzle. I told the police, Army CID, and the FBI that they could stop looking for a red pickup truck. They thanked me, sort of. But the fact that it was house paint didn't answer the question of where it had come from, and when. There were scratches on Cross's car to go with the paint. The pusher didn't need to be a red car or truck, but something had pushed or bumped against it, and the red paint, whatever kind it was, probably came from the vehicle or tractor or whatever that did the pushing or bumping. The question was, when. Did it happen when the car was being pushed off the pier? I still needed to talk to Jack McGrievey. I made the trip.

The canoe shop consists of his house, a big lot, and a small outbuilding. The lot is filled with old trees. To get to the shop, I had to make my way through a dozen or more wooden boats under the trees, resting there in various stages of repair. McGrievey is highly articulate, an interesting man. He was pursuing a Ph.D. in English literature when he decided to build canoes. A rational choice. He's big, about my height, and probably a little heavier. He has all his hair. I found him scraping the gunwales of a new canoe with a piece of broken glass. He deftly manipulated the glass to suit the curves in the gunwale.

I said, "Glass?"

He said, "Makes a good scraper."

"Why not just use sandpaper?"

"In finishing wood, you want to use a scraper. Sandpaper, no matter how fine it is, just fuzzes up the fibers of the wood. It doesn't cut them cleanly. You use a scraper to cut the fibers. Fancy canoe shops use stainless steel scrapers, but a sharp piece of glass works better."

"Is broken glass harder on your hands?"

"Have to know what you're doing."

The canoe was beautiful. The gunwales, decks, and thwarts were made of cherry and the planking was cedar. Pacific red cedar. I asked him why he used cedar from the other coast. He said it was more dimensionally stable than Eastern white cedar, which absorbs more water. The canvas would be painted blue. It was a work of art.

I asked him about the red paint on the car. At first, he didn't recall it. The car had been gone for several months, and he'd been paid by the insurance company. The State Police told him that the car was found, but they also told him that it was a total loss. He wasn't trying to get it back.

Then he remembered. A part-time employee at his shop, a handyman, had backed a truck into the rear of McGrievey's car. The handyman's truck was old and rusty, and the man, being a practical sort, had covered the rust with red paint. He used the paint he had available. Some of that got onto McGrievey's rear bumper and the panel above it. No big deal. The red pickup truck was a red herring.

* * *

Hastings and I assessed the situation. Essentially, we were back to the question of how the car happened to go off the end of the pier with Alan Cross in it. Since he had lake water in his lungs, he was almost certainly alive when the car entered the lake, but not necessarily conscious. He had injuries to his head, but expert opinion did not exclude the possibility that those had been caused by crashing through the fence on the end of the pier, or by the impact of the car hitting the water. in short, he could have committed suicide. We hadn't made progress on any of that, and I wanted to know more about whether he had a reason to take his own life. I especially wanted to know whether he had contact with a Soviet spy.

The weather was cold and wet, and it was now dark earlier in the day. It wasn't a pleasant time of year to be moving about. The colorful leaves were off the trees. There'd already been snow in Lake Placid, and there would soon be snow all over the Adirondacks. The snow would be welcome, both for downhill skiing and for cross-country. The snow was good for both tourists and locals.

There was no alternative but to go back to Camp Drum and environs and have more conversations with soldiers. I noticed that security at the entry gate was tighter than it had been on our last visit. The commander of CID at the base told me that the three deaths had put the whole place onto high alert. The deaths were coming fast. There was a certain amount of panic in the command offices, and there were a lot of cooks working on spoiling the broth — several investigative agencies were competing and conflicting. It was an Army problem, of course, and the Army was eager to solve it, itself, but the FBI was also claiming jurisdiction and so was the State of New York. The CIA's stirring of the pot was not welcome. My presence on the base was barely tolerated and the questions asked by a Brit with a vaguely military manner were regarded with grave suspicion and not a little resentment. Drum couldn't figure out what Hastings was doing there. For that matter, I had some questions about him myself.

We heard several theories about Cross and his motivations. A popular hypothesis was that Cross, like Major Bradley and Sergeant Rafferty, had been killed by a Soviet operative on the base, the spy who stole the contingency plans for the defense of Alaska. Proponents of this view, many of them in the Army chain of command, suggested that the three dead men were threats to the Soviet spy — that they, either individually or together (depending on the version of the theory), had discovered the spy's treachery, or at least suspected it — so the spy eliminated them. Hastings was trying to determine whether the operative might have been his son, Monty, or Monty's girlfriend, Alice/Alina, acting as messengers relaying the documents to Moscow.

Another popular version was that Cross had killed the major and the sergeant, and then either Cross committed suicide or someone killed him in retaliation for his murders. If it was the latter, I couldn't figure out how Cross's killer knew that he was guilty. Several law enforcement agencies had not been able to determine that, but maybe the killer knew something we missed.

The CID commander on base told me that Cross was on their list of suspects. He said Cross was a "bad actor," had access to the stolen documents, and that CID was "watching him." But they weren't watching when he drove or was pushed off the pier.

A third theory was that there was a homicidal soldier loose on the base, a serial killer unrelated to the espionage. I referred to this as the "random terror" theory. Proponents of this view tended to be jumpy. People who advocated it and knew about the stolen contingency plans argued that the killings and the spying were two separate problems. Alaska didn't enter into it. But more often the view was held by people who were unaware of the espionage, as they should have been. It was not supposed to be public knowledge.

I saw no convincing or even especially meritorious reason to prefer one of these theories. They were all plausible, or at least possible. We needed to figure out how to start excluding possibilities.

We already knew that Major Bradley and Sergeant Rafferty had given Cross bad ratings and that he had complained about them. Two soldiers told us that Cross was bitter about Bradley and Rafferty and had made insulting remarks about the officers, but the soldiers regarded that as "no big deal." They said Cross was always complaining about something, "It was just his personality," and they didn't take him seriously. They also told me that he only recently bought the car in which he died. They were aware that he had it, but he wasn't permitted to keep a car on the base, so he parked it in a garage in a town nearby. I asked them how much he paid for the car. They said they didn't know.

I thought that, if he had enough money to buy a car, the money might have come from the Soviet Union. But a hot car probably didn't cost much on the stolen car market. In any event, his purchase was untraceable, so I wasn't going to find out how much it cost.

Eventually, Hastings, in his intrepid research in the neighborhood, found (note that I don't say "uncovered") a prostitute who gave us useful information about Cross. When I kidded Hastings about his dealings with the prostitute, he pled innocence and protested that he was a happily married man.

I said, "Yes, a happily married man a long way away from his wife for an extended period of time."

"I'm an assassin, not an adulterer. One of my favorite Thornton Wilder observations is that it's your combination sinners who give vice a bad name."

"Have you used that line before?"

"Perhaps."

In any event, the prostitute told Hastings that Cross, an

occasional customer, was an angry man, erratic, and "probably nuts."

Hastings said, "In my line of work, young Joseph, I have found it useful to have insight into male psychology, but I yield to prostitutes in that area of expertise. I think they are even more needful of such knowledge than I. The woman told me that she had last ministered to Cross about a week before his untimely demise. She said he was, on that occasion, so nervous that he was almost, but not quite, unable to perform."

"Did you pay the prostitute? Will it be on your expense account?"

"I thought that would insult the kind lady. She didn't request payment, and the service provided was not in her line of work. Besides, she said that she liked my accent." He straightened his necktie. "And, by the way, in an assassin's accounting, such expenses are customarily listed as 'reference books,' or sometimes as 'communion wine.'"

In working with Hastings, I picked up many odd bits of information, but I seldom knew which of them to believe. It was like an education at a highly idiosyncratic school. One could never be sure that the formulas would work.

I said, "The prostitute found Cross to be especially nervous a week before he died, which suggests that something or someone was putting pressure on him. The pressure could have come from law enforcement, or it could have come from a Soviet handler. Where do we start?" I turned up the collar of my jacket. It was getting colder. "Technically, Cross was AWOL when he died—he was off the base, and he was at a place where he didn't have permission to be. Did he have a particular purpose to be near Lake Bonaparte, or was he just looking for trouble, or looking for escape?"

"Many young men don't like the Army; that isn't unusual. Perhaps he was planning to meet someone. Monty? or Alice? Do we have other candidates? The nice lady told me that she didn't meet clients on the shore of Lake Bonaparte. It doesn't seem like a promising place for that sort of business."

I went back to his motivation. "It hadn't been reported yet, but he was definitely AWOL. If he got caught, that would get him serious punishment. A sane man wouldn't do that without a good reason."

Hastings said, "The vehicle identification number wasn't altered or eradicated. That's odd. The fact that the VIN was still legible is probably significant. It suggests that the car was not intended for sale, so there'd be no transfer of title, which means that the car was either a junker—parts would be harvested, and the remainder would be sold for scrap—or it would be used as an escape car in a hit-and-run crime, like a bank robbery or a killing, and then abandoned. Assassins often use stolen cars. I seldom have, but others do.

"Cross might have stolen the car for use in killing either the major or the sergeant. But neither of them appears to have been transported after they were killed. Their bodies were found where they died, but one or both could have been picked up elsewhere and then driven to the kill site. Was the interior of the car searched for evidence of other passengers?"

"I don't know. There was nothing about that in the State Police report. The car was pretty wet." I stamped my feet because they were freezing. "In your story, Cross could have found the car after it had been abandoned by the thief. Or he could have bought it from someone who got it that way. There's probably a pretty steep discount in the market for cars that don't have a title. But I don't think it was a junker. The car looked clean."

He said, "Why drive off a pier? Why didn't he just shoot himself, preferably in the head?" One of the people walking toward us flinched and moved aside after "Just shoot himself, preferably in the head." Hastings went on, "It's a military base; there are guns around. The Army controls access to the guns and ammunition, but those can come from outside, off the base. If the theory is that Cross shot both Major Bradley and Sergeant Rafferty, and maybe he did, then why couldn't he also shoot himself? And, if he was determined to use his car to kill himself, driving off a pier is an unusual, uncertain way to do it. Driving head-on into a heavy truck usually works, but that endangers the truck driver, and he might not have wanted to do that. Or there's always driving at a high rate of speed into an immovable object, like a bridge abutment or a big tree. Those are more likely to work than driving off a pier. So why did he choose the nice, soft water? Did he not want to hurt himself?"

"Yeah, I get it. But as you pointed out to me on the day it happened, it's also not the way that a good, sensible assassin would choose to kill somebody."

I thought our best lead was the car. It was a solid fact

that Cross got it recently. That was something we might be able to trace. It was unlikely that he found his way over to McGrievey's canoe shop and stole the car himself. The shop is a long hike from Drum and is off the beaten path. To get there, he would have needed a ride from someone. I was betting that Cross bought the car near Drum. Hastings thought there would be an established stolen car market (he said there usually is) and he thought he could probably find it.

We went back to Saranac. We had already talked to a lot of people at Drum — ranking officers, enlisted men, civilian employees — and also to townspeople in the surrounding communities. It was possible that some of them knew things we hadn't been told, but we were well-past the point of diminishing returns. We thought we could investigate this as well at Saranac as we could at Drum. Which is to say, not very well. Besides, Linda still needed my help with the school board.

15

When I got back to Saranac, John was at our house. Linda was still at the school. John and William were cutting open a cardboard box that held a large number of printed signs suitable for display in store windows. The signs said, "Elect Linda for Our Schools." This came as news to me. I suppose I looked surprised.

William said, "I'm her campaign manager." He beamed.

I looked at John. I said, "And what are you?"

John was all innocence. "I'm just her lawyer."

I said, "Mac will be upset."

"Mac the dog or Mac the banker?"

I said, "Probably both, but you can tell the difference. The dog is much nicer and doesn't wear cufflinks."

William laughed. That helped.

I said, "What happened?"

John replied. "People started talking. I think Ellie Castwell had something to do with it. In her newsgathering rounds, she started asking people, 'Do you think Linda Boudreau should run for the school board?' A lot of them said, 'Sure, that's a great idea.' Then Ellie reported in the newspaper that there was public enthusiasm for Linda's candidacy, a groundswell of public support. But Ellie started it."

I was unhappy. I couldn't tell John or William that the CIA had instructed me to avoid attracting attention and that the rule also applied to wives. Rabbit would be angry.

This was a problem. I needed to put on the brakes without causing a family crisis. I couldn't tell Linda not to run—she wouldn't like that—and it would provide another opening for John, another opportunity for him to appear to be the good guy. William was also a worry. Being the campaign manager was the biggest thing that had happened to him since we built a soapbox racer. He had a very imprecise idea of what an election campaign was, but he'd never been the manager of anything before and he liked the title.

I said, "William, we are going to plan our campaign strategy."

He was eager to get started, but I told him, "He who watches and waits, lives to fight another day."

He could hear the quotation marks around it. "Who said that?"

"Thousands of old geezers."

He smiled but he still wanted action.

I said it would be better for us to bide our time, take the opposition by surprise.

William liked the idea of surprise. John, mercifully, kept his mouth shut.

When Linda got home, I talked to her about it. I asked, "Has there ever been a teacher on the school board before?"

"No, I don't think so. Not that anyone can remember."

"Won't some people think it's a conflict of interest? They may think that the board should be supervising the teachers, holding them responsible, rather than having the teachers supervising teachers."

"I talked to John about that. He said that in a lot of companies, some employees of the company serve on the board of directors."

"There are also employee-owned companies, but the teachers don't own the schools. The public does."

She said, "John also pointed out that the school board is elected. If the voters think a teacher shouldn't be on the school board, they don't have to vote for me. I'm still a citizen and I should have as much right to run for office as any other citizen. Let the voters decide."

I said, "John is very helpful." I opened a beer, poured it into a glass (I'm a formal sort of guy), and let the foam settle. I said, "That sounds right to me." I'm nothing if not reasonable. I added, "As you probably know, however, Rabbit isn't going to like it."

"Yes, I thought of that, but I'll be damned if I'm going to let the Agency run my life. They run yours, that's bad enough. They ought to be satisfied."

This was a bigger topic than I wanted to get into. If Linda and I had high visibility, it would make it impossible for me to work for the Agency. The CIA is supposed to have only a very limited role within the US, very limited jurisdiction, and that's why Rabbit's job as director of domestic operations is so politically tricky. It's sensitive. If Mac Denleigh started spending his money to investigate exactly what it is I do in my work, that would make it impossible for me to do the job. Rabbit would have to get rid of me.

I said to Linda, "Have you talked about this with the principal, Rusty Hesseldenz?"

"No, I haven't. He's a bozo."

"Yeah, but sometimes it's helpful to have a bozo on your side. Let me talk to him."

"Okay. Have fun."

As Ellie Castwell had suggested, Hesseldenz was not a ball of fire. It immediately became clear that he was frightened of Mac Denleigh. Or maybe, as John had predicted, Rusty just wanted to back a winner and he'd been told that Denleigh had the vote sewed up. Hesseldenz had two goals, reappointment as principal and an increase in salary, so the winner of the election was going to be much more important in those decisions than the loser. I asked him to make a public statement, such as a letter to the newspaper saying that the proposed rule would make it harder to hire teachers or might even cause some of them to resign. He told me that he didn't think it would be appropriate for him to "intervene" in a board decision. I pointed out to him that he routinely took part in board decisions by attending the meetings and making comments during the discussions. He said that was different.

Linda was not surprised by my lack of success. She said, "Rusty doesn't have a lot of horsepower. I don't think he has much courage." She paused. "Maybe I could bulldoze him. I could tell him that, if I'm elected, he'll have a hard time."

I said, "Well, that's honest, straightforward, but I don't think it's the best way to handle it. I suggest adopting your 'butter wouldn't melt in my mouth' personality. Say something like you hope that he won't support the Denleigh proposal. If he seems to be too dense to get the point, you might say, 'If I'm elected, it would be awkward for both of us' or 'it would put both of us in an awkward position.' But if he has any sense, you shouldn't need to go that far. The more subtle and low key you are, the better it will be. There's never a reason to make enemies if you don't have to."

She gave it a try with Hesseldenz, but I don't think she had any more success than I did. At most, she may have persuaded him to keep quiet instead of speaking up in favor of the Denleigh proposal.

So, Linda, John, and I had another strategy session. The school board still hadn't voted on the proposed rule. John pointed out that, as far as the court was concerned, the legal situation hadn't changed, and an injunction would still be premature. There was nothing more to be done on that front.

Linda said, "I could take my campaign posters to Rassmussen's Hardware and Flori's barbershop and ask them to put the signs in their windows and see what reaction I get."

John was dismissive. He said, "That isn't going to accomplish anything except to piss them off."

John was probably right, but Linda was tired and tense. She didn't like being a candidate. Some people are built for politics, and some aren't. Or maybe this was just part of the divorce process. She shot back at him. "Go home, John."

He was taken aback. "We had a child together."

"I don't regret the child. I regret the father."

"I'm trying to help you."

"Too little, too late."

It was a scene inside their marriage. It was uncomfortable, I didn't like seeing it, and I knew that, if Linda ran for office and Denleigh went after us, I'd lose my job at the Agency.

After a pause, I said, "I have an idea. Let me talk to Denleigh. Linda, I don't think you'd really like running for office, and I also think it may not be necessary. It may be that all you need to do is threaten to run. Mac Denleigh won't want to lose."

I could see the relief in Linda's face. John could see it too, and he didn't want to cross her, not again. He said, "It's worth a try." Linda nodded.

Then Thanksgiving happened. The schools were closed for a long weekend and Denleigh gave himself a golf holiday in Boca Raton. There was nothing new from Camp Drum. I did the only thing I could—I called Denleigh's office and made an appointment to see him on the day after he returned.

His office was still on the top floor of the bank building, where I'd seen him before. I walked through the lobby straight to the elevator, pushed the up button, and took the car to the top. There are only three floors in the building. Denleigh's receptionist remembered me, and I had made an appointment. She buzzed him and said, "Mr. Boudreau is here." She didn't say "Captain," which pleased me. That rank was getting a bit shopworn. I thought I'd need to do something about it.

Denleigh was seated behind his big mahogany desk, wearing a dark gray banker's suit, maybe the same one he wore when I saw him before. Or maybe it was just the same Brooks Brothers special, with crisp white shirt, tasteful tie, and the same gold cufflinks. He didn't look like the Adirondacks. I'll give him credit for independence. His face was red. Round and red. Hypertension. Maybe too much meat in his diet, maybe too much scotch, or too many mortgage foreclosures. He didn't stand when I entered the room. Our prior conversations had not been cordial. There were guest chairs, but I wasn't invited to sit. I sat.

He said, "Good afternoon, Captain Boudreau. I hope you've been well." He smiled when he said captain.

"I have, thank you, sir." I laid heavy on the sir. "I hope the bank is doing well."

"It's prospering nicely. The Nixon administration will be good for business."

I thought about saying that it would be good for the Pentagon also, but I thought we had already fulfilled the hypocrisy quota for the day.

I said, "I'm here on school board business. Have you thought further about your proposed rule regarding pregnancy in the schools?"

"I have, yes."

"Do you plan to proceed with it? I hear the board hasn't yet been asked to vote on it."

"Yes, of course. We do plan to proceed. I think the board will adopt the rule."

"You're likely to lose some teachers if you do that."

"Mr. Hesseldenz tells me he thinks that will not be the

case. We believe the rule will be popular, both in the school and in the community."

"The local president of the American Federation of Teachers tells me that most teachers don't like the proposed rule and those who are of child-bearing age and want children are likely to resign."

"The Union doesn't represent our teachers."

"I know it's not the bargaining agent, but it reflects the views and the interests of teachers."

"Many people are opposed to the unionization of public employees. You don't have a union in the Air Force do you, Captain?"

"Please feel free to call me Joe." I was wearing civilian clothes. "If you don't want to have a union representing the teachers, you might want to think again about the proposed rule. The union leader told me that he thought the rule would be a great organizing tool, a gift to the union. Many people, and I'm one of them, see the rule as discriminating against women. Most of the teachers are women. Since only women become pregnant, only women and girls will be hurt by this rule."

"I'm not responsible for biology. I can't change that."

"No, but you can make the consequences of it worse, or better." I stood, took off my overcoat, and put it on the chair next to me. I planned to stay a while. "Excluding students from school, suspending them, depriving them of an education, is ordinarily a punishment. Girls who become pregnant will, in effect, be punished for becoming pregnant. The boy who did it will not be punished."

"Maybe wayward girls should be punished. Perhaps

their example will lead to self-restraint, self-discipline. We expect a higher standard of morality from girls than we do from boys. That's probably partly because of biology, but again I'm not responsible for that."

I was getting nowhere. His desk chair was some sort of semi-recliner, made so that he could lean back without falling over. He did that, showing me that he was comfortable. I reacted by turning up the heat.

I said, "If the rule is adopted, we'll go back to the court and renew our request for an injunction. You should ask lawyer Greathouse what he thinks your chances would be. Our reading of the judge is that you would lose. What would that get you? It would cost money and you'd have nothing to show for it."

"I think we have more money to finance this case than you do, Captain."

"Just Joe."

"I prefer to call you Captain. That shows, at least, that I have a sense of humor." He adjusted his chair and leaned forward a bit. "Where are your captain's bars?"

"I'm having them made into cufflinks." Denleigh tried to laugh, but failed. I said, "When we move for the injunction, there'll be a hearing. We'll call Earl Flori and Wesley Rasmussen to testify, and our lawyer will question them about the circumstances that caused them to vote for the rule. They won't lie for you when they're under oath. Perjury is serious business. We'll ask Flori how it happened that his granddaughter was given a job as a teller at the bank, and we'll ask Rasmussen how it came about that he got a big loan to expand his hardware business. They won't like being put on the spot. They'll be embarrassed, and their families will be embarrassed. The families won't like it. And it will be you that put them in that position."

He sat up straight and his red face got redder. He said, "They'll be mad at you."

"Yeah, maybe they'll be mad at me too, but I work for the government, Mac. I'm not asking folks to deposit money in my bank." I figured that, even if he wouldn't call me Joe, I could call him Mac.

"You work for the CIA! I can prove it." He almost shouted.

"In the hearing on our motion for an injunction, it won't be relevant who I work for. You won't get an opportunity to ask about it. The circumstances that caused the board to adopt the rule—specifically, whether the vote was improperly procured and therefore was illegal—will be relevant, but my employment will not."

He jumped up from his chair, strode over to the windows, and looked out over the business district of Saranac Lake. I had seen this move before. He was the lord of the manor surveying the domain he ruled.

He turned toward me. His voice was cold, controlled. "It doesn't matter whether I can question you in court, I can shout it from the rooftops that you work for the CIA. It won't be a secret anymore."

"Yes, you could do that. And, if you did, Linda would run against you in the election. People have been urging her to run. There've been stories in the newspaper about it. Campaign signs have even been printed. She has a lot of support. She'd defeat you and you'd be humiliated."

"I don't know about that. I'd be better financed, and the CIA isn't all that popular. The Vietnam War isn't going well."

"That's true, but which do you think people dislike more, the CIA or Mac Denleigh?" I stood and put on my overcoat. "You're an insider at the country club, Mac, but you're an outsider in the town. You didn't grow up here. Linda did. Her parents and grandparents and aunts and uncles all lived in Saranac. My family too. There are lots of Coyles here and lots of Boudreaus. And other families like us. This town is our people, Mac, not yours. You're not even a downstater, as bad as that would be, not even from the Big Apple, as they like to call it. You're from New Jersey, or some such foreign place. Look around you, Mac, the town will close ranks."

Denleigh stumbled on his way back to his desk. I caught hold of his right arm to prevent him from falling.

The unspoken agreement was that he wouldn't call for a vote on the proposed rule—nobody but him was pushing it—and Linda wouldn't be a candidate for election to the board. It was a standoff. We had the power to humiliate him, and he had the power to make me lose my job. It was essentially like our foreign policy since the end of World War II, mutually assured destruction.

William was disappointed.

16

It was mid-morning at the Full Moon. A few customers were still finishing breakfast, and a few more were drinking coffee and reading the newspapers. John had a table to himself. He was wearing his lawyer clothes, a gray business suit, a white shirt, and a silk tie with regimental stripes. Like most Americans, he had no idea what the regiment was or whether any regiment had such stripes. There was a young man sitting at the counter drinking coffee—wearing jeans and a forest green sweatshirt, with a backpack slung over one shoulder. John caught the kid looking at him. The young man stood, walked over to John's table, and said, "I see you were Scots Guards." He had a British accent of a type John couldn't identify.

John said, "What?"

"Scots Guards. Where did you serve?"

"I don't know what you're talking about."

"The tie. Scots Guards. Can't wear the tie if you weren't in the regiment."

"Maybe that's the UK rule. This is the US. All rules are waived here."

"Where'd you get it?"

"At a clothing store in Albany. Had a stack of them."

The young man said, "Haberdasher should be shot."

"Seems a rather drastic punishment for selling a tie."

The kid pulled out one of the chairs at John's table and sat, uninvited. He said, "I know who you are. You run with people who do killing."

John said, "What?" again.

"Joe Boudreau and his buddy, Evelyn Hastings. They're killers."

For a third time, John said, "What?" This time it had become shrill.

The young man turned his chair so that he was with his back to the counter, fully facing John. He had the backpack in his lap, and he opened the top of it. He leaned forward and put his hand into the backpack and lifted a pistol far enough that John could see it. He said, "This is for them. Don't get in the way."

John wondered whether the kid was drunk or maybe on drugs. He didn't seem to be, but who knew? John said, "I don't understand."

The young man closed his backpack and said, "Hastings and Boudreau are killers. Your government knows about both of them. Boudreau works for the US government and Hastings probably does too."

"Who's this Hastings you're talking about? There's a British military officer Joe knows. I've seen him around." John had stopped eating. He'd lost his appetite.

"He's no British military officer. He's a profession-al trigger man, a killer for hire. He's semi-famous. If you know anyone in law enforcement, anyone who can search records, ask them about Ev Hastings."

"Who are you?"

"I'm his son. My name is Ibbetson now. I'm going to kill the fucker."

The young man pushed back his chair with a considerable scraping noise, stood, and went out the door. John continued sitting at the table, stunned, catching his breath. A waitress came over and said, "Is everything okay, sir?"

John shook his head. "I'll be damned if I know. I hope everything's okay, but I guess I better work on it."

* * *

John had intended to leave that day to drive back to his job at Ballston Spa, but he stayed at Saranac to tell me about the confrontation. He called me at my office, and I told him that I wanted to see him at home. We met an hour later. John was nervous, understandably. He gave me a full account of the unwelcome encounter at the Full Moon.

Then he said, "Joe, if you're doing stuff that's fucking well going to endanger Linda or William, you'll answer to me. It won't be pretty. They'd goddamn hell better not be hurt."

I looked him in the eyes, level and steady. "John, I understand your concern. To be completely honest with you, I'm not entirely able to control the situation. The man who came to your table isn't under my control. I love Linda and William, and I'm doing everything I possibly can to protect them and insulate them, and the resources of the US government are behind me. I'll put my body out in front."

John said, "What the hell is going on? Who the hell is Hastings?"

I told John as much as I could. "Hastings is a professional who has worked in international security ever since World War II. He's been employed by various governments, including ours, mostly undercover. To the best of my knowledge, he's now working for the US government on a secret assignment. The young man who met with you, calling himself Ibbetson, is Hastings's son. That part is true. The son apparently hates his father. I don't know if this is just a personal thing, or whether he's working for someone else. I'm not sure which would be worse. It might be better, safer for us, if a foreign government controlled him."

John said, "It would be safer if Linda and William left Saranac, came to live with me in Ballston Spa."

I think there was a part of John that envied the risk in my job. He bought, to some degree at least, the story that CIA work is glamorous, romantic. He probably thought Linda was attracted by that. Maybe she was. John didn't see the tasks like alphabetizing the Rolodex.

* * *

Then I talked to Linda. We started in the kitchen. "There's something about this that doesn't make sense. If you were trying to kill Hastings and you were serious about it, you'd ambush him. You wouldn't be coming out into the open. But Monty went to the Sisters camp and confronted Hastings, and now he presents himself to John, and Alice confronted you in the gym. Why? A serious killer would use stealth. You'd strike without warning. Hastings is a pro with a long history of staying alive, winning gun battles. You wouldn't be asking for a shootout with him. Monty and Alice started out right by shooting at him on the path off the Coreys Road. That made sense. If you want to kill him, you'd wait for him at a place where you knew he'd be, and you wouldn't be visible. But now they're letting us see them. Why? What are they trying to do?"

I got up from the chair at the kitchen table and moved to a more comfortable one in the living room. Linda came with me. I said, "I remember the first time I ever saw Hastings, five years ago. It was at the Full Moon. He came over to my table and introduced himself. He let me see that he had a gun. That's exactly what Monty did with John. It looks like Monty's copying his father. Shooting from cover on the path at Coreys was the way to do it. But maybe the important thing is that the shots missed. Maybe they intended to miss. Maybe those were warning shots."

Linda said, "Maybe, maybe, maybe. As usual, you're full of maybes. Am I really supposed to answer this?" She stood and paced. "Okay, I will. I think it's a game, at least in part. Maybe they don't want to kill him, they just want to frighten him."

I said, "Why would they do that?"

"To get him to retire, to stop being an assassin, to start being a father, to go home to his wife and family. He has children at home."

"Yeah, two daughters and a young son."

"Maybe this is Monty's gift to them."

"It's a very dangerous game."

"Yeah, but maybe that's like father, like son. Maybe the taste for danger is in the genes."

"Now you're full of maybes."

"Two can play the maybe game."

"Hastings can't go home. The KGB is after him, and they're not going to just let him retire. They'll hunt him down and kill him. If he goes home, it'll endanger his entire family. Monty must know that."

While I thought, I went back to the kitchen and poured a cup of coffee from the pot. I continued talking when I got back to the living room. "Monty's approach to John is too much like Hastings's approach to me five years before. The same m.o., at the same place, at almost the same time of day. Surely Ev didn't tell Monty about it, didn't describe it in detail. It wasn't a big event, not something that he'd tell his son. So how does something so similar happen again? It's uncanny. Are the impulses, the inclinations of the two men, father and son, duplicates? Do they think the same way to that extent? Human motivation is a mysterious thing. Maybe that's why Monty hates his father. He hates what he sees in himself that's the same as his father, the same destructive urges. He sees himself as cursed by his personality, inherited from his father."

Linda exploded. "Jesus Christ, Joe. Too much claptrap psychology. This isn't like you. Let's stick to facts, to what we know, instead of this half-baked psychologizing."

"If you want a significant fact, one is that Monty is Ev's

son. Surely that has some bearing on what he's doing. I'm trying to understand the boy, to get inside his head. You're right that I don't know what he's thinking, but I'd sure like to know. That might help us see the next move. " I walked over to Linda and put my hands lightly on her shoulders. "I'm essentially a detective. I'm supposed to figure out who committed crimes and why, but also and maybe even more important, my job is to prevent crimes, the ones that haven't happened yet. To do that, it would be very helpful to understand his motives."

Linda said, "You're a practical man, Joe. The best prediction of what's going to happen is what's already happened. I've heard you say that."

She had a point, and I retreated a bit. "Maybe the two of them just think the same way. For example, contacting your target, talking to him. That could just be a strategy intended to rattle the target, unsettle him, or intended to mislead him. Maybe it's even taught in KGB school. It's not a dumb move. I'm just upset by the father and son business, the copycat part of it. How much of what we do comes from what we inherited? Did you ever hear 'the apple doesn't fall far from the tree'? I think it's true."

"Maybe it is. So what? The things people do usually make sense, usually serve their interests. So just figure out what they want."

I said, "Sometimes motives seem clear. If a man holds up a bank, he probably did it because he wanted the money. But other times people do things that are self-defeating, that are contrary to their interests. Why do they do it? It's very hard to know what's going on in someone else's head.

Hastings is unpredictable, or maybe the word is capricious. He does things on a whim. Maybe Monty is the same."

Linda said, "Or, maybe the son is competing with the father. Hastings is about as famous as you can be in a secret occupation. Maybe Monty wants to prove that he's better than his father. He wants to win the game."

"Now who's psychologizing?" I said it with a smile. "If you think it's a game, does that mean you don't think he's working for the KGB?"

She said, "It doesn't necessarily mean that. I think it could be partly a game—a game with serious stuff behind it. He could be KGB but still be his father's son."

* * *

Three days passed. Mac the dog, Hastings, and I were walking along the lakefront in Tupper. Linda was teaching. There was a brisk onshore breeze and small whitecaps. The big lake was not yet frozen solid. As usual, the wind was coming from the southwest and real waves were lapping the shore. Mac approached the waves and then jumped back before they could get him. I think it was a contest, a game of skill. Mac knew it was too cold to get wet, and he doesn't like the water, even in summertime. He thinks water is only for drinking—no swimming, no bathing. Since he refuses to swim, he sensibly also avoids riding in canoes or rowboats. He does, however, ride on the Lake Champlain ferries, which are substantial. He walks around on them. He has likes and dislikes, of course, and he tells you about them. But everything I've ever asked Mac to do, he's mastered. I haven't tried him on mathematics. He certainly knows what is more and what is less.

The wind blew away Hastings's words, but his voice was strong, and I heard him. "Sergeant Rafferty was killed on the day that Monty returned the rental car to Thrifty in Plattsburgh. He couldn't have been in both places at the same time, but Alice could have done the killing at Drum, or she could have returned the car while he used their truck to go to Drum. But it's likely they took the car back to Thrifty when both of them were available, so they could leave it there and then both go home in the truck." He paused. "If they were killing someone that day, I think it would crowd their schedule to deal with the rental car at the same time, but maybe they wanted to get rid of the car because it was seen at Coreys … I think it's likely someone else did the killing."

I said, "Cross?"

"Maybe. Probably."

We saw a float plane approaching from the south, in the direction of Long Lake, where there are planes that take tourists for sightseeing rides over the lakes and mountains. The plane was flying low. I thought it was coming in for a landing. But it kept coming. It rose slightly as it approached the shore and headed toward us. The plane flew over our heads, just barely. It may have been fifteen feet off the ground. The people in the cockpit got a good look at us. Maybe that was their goal — to identify us. Mac didn't like it. He growled and barked, which he seldom does.

Hastings said, "Monty."

"What?"

"Monty. In the plane. Take cover."

The plane wheeled, executed a tight turn over the parking lot across the road, and came back toward us over the ballfield, even lower. I thought they were going to crash the plane into us. They came straight for us.

But by that time, we were running toward the nearest cover, which was the restroom building. Unfortunately, that took us closer to the plane. Or maybe that was a good thing—it gave them less time to aim at us, and the pilot had to pull up a bit to avoid lamp posts between the restrooms and the shore.

Bullets hit the ground next to us. And then the plane was beyond us again. They'd missed on that pass.

Mac was the fastest. He got to the restrooms first and ran into the Ladies. Hastings and I didn't argue with him. We followed.

Hastings had his Webley, his daytime gun. I was unarmed, as usual. Mac, sensible fellow that he is, crawled under the sink.

Instead of staying away from the windows, as I did, Hastings used the Webley to break the frosted glass out of one of the side windows and steadied the gun on the sill. It wasn't the tourist season and there was no one else on the lakefront, but the gunfire had attracted the attention of people across the street. Those in the parking lot in front of the stores ran inside for cover, and a few damn fools who'd been inside came out to see what was going on.

It was quiet in the Ladies room. I thought the plane had given up and was going back out over the lake. But then I heard the sound of its engine. It was coming back.

Hastings was ready. When the plane got within range, he took careful aim at the pilot. The windshield shattered and the plane veered suddenly to the left, rose sharply, and then dipped, and swerved again. Bullets hit the building next to the window that Hastings was using. We heard them hit and a couple of them came inside. The walls were only one board thick.

Hastings said, "I think I got him."

"Monty?"

"No, the pilot."

The plane looked like it was going to crash into the motel across the street, burn, and kill several people. But it pulled up at the last minute, rose to a higher altitude, and disappeared over the lake. We don't know where it went from there.

Hastings said, "Must have only winged him. Or maybe glass from the windshield cut him. He could be in bad shape if he wasn't wearing goggles or military glasses."

I said, "We were lucky."

"No, we weren't." He was contemptuous. "It was bloody goddamn nonsense. As soon as we were under cover, we had the advantage. We could see them, and they couldn't see us. Bloody goddamn fools. They're lucky to be alive. Amateurs. KGB is hiring clowns. Children and clowns. What the hell do they think they're playing at? I'm Ev Hastings!"

I said, "Somebody must be watching us, tracking us. That plane didn't just happen to spot us walking along the lakefront. The shooter was told where we were, told by somebody in Tupper, near here, who could see us."

"And communicate with the plane by radio telephone."

"A walkie-talkie."

Hastings grimaced. "A very American term. Almost Disney-like."

I would've laughed if I hadn't still been thinking about being shot at. I said, "We need to locate them so we can track them instead of having them track us. Knowing where the other side is and what they're doing is a big advantage, maybe essential."

Hastings said, "Who was flying the plane? I'm quite sure I saw Monty leaning out of the window, shooting at us. And the last I knew, which unfortunately is not very recently, he didn't know how to fly a plane."

"Maybe the pilot was his girlfriend."

"Maybe. A regular Amelia Earhart. But if she was the pilot, then who was on the ground here doing the spotting for them? How many people do they have here? It's not like the KGB to send an army."

I said, "Maybe Monty and his girl just used money to hire local talent, including a pilot for hire."

"A pilot who ended up with holes in his plane, a shattered windshield, and lucky to be alive. He flew like a pro. I don't think just any old pilot would let his passengers take potshots at people on the ground. This was a very special hire."

"When the pilot reports to his buddies that he limped back home all shot up, that may make it harder for Monty to hire another one."

"Speaking of reporting, there will certainly be a story in the newspapers about the gunfire here. How do you plan to handle that?"

I said, "I think the best you and I can do is play dumb, say we have no idea who was shooting, say that maybe some drunks mistook Mac for a wolf. Rabbit might be able to persuade the newspapers to downplay it because of 'national security,' but he won't like it. And it will reinforce his view that you and I are too visible. Also clumsy."

"In fairness, all we did was go for a quiet, leisurely stroll on the lakefront, an almost deserted lakefront."

"I'll let you make that point."

Hastings said, "Does he want us to go into hiding?"

"Yes, he probably does. He still doesn't know what you're doing here."

"Tell him to talk to the Army. Tell him to talk to counterintelligence. But, in truth, I'm here because the KGB is hunting me, and I'd rather be under your protection than floating loose with nowhere to go."

"You could disappear, as you have in the past."

"It becomes more difficult, the more times you do it. You run out of options."

I said, "I'm going to recruit Linda to help us. We need another set of eyes, especially if Rabbit wants you to be less visible."

The Tupper Lake authorities complained to us about the damage. I assured them that we would have preferred that we not be shot at. I think Rabbit had to pay the city some money for repairs to keep them quiet.

17

When Mac and I got home, William was excited because there was going to be a pageant on the ice in connection with the Winter Carnival and he had been selected to skate with a lighted torch. He wasn't sure whether he was supposed to be a messenger or an elf, but it was a big deal that the torch would be burning. He's a good skater. Unfortunately, I broke the celebratory mood because I had to tell Linda that I was shot at before she heard it from Ellie Castwell or a Tupper Lake teacher. And, of course, there was no way to tell Linda without telling William. I tried to make light of it, but it was hard to make having an airplane fly at us and shoot at us sound like an ordinary everyday outing.

Linda was sure that it was Hastings's fault. I said he wasn't any more at fault than I was, or Mac. Mac raised his head and looked at me. Did he shake his head, or did I imagine it?

Linda said, "If Monty was in the airplane, that means they were hunting Hastings and shooting at him. Having him around here is endangering you. I don't want him here. You can't deny that you're in danger."

"I don't deny it, but I would've been in more danger today if Hastings hadn't been with me. He's the one who made them go away. And a certain amount of danger is part of my job. I work for the Agency. You knew that when you married me, and in international security the stakes are high. Both sides are willing to take risks."

"I want you to send Hastings away."

"I can't do that. I'm working with him on the Camp Drum killings and a possible breach of security there, an important breach. I have a duty to protect him and defend us against the KGB."

"A son shooting at his father isn't a matter of national security and Monty isn't the KGB."

"Hastings thinks he is. So does US intelligence. Maybe KGB was able to recruit Monty because he hates his father, but that suits the KGB's purposes and now he's working for them. They're happy to use him. And what about the woman who contacted you at the gym? Langley thinks she's almost certainly KGB."

"How do they know?"

"They're an intelligence gathering organization, a very big one and a very good one. With all respect, Linda, they know more about it than you do." I paused. "When things begin to get a little dangerous, it's time for me to do my job."

She said, "And get shot at." She left the room.

I thought it wasn't wise to press the argument any further that day. She was upset, understandably. Being shot at was an even bigger deal than William's carrying a lighted torch while on ice skates.

The next day I told Linda that, if she wanted to protect me, she could help by gathering information. I pointed out that we didn't know where Monty and his girlfriend were, that there was also a pilot involved, and that there had to be a spotter on the ground to direct the plane. We didn't know how many agents the KGB sent to the Adirondacks, but there seemed to be several. Hastings and I were only two men. We needed another set of eyes.

She was reluctant, but I think she was also intrigued by the challenge and maybe the romance of it, the thrill. She has a taste for risk. I saw it in her tennis. It was one of the things that attracted me to her. And she has a lot of courage.

She considered the request. Half an hour later she said, "I think I've seen that blue pickup truck around town." I said, "The same truck, the one the KGB woman was driving?"

"Pretty sure."

"Sure enough to devote time to watching, following it?"

"Think so."

"Good enough for me. Try it." I put on my coat. "Where'd you see it?"

"Driving by the line of motels along Lake Flower."

"Since that's between here and my office, it'd be a good place for them to watch us. I go that way all the time. They could be keeping notes, trying to figure out whether we follow a regular schedule. I mostly don't, but you're tied to school hours."

She said, "I think they're a lot more interested in you and Hastings than they are in me."

"That sounds right. I sure hope it is. I'm going out to Coreys to see Hastings. We need to have a plan for how to find Monty and the girl. You watching for the pickup will help. It sounds like Hastings and I should watch the motels by Lake Flower."

"What names are Monty and the girl using?"

"The woman gave you a name, Alice Henderson, but they won't be using that one if they're trying to hide. I wonder whether she had a purpose for giving that to you. And they probably won't use the Ibbetson name since Hastings knows that one and Monty announced it to John. But both Ibbetson and Henderson are English names, and Monty has a Tyneside accent."

Linda interrupted at that point. "What kind of accent?"

"Tyneside. North England. Newcastle-upon-Tyne. The accent is distinctive. As is Newcastle Brown ale.... See what I learn from hanging around with Hastings."

"Yeah. Very useful stuff."

"I think it tells us that they'll be using English names. But the woman could choose to be a German or anything central European, if she wanted to."

She said, "Doesn't narrow it down much."

"I think I'll also try the Adirondack Hotel in Long Lake. Her father stayed there, and so did the late, departed, Vasily Rostov. The hotel seems to be on the KGB's approved list."

"I'll bet they have a little guidebook."

* * *

I had arranged to meet Hastings at the Sisters camp. He was expecting me, and I received an unusual greeting.

"Joseph, my dear boy! What a treat! Don't bother to find a comfortable chair. We'll be going out." He was at his most ebullient.

I looked at him with raised eyebrows and hands forward, palms up. This was a departure from even his Colonel Blimp mode.

He pointed a finger of his right hand at a table lamp and held one finger of his left across his lips. I nodded. He walked to the lamp and picked it up while saying, "I'm told by the wireless that there may be snow tonight."

I saw that, under the base of the lamp, there was a miniature microphone attached with a magnet. I said, "It looks to me like there will probably be sleet."

"I hope not. Now that we know where they are, I want to go finish them as soon as possible. Let's move in fast… Here, take this shotgun. You won't miss with this. It has a scatter pattern, but if you're in close on them you'll cut them in half." He smiled and pointed at the outside door.

I walked toward the door and said, "I haven't done this often, but I'm ready for action!" And we both went out.

He barely restrained his laughter long enough for us to get out the door. He said, "Well, that ought to worry them. Their motel room will look like a fortress."

I wasn't sure. I said, "Will they hide and take a defensive position or will being scared make them more aggressive, more ready to come after us?"

"Either way we win; if we play it right. If they're in

hiding, we can't get hurt and they can't arrange anything big. And if they decide to come after us, that brings them out into the open and we'll be able to see them. I'm ready for either."

"But what do we do now? Do we just wait and see? It seems like a standoff."

Hastings said, "Maybe it is. There isn't necessarily a first-mover advantage because the first to move is also the first to commit."

"Yes, unless it's a feint—and we saw the KGB use that five years ago."

"As you say, young Joseph, there is that possibility. I think it would be well for us to be alert. You might even want to consider being armed."

"It's hunting season. Linda usually has a rifle in the car."

"A handgun is more accessible."

"Linda is very good with a rifle, knows what she's do-ing."

I was getting cold. I said, "We can't talk in the house unless we ditch the bug."

"Don't want to do that. We may be able to use it again."

"Okay, let's go down to look at the river, see if it's frozen solid. We can take my car. It has a heater. We'll talk on the way."

As we turned toward Axton, I said, "I received a message from Captain Jencks in CID at Camp Drum. He says the local police have rolled up a stolen car enterprise operating in Syracuse and Watertown and in-between. Jencks says they think that's where Cross got his car, that he bought it from the dealer. Turns out some of the other soldiers at Drum knew about the business."

"Knew that Cross did business with them?"

"No, I don't think so. They just knew that cars were available there at bargain prices."

Hastings said, "If Cross bought from the felons, it might be possible to squeeze them to get more information about Cross and how much he paid. They'll want to plea bargain."

"Where did he store the car near Drum? Maybe I should make another trip there to do more digging."

Hastings agreed. "You could do that while I stay here and look for Monty. Linda will help."

I said, "Be careful. Linda will want to help, but she's going to need to teach and look after William. And she's pregnant. I'm not sure how active she should be."

"I have all that firmly in mind. But she doesn't take orders from me."

I said, "Nor from me."

So, I made the drive west and a bit north once again. The landscape was snow-covered and the lakes were frozen. I stopped about halfway for a hot cup of coffee at the general store in Wanakena, on the shore of Cranberry Lake.

The big subject of talk at the store was the rescue of an iced-in loon. A young adult female had become stranded by the rapid freezing of the lake. She was diving in a small area of open water, but the freezing closed it in and there wasn't enough opening left for her to get airborne. Loons have heavy bones, and they need a long runway in order to take off, maybe a quarter mile. A team from the

Ranger school went to rescue her. It was dangerous work because ice that can support a loon won't necessarily hold a man. But they caught her with a net. They planned to take her over to open water on Lake Champlain and release her—giving her another chance to migrate.

It was a blustery day. The big lake was covered with rough ice. There were dark clouds that promised more snow, maybe with thunder. I didn't stay there long. I went straight to the State police office in Watertown, identified myself, and asked about the stolen car gang. I got the name of the lawyer who was representing the ringleader, and I went to see him. He was a solo practitioner in his early fifties with an office in a nice, small white frame house on a corner in a primarily residential neighborhood. The framed certificates on his office walls told me that, in addition to several bar associations, he belonged to the local Rotary Club. I assumed that stolen cars were profitable and that the lawyer was well-paid. He was not *pro bono* counsel.

I explained I was not a lawyer, I was a government investigator, and that I was looking into the circumstances associated with the death of a soldier named Alan Cross, an apparent suicide. The lawyer was appropriately cautious. He assured me there was no reason to believe that his clients had anything to do with Cross's death. (He apparently represented more than one of the men.) I told him I didn't think they did, but that the police had said Cross bought the car from one or more of the clients, and all I really wanted was background information on Cross. I also told him I didn't work for the prosecution, and I wasn't empowered to make any deals, but I would appreciate his cooperation and would be willing to tell the prosecutor he had been helpful if that in fact was the case. The lawyer told me he knew the prosecutor—indeed, they were old friends. The lawyer had started his career in the prosecutor's office. I said I thought the car thieves were fortunate in their choice of counsel. He said, "Alleged thieves." I acknowledged the correction. We both laughed, a little.

I said I would like to talk to the principal in the auto business and that I would be happy to have the lawyer present. He said he thought his presence wasn't necessary—his client had been arrested, his name was public knowledge, he was now out on bail, and it would be up to the client whether he wanted to talk. He took one of his business cards from a box on his desk, wrote the name and address of the client on the back of the card, and gave it to me.

I went to see the man that same afternoon. I told him I had talked to his lawyer, and I handed him the lawyer's card. The man handed the card back to me and shut his door in my face. That was probably a good decision. I think the lawyer knew he'd do that.

By then it was late in the day. I had a barbecue and a chocolate milkshake at the Dairy Queen and found a motel that gave a discount to military personnel. The Air Force ID has its uses.

The next day I talked to Captain Jencks. The most useful piece of information he gave me was that the thieves had stored their cars in an old warehouse in Watertown. I asked if I could see it, and he offered to take me there.

The warehouse was in a rundown neighborhood with

a takeout pizza place, a laundry, and a gun repair shop. It was on a particularly dismal stretch of the Black River. Our timing was good—we arrived just as a custodian was coming out of the building and locking the door. He was an old man from the neighborhood who was hired by the car business to look after the place. Since the police were threatening to charge him with being an accessory or a co-conspirator or some such, he was eager to cooperate. Captain Jencks was in uniform.

The man remembered "Mr. Cross." Jencks told him that Cross had been a soldier stationed at Camp Drum and that we were investigating his death. It was a serious matter. The old man was nervous. He confirmed that Cross had parked his car there, and he said that Cross had left some "stuff" there. I asked to see it.

Apparently, Cross had an assigned parking space in the building. The custodian led me to it, and he showed me a small, wood-frame storage enclosure on the wall at the end of the parking place. The man referred to it as a "closet." It had a padlock. I asked whether he could unlock it. From a large side-pocket of his overalls, he pulled out a ring of keys and promptly demonstrated his competence. It didn't take him long to find the key and I wondered how many of the lockers used the same one.

The shelves held a forlorn collection of junk—a vintage Olivetti typewriter with broken keys, a heavily used, torn catcher's mitt, a small stack of back issues of *Playboy*, and a hammer with a wood handle. On the floor, there was also an Army-issue footlocker. I asked Jencks whether the footlocker came from Drum.

He said, "It isn't marked."

I said, "Let's investigate."

Unless a footlocker is padlocked, it's easy to pry it open with a screwdriver. I asked the custodian to supply the tool. He said, "Yes, sir," and produced one from his tool belt. Cross was dead and no one was going to complain. It opened with only a little effort.

The footlocker held some civilian clothes—a wool sweater, a ball cap (Boston Red Sox), old jeans, worn tennis shoes—but at the bottom there was a lined notebook.

I did a quick reading of a few pages that were filled by a crude but legible scrawl written with a blue ballpoint. It appeared to be drafts of complaints about the conduct of officers at Camp Drum. Jencks and I decided that the notebook was evidence and we took it into custody.

I said, "Where's the gun?"

"Gun?"

"The murder weapon that killed Major Bradley and Sergeant Rafferty. Cross didn't have a gun on his body or in the car when it went off the pier. I was hoping to find it here."

"The murder weapon hasn't been found, but the fact that it isn't here doesn't tell us much. There are a lot of deep bodies of water. The pistol could be in any one of them. Or the other big possibility is that Cross didn't kill them. The gun could be one of the many at Drum. We can't know that for sure without ballistics."

I said, "Right. So do you think those murders will ever be solved?"

"CID sure hopes so. But we don't seem to be making much progress on it. Maybe the notebook will help."

He drove me back to the CID office at the base. Jencks then dealt with another matter, and I had time to read the notebook closely. It was extraordinary. It accused Major Bradley and Sergeant Rafferty of serious misconduct, but it was impossible for me to tell whether the facts were true, exaggerated stories, or pure fantasy. There were allegations of sexual misconduct as well as of specific bias against Cross. I had no way to investigate any of it. I left that for CID to do if they thought it was warranted, but Bradley and Rafferty could not refute the charges or offer contrary evidence. Significantly, especially for CIA purposes, there was no mention of the stolen contingency plans, no evidence that Cross was even aware of the plans. And there was no talk about killing the major or sergeant or about any such intention.

I made Xerox copies of all the pages. The original stayed at Drum. When I got back to Saranac, I sent the material to Langley. I'm not a psychiatrist or anything remotely like one, but the Agency has plenty of them. They referred it to one of their top people, Leslie Dusseault.

We exchanged telexes. I asked her, "What's the diagnosis?"

She sent a one-word reply. "Bananas."

My next message was, "Is that the clinical term?"

"Close enough."

"Homicidal bananas?"

"It's not possible to be certain without more, but there are unmistakable signs that the man was seriously mentally ill. He was out of touch with reality, at least some of the time. It's possible that, in the grip of one of his delusions, he might have become homicidal. Can't say for sure, but it's certainly possible."

I replied, "Close enough for government work."

She said, "Thanks."

18

Linda went to the grocery store to pick up a few things. Mac went with her, as usual. On their return trip, she spotted the blue pickup truck and seized the opportunity to follow it. The snow overnight had not yet been plowed, and the roads were a bit slick, but Linda is experienced in winter driving. She was determined not to lose sight of the pickup. The sun was bright, and vision was good.

From the stoplight at the city hall intersection, the pickup took route 3, the main road, west toward Tupper Lake. Since the airplane attack had taken place in Tupper, Linda thought Monty and Alice were probably staying there or somewhere near there. She didn't know who was driving the truck—she wasn't able to see the driver or whether there was a passenger. It was possible that Monty and Alice were both in the pickup.

Just after the access road for the Indian Carry, however, the pickup turned off route 3 onto the Coreys Road. Linda knew that only the paved portion of the road is plowed in the winter, and that the paved portion ends about a mile in, at the snowplow turnaround near the Rockefellers' storage building. It continues unpaved on past Axton Landing and an access point for the Seward Range, ending at the Rockefellers' camp on Ampersand Pond. Linda thought that, if the pickup had four-wheel drive, it might be able to go farther on the road than she could. She followed the truck cautiously.

The pickup, however, didn't try to go farther. It parked at the turnaround, which is just above the road's slow descent to Axton and the Stony Creek valley. Linda observed from a distance. The driver, who appeared to be Alice, took cross-country skis from the truck, and strapped them on. She was alone.

Linda knew that there was a trail from the top of the hill, through hemlocks, firs, and pines, down to the bridge over the Stony Creek. The new snow and the bright sun made it a beautiful day for cross-country skiing. But Linda also knew that there was an old camp just off the Coreys Road, about halfway between the turnaround and Axton. It occurred to her that Alice could be heading toward the camp. Perhaps she and Monty were both staying there. The camp is concealed in the woods, the road was closed to traffic, and the location is not far from the Sisters camp, the house Hastings had rented. It would be a convenient place from which to strike quickly and to which to disappear quickly.

Linda wanted to follow Alice, but she didn't have skis in the car. She did, however, have her deer rifle. The ski tracks in the new snow made Alice easy to follow. Linda took the rifle. Mac, of course, joined her.

The trail leaves the Coreys Road about a hundred yards

beyond where the pickup was parked and it goes through the trees along the ridge, straight and level, for another hundred yards or more, but then it turns sharply left and plunges down the hill. There was erosion of the trail at that point. The clearing of the underbrush and the sharp descent had created a path for runoff water, which cut a ditch down the hill. It might have been easy to glide over this on skis, but it was tough going on foot. Linda stumbled and fell. She held onto the rifle. Mac licked her face. It was an expression of concern, sympathy, and encouragement, but the moisture was not welcome in the cold weather.

At the bottom of the hill, there was marshland and fewer trees. Linda could see farther ahead. Alice's ski tracks were there but Linda didn't see her. And then, suddenly, there she was, only about twenty yards ahead. She had probably heard the noise of Linda's fall and then turned back to see who was coming.

Alice was looking straight at Linda and had a pistol in her hand. The two women could see each other's eyes. Mac sensed the tension. He started to chase his tail. He spun around and around very fast. Alice fired the pistol and a bullet hit an old white pine only a foot away from Linda's head. Linda didn't hesitate. She didn't raise the rifle and sight along it at shoulder height. She fired with the rifle at waist level, like John Wayne in "Stagecoach." Alice dropped. She'd been hit in the center of the chest. The rifle's load was intended for deer. It was more than adequate for this task.

Linda knew that she needed to call the police. To do that, however, she first had to find a house at Coreys that was occupied, one that had a telephone. Most of the houses there are summer camps, owned by summer people, but the Van Puttens were at home, and they had a phone. Linda gave the police a quick version of what had happened. They told her to stay put and wait for them. She did.

The Van Puttens were upset, of course, but they were accommodating. A squad car soon arrived, shortly followed by an ambulance. Linda led them to Alina Kuznetsov, who had been using the name Alice Henderson, and who was now duly pronounced dead. The body was loaded into the ambulance, taken to the Adirondack Medical Center, and then to the morgue. Crime scene tape was strung in a circle enclosing many square feet of wooded forest and a section of the trail.

Linda was driven to town in the squad car, while a deputy and Mac followed in our car. Mac wanted to ride with Linda, but he doesn't argue with police officers. He respects the uniform, or maybe the gun. Since our run-in with the float plane at Tupper, Mac had become acquainted with a few officers. They gave him treats.

Linda would probably have been in big trouble with the authorities had it not been that Alice was a Soviet agent who had entered this country illegally on a forged passport, and a paraffin test on her hand showed that she had fired a weapon, and a bullet that ballistics matched to Alice's pistol was found in the pine tree at the level of Linda's head, and Linda was a pregnant schoolteacher and a mother. The authorities were satisfied, even without Rabbit's help, but he persuaded the newspapers to be vague about the details.

I wasn't surprised at the way Linda handled it. When

we were in high school, she was a championship tennis player, and she went to college on a tennis scholarship. Her reflexes are excellent. And she learned to shoot at the age of twelve and spent many hours with her father hunting in the Adirondack woods. She knows what she's doing. Five years ago, when Hastings shot a flashlight out of my hand in a mine tunnel, it was Linda who returned his fire. Her shot sprayed his face with rock chips. He was lucky that it was dark in the tunnel.

Linda called me from the police station, told me I would need to pick up William from school, and gave me a brief account of what happened. I was pretty much speechless, which was probably a good thing. When she got home, she told me the full story and I asked questions. My telling of it, of course, was based on what she told me, maybe supplemented a bit by what I heard from the police.

I asked her, "Were you frightened?"

"There wasn't time for that. It all happened too fast."

I thought following Alice through the woods was reckless, but this wasn't the time for criticism. Linda needed my support. She might not have been frightened when the shooting was going on, but by the time of our conversation she fully understood how close she had come to checking out. She was shaken. She needed comforting. I also told her that I loved her, and that William and I needed her.

Then I called Rabbit. I had to report to him as soon as possible, before he got the story from the FBI or the news media. Rabbit, as I expected he would be, was angry. He said it was foolish for Linda to "chase" Alice. I didn't argue with that. I explained that Hastings and I needed help in watching Monty and Alice, and that the Adirondacks is a big place with lots of trees to hide behind. He asked me to explain, once again, why Hastings's son and the boy's girlfriend were persons of interest to the US government. I told him, as I had before, that US intelligence said both Monty and Alice were working for the KGB and our theory was that they were connected to the theft of the secret contingency plans from Camp Drum and possibly to the murders of two soldiers there and the mysterious death of a third soldier.

Rabbit shifted his ground. He said, "Linda is your wife, not an operative. You are not free to delegate official duties to her. Is that clear?"

I said, "Yes, sir. May I have some help?"

He said, "Hmph." And hung up.

That night, Linda, Hastings, and I had a conversation in our living room. William wanted to be there, but we banished him. We debated about whether it would be better for him to know the true facts rather than be open to wild speculation, but we decided that the reality was truly frightening. Linda said it was just too much. There wasn't much room for speculation to be worse.

The conversation was wide ranging. Linda thought Mac had distracted Alice and spoiled her aim. Hastings enthusiastically endorsed that. He hadn't seen it happen, but he spoke as if he had.

He said, "Mac saw what was going on, and he understood the problem. He reacted to it. And he solved the problem. He attracted attention to himself, a dangerous thing to do, and that gave Linda the opportunity she need-ed. Mac could work for me any time."

Linda said, "You can't have him."

I said, "Mac always does that when he's nervous."

Hastings petted Mac, scratched behind his ears, and said, "He did what you would have done — he put himself in harm's way in order to save Linda. At least give Mac credit for having as much sense and courage as you have."

I couldn't argue with it, so I laughed. Linda didn't.

I said, "Why didn't you laugh?"

"I killed a woman! It's hard for me to believe, but I did it."

Hastings said, "She was trying to kill you; she almost did. You had to shoot."

"That doesn't change it."

And then she started crying and wouldn't stop. Crying uncontrollably. I tried to comfort her, but it didn't help.

After a time, Hastings said, "You go sleep in William's room, Joe. Linda and I are going to attack a bottle of scotch."

Linda told me about it later. "Hastings didn't say much. We drank, and we both cried. He said I won't get over it. He said you don't get over it, you have to live with it. It'll always be there. He said when I shot her, I had a choice. I could have died; I could have left William and you be-hind. He said I made the right choice, but we have to live with our choices. I realized he was right. I'm glad I made that choice. I can live with it." She raised her head and looked at me squarely. "You either go on with your life or you just shut down in one way or another. I couldn't do that to William.... I confess I would have felt more guilt about William than about you, Joe."

My reaction to Linda's remarks was not entirely positive. It set me back on my heels. Initially, I was startled that she chose to tell me that she felt a greater concern for, maybe a greater attachment to, William than she did to me. Then I thought my reaction was selfish. She had borne him; she had shared a bloodstream with him. And she was pregnant again, which probably heightened her consciousness of motherhood. I was a big boy, William was not. I could take care of myself. I also thought then, and I think now, that she may have held me responsible (as, in fairness, I was) for getting her involved in dangerous international conflict, seriously dangerous.

I had asked for her help in watching Alice/Alina. I didn't know how dangerous it would turn out to be, or how aggressive Linda would be about taking risks. She realized she had made a mistake, but I bore some responsibility for it and Linda felt that. There's little with practical value that can be done to atone for past sins. You can wear the hair shirt or engage in self-flagellation, but it seldom makes other people feel better. As Hastings had said to her, we sometimes face choices we would rather not have faced, and we find it painful to face them again, in retrospect. Some choices are awful. To say that this one was regrettable understates the case, but the regret was real. When it came down to it, Linda's regret was only a more extreme version of many things in this life. We have to get on with it.

* * *

Two days later, I got a call from Rabbit.

He said, "The story was made-to-order for the national media. The headlines were almost set in type: 'Schoolteacher Kills Soviet Spy.' Linda was about to get calls from *Time* and *Newsweek* and an invitation to appear on the *Tonight Show*. It would have been a disaster, and your usefulness to the Agency would have ended. I had to cash in many chips to spike the story. It takes years to build up our balance on the credit side of the ledger, but you've wiped it out overnight. I now owe every publisher and broadcaster in town."

"She almost got killed, Rabbit."

"Yes, yes, I know. And I'm grateful that she survived."

"You don't sound like it."

"She must surely be the most lethal mother teaching at the high school."

I paused, "She's also good at tennis."

Rabbit made a noise like someone was strangling him. Then, "Maybe we should hire Linda and you could teach history."

"I don't think she'd like that."

I could hear Rabbit shuffling papers on his desk. He said, "Our sources in Moscow tell us that the KGB was upset about the botched airplane attack. They didn't like the publicity and they didn't like that it was ineffective, that the targets were missed. Monty is not in good standing with the KGB at present. As they see it, all he's accomplished is the further enhancement of his father's legend. You are, I'm pleased to say, simply irrelevant in Moscow's view — had you been killed in the attack, you would've been collateral damage."

I did not respond.

Rabbit grumbled and said something unintelligible. Then he said, "I'm told you had your dog with you."

I said, "Yes, they also seemed to be shooting at the dog."

"Then you both would have been collateral damage, you and the dog."

"Which one of us would have been the greater loss?"

"Don't press me."

19

The police searched the cabin off the Coreys Road, the one near the place where Alice died, but they found no evidence that Monty or Alice had been there. The owners of the cabin confirmed that it appeared to be undisturbed. The blue pickup truck Alice/Alina had driven to Coreys was still parked by the snowplow turnaround and the state police traced ownership of it. They discovered that the truck had been sold by a dealer to one "M. Ibbetson," who claimed to live at an address that didn't exist.

Hastings wasn't satisfied to rely on the search of the cabin done by the local police, so he did his own search. I'm not sure whether he picked the lock or found an open window, but in either case the search was not productive. He didn't find anything to make him think Monty had been there. He noted, however, that the cabin wasn't visible from the road and that its sight lines would make it an excellent hideout, should the need arise. He remembers such things.

The Christmas holidays happened about then. I'm a little vague about the exact sequence because things were coming so fast that it all became a blur, and I was more concerned with everyone's safety and welfare than I was with Christmas. Linda and William did the decorating; and we had a ten-foot tree, as tall as our ceiling would permit. It was cut at the Coyle farm, owned by one of Linda's uncles. In my stocking, Santa gave me a new stapler for the office.

Just before the new year, I received a coded telex from Rabbit. Decoded, it said: "Moscow sending more agents to Adirondacks. Two experienced men ordered to terminate target. KGB angered by death of Alina Kuznetsov and dissatisfied with Ibbetson. Expect increased pressure and professional tactics. D D O." The initials stand for Director of Domestic Operations.

Hastings and I talked about how to react. Linda and William were in school, so we took our coffee to the living room.

I said, "I think we can ask Linda to activate her waitress network. We should use the assets we have. She's still in touch with waitress friends. They helped us with Colonel Kuznetsov and Bill Reilly five years ago, and I'll bet they would help us again."

"How do we tell them what to look for?"

"Linda could just ask them to be on the lookout for two Russian men, traveling together, maybe claiming to be Germans or Bulgarians or anything central European."

"KGB men don't always travel in pairs. They aren't nuns."

"I'll make a note of that and tell Linda." I refilled his coffee cup. "Maybe Langley can get the approximate ages of the men who were sent."

Hastings said, "Yes, that would help. Age, height, weight, languages, any description."

"I'll try."

And I did that as soon as I got back to my office and had a secure line. But Rabbit told me our source in Moscow was not strong. The intelligence we got was good, but not detailed, which suggested to me that the source was not inside KGB or not high up.

Rabbit said, "Don't tell Hastings this. I don't trust him. I don't want him to know anything about the source. That's an order."

So I told Hastings that the only thing we knew was that there would be two men.

He said, "Not much to go on."

I said, "Since it's winter and the slow season, and there aren't many people around except for skiers, the two agents will stand out more and be more visible. Unless they disguise themselves as skiers."

Then I talked to Linda. I told her we were looking for two KGB agents, two men. I didn't want to scare her, but I thought she might, possibly, be a target. KGB's sources pay attention. It was likely they would know who killed Alice/Alina. I had to warn Linda.

We had a longer discussion. I said, "What we know is that KGB's target here is Hastings. I don't think they're really interested in you or me. But since you got in the way of their operation by defending yourself against Alice, they will regard you as an enemy."

"What can I do? I don't want to start carrying a gun all the time. I'm a teacher."

"Yeah. It's a problem. I should probably consult Rabbit. He won't be happy."

"What about William?"

"KGB won't threaten him. If they did, that would start an all-out war between the two intelligence services. KGB won't want that."

"But what if William is next to me? He'll be in danger." Linda hugged Mac, a substitute. "And what about my students?"

"We shouldn't overreact. If the probability that you are in danger is near zero, then we may not need to change your routines."

"Who knows whether it's near zero? Does anybody know how much danger there really is? We can't put the students in danger."

"No. You're right. Of course, we can't. But, if we tell the high school to be on the lookout for KGB agents, that'll start a panic in the town. For the same reason, we can't provide an armed guard to follow you around, including at the school. Rabbit won't want to publicize the Agency's presence here, my role."

"He'll like it even less if the KGB shoots up the high school and some poor kid gets killed. Congress would have Rabbit for breakfast, lunch, and dinner."

"Yeah, even worse."

"It sounds to me like I shouldn't be at the high school."

"Maybe not."

Linda patted her stomach. "I'm pregnant. Maybe I could have a problem pregnancy. I'm sure the Agency's doctors could cook something up."

I said, "Mac Denleigh would be happy. He doesn't want pregnant teachers at the school."

"It took the KGB to get him what he wanted."

"I don't think we can tell him that."

Linda said, "No, I suppose not, but it would be fun."

"If the doctors' advice is that the pregnancy problems require bed rest, that would mean you couldn't go out of the house. In effect, you'd be locked up."

"Maybe the problem wouldn't need to be so serious. Maybe it would just require me to go spend a few weeks in the Bahamas."

"Dreamer."

"Or I'm sure that John would be happy to have me, and William, come to stay with him at Ballston Spa. That would get me out of sight here. He's already invited me."

"I wouldn't like that."

"I wouldn't either, but it might be safer."

"I'm going to have to call Rabbit about this. It'll be painful, but it's necessary."

* * *

I went to the office to call Rabbit on a line that was constantly monitored for taps. "Rabbit, I need your help and maybe your action. Our intel says that two KGB men are being sent here to kill Hastings, but I think it's possible Linda is in danger. Alina Kuznetsov was the daughter of Colonel Kuznetsov. Linda acted in self-defense, but that might not make much difference to the KGB."

"Yes, I'm afraid that's probably right, I'm very sorry to

say. You put Linda in that danger, Joe, by involving her in our work, and you did so contrary to my advice."

"I plead guilty, and I apologize for causing trouble. I didn't think far enough ahead. I'm sorry. But now we have to decide what to do. I don't want to resign from the Agency and move with Linda and William to a remote location, but that will be your call. What are your orders?"

"Apology accepted. Spilt milk…What are my orders? First, it's very important to avoid publicity. We can't fight a war with KGB out in the open. We can fight it covertly, if we need to, but not in the open. What that means is we have to hide Linda. We have to get her out of the high school. Can Linda take a vacation or a leave of absence?"

I said, "The chairman of the school board wanted to force her to take a leave because she's pregnant. We fought that and we won, so she's still teaching."

Rabbit said, "Maybe she has a problem with her pregnancy or another health problem, so she has to take a leave for the time being."

"How long?" I didn't tell him that we had the same thought.

"Who knows? That's up to KGB. If they make their move against Hastings quickly, it might bring the matter to a resolution, one way or another. Either they would kill Hastings and that would finish it, or Hastings would kill them and that would probably also be the end of it."

I said, "You don't think the KGB would pursue it further?"

"If KGB is losing agents right and left, at some point they're going to give up. How many agents is Hastings worth? How many can they afford to lose by continuing to go after him? At some point, I think they'd have to give up. I certainly would if I were in their shoes."

"Okay, but what if they don't move quickly against Hastings and it doesn't get resolved."

"Then we would be left in a state of uncertainty. That would be inconvenient for you and Linda, but unless you want to resign from the Agency and move to a Pacific island, that may be what we're stuck with." There was a pause and once again I could hear a rustling of papers. "Our files tell me that Linda's ex-husband is the boy's father. What's the custody arrangement? Do they have joint custody? The ex is John, I see. Does John have parental rights? If so, then it would be relatively straightforward if William went to live with him."

"I don't like that."

Rabbit said, "Would you prefer to have him shot at?"

"If William goes to John, Linda would have to go with him."

"And you hope she wouldn't do that."

"Yes." I lowered my voice, almost to a whisper. "One thing is clear. I'll need to talk to Linda. I'm not sure what she will accept."

"Well, for the good of both her and the Agency, we have to get her out of the line of fire. That's also clear."

* * *

That evening, after Linda got home from school, we talked while we were getting dinner.

I said, "Rabbit thought maybe you and William could go stay with John for a little while."

"Oh, he did, did he? That isn't going to happen."

"Don't hold it against Rabbit—you and I had the same idea."

"Not seriously, I didn't. There were reasons why I got divorced and those reasons are still good ones. Are you trying to get rid of me?"

"Of course not! That's ridiculous. I love you."

"I'm glad to hear it." She cut the head off a turnip. "You're okay too, I guess." She smiled.

"Thanks…Okay, so what are our options? Are there people in the Coyle family that you and William could go live with?"

Linda said, "That's going to look like we're separating and everyone in town will think we're on our way to a divorce."

"Yeah, but it's not as bad as you and William being in danger."

"My mother would be happy to help, but she isn't well enough to do much and there isn't room at the house. But, there are lots of Coyles. I have family in Tupper, Long Lake, and Canton. My Aunt Sophie lives in Canton. She's very friendly and a nice lady, and Canton would have more options for school for William."

"You started graduate work in American history. Maybe you could continue your studies."

"Maybe. When I was doing research on the old iron mine at Tahawus, working in the archives at St. Lawrence U., I met a professor in the English department. His name is Angus. I think he'd remember me. Maybe he could use a research assistant."

"Would the high school pay you when you're on a leave of absence?"

"I don't know, but I don't think so."

"Well, a job as a researcher would be helpful. Without your teaching salary, we would need the money."

"I'll call Professor Angus and sound him out. He was writing a book about Nova Scotia. Maybe he needs some Nova Scotia history."

"Sounds like a plan."

Linda said, "But William will be heartbroken if he misses the opportunity to skate with the lighted torch. It's an honor, and it'll be fun. He'll want to come back here for the Winter Carnival and the Ice Palace. If you make him miss that, your popularity will take a big hit. It may not recover."

"Right. Canton isn't far away—about an hour and a quarter. In the big city, people do commutes that long every day."

"I don't think you're planning on driving within the speed limit."

"Maybe not. I'm a public official, on official business."

"Coming to visit me official business."

"Absolutely. You and William. What could be more official than that?"

"I have another question. What are we going to tell William about the reason why we have to leave town?"

"Good question."

A part of it was already public knowledge. There had

been a story in the newspaper about a shooting in the woods near Coreys where, it said, "a woman died." The woman was described as "so far unidentified, but definitely not local." The report was brief and vague enough that the death might possibly have been a hunting accident.

I said, "Rabbit has done a good job of keeping your name out of the paper, but there are police who know you were involved, and one or two Coreys residents know. It wouldn't be surprising for the full story to leak. The people who know have been asked—maybe 'ordered' is the right word—to keep quiet for reasons of national security. Most of them will obey. But it only takes one leak to start talk."

"We'll know if William's friends start teasing or asking him about it."

"Yes, and that will raise questions in his mind. He'll need something to tell his friends that won't scare the hell out of them and upset their parents and their parents' friends and won't cause a security breach."

Linda said, "It would also be nice if it didn't scare the hell out of William. Having his mother shot at and having his mother shoot and kill another woman is pretty strong stuff to ask any ten-year old kid to handle. He's got his head screwed on tight, but there are limits."

"Yes, damn it. What can we tell him? We can't just put the genie back in the bottle."

"What if we tell William we have to leave because you're going to be working on super-secret Air Force business? He thinks you're an Air Force officer—as you really are. That part of the story has the advantage of being true."

"That's good so far, but what could we tell him about what I'm working on? We can't tell him about the KGB."

"We can tell him that the reason he can't know about the business is because it's super-secret. That's what secret means."

"Do you think he'll accept that?"

"Maybe he'll have to."

"But why would you and William need to leave? Why wouldn't I just go to work as usual and do secret stuff at the office? He's sure to ask that."

"I'd say it's because you're going to be bringing secret work home. In a very real sense, that's also true."

"Okay." I put the plates, glasses, and silverware on the table. The noise helped. "What about the killing of Alice?"

Linda said, "I suppose we'll just have to hope that Rabbit can continue to keep that bottled up."

I said, "You're a good planner. You'd make a good spy."

"I'd rather be a good mother."

"You are that."

"I also help you."

"That's true too."

Linda rearranged my place settings. "If John gets word of this, he'll blow a gasket. He'll use it to try for custody."

I said, "I can handle John." I hoped that was true. Actually, I don't think John and his new wife really wanted William around. Having William would have meant doing much more negotiating with Linda. They didn't really want that.

* * *

Then I got a wild telephone call from Monty. He was either drunk or demented, maybe both. One thing was clear: he was very upset about the death of his girlfriend, Alice/Alina. That was, of course, to be expected. Monty threatened to kill Linda, me, and Hastings. That was scary, as it was clearly intended to be. Oddly, however, it wasn't nearly as scary as it should have been. My reading of Monty was that he was a lost little boy. He didn't know what to do, and he was frightened. But my reading might have been wrong. Hastings and I wanted to make moves to protect all of us against him, but there wasn't much we could do until we knew where he was. He was in hiding.

20

I decided to ask questions about what became of the corpse of Alice Henderson/Alina Kuznetsov. An ambulance had hauled her away from Coreys, but I didn't know whether anyone claimed her.

It seemed to me that the KGB had a problem. On the one hand, they might want to give her a proper burial. She was one of theirs and she was the daughter of the late Colonel Kuznetsov, who was also one of theirs, and no doubt she had friends in the service. Monty would surely want the remains to be treated with dignity and respect. And there is a certain amount of popular nonsense about not leaving a fallen comrade on the battlefield.

On the other, she was an embarrassment to KGB. If they sought to return the body to Russia, she would be revealed as a secret agent of a foreign government, an agent who had entered our country illegally, using forged documents, and who was engaged here in clandestine work, almost certainly criminal work. How much of that would the Soviets want to admit? The corpse had the potential to cause a serious international incident, a diplomatic breach.

My bet was that the Russians would want to keep quiet about it, say as little as possible. Rabbit made the same bet. He said, "The Soviets will say, 'what girl?'"

Then he said, "But what about the boy?"

"Hastings's son? Monty?"

"Yes. If Moscow tells him to walk away from it and keep his mouth shut, will he play the game by Moscow's rules?"

"I don't know. He's unpredictable, maybe unstable."

"It could be that one of the reasons KGB is sending more agents at this point is to ride herd on the boy, to keep him in line now that Kuznetsov's daughter can no longer play that role. Perhaps the new agents will be helpful, will make the situation less incendiary."

"I never like to count on the KGB for help."

"No. Don't let the boy have much running room."

A few hours later, I found that Rabbit had nailed it. Sometimes I think experience really does have value. The next morning, Hastings arrived at our house before breakfast. He didn't take his coat off, and he declined a cup of coffee.

He said, "We had some excitement last night. It was two o'clock in the morning and Edna White was visiting Steve Hallbauer." I must have raised my eyebrows at that. "Oh, don't look so shocked. I'm sure it was perfectly proper—they're married, just not to each other. In any event, they were still awake. No doubt reading the Bible, probably some especially compelling verses from Deuteronomy.

Then they were disturbed by a noise, and Mr. Hallbauer apparently thought it was Mrs. Hallbauer returning early from her shuffle off to Buffalo. The noise interrupted their devotions — there's a Latin phrase for that, I believe. Well, in the event, it was Monty. He was looking for me, but he had the wrong house. An understandable error. There was no moon, and it was very dark. He may also have been inebriated. But I think the mistake indicates that he's getting restive. Mrs. White came to fetch me. I must say, she was somewhat distraught. I apologized for Monty and assured her that such intrusive behavior is one of the quaint local customs in the north of England, perfectly normal."

"Did you see him?"

"No. I wanted to have a conversation with him, but he'd gone by the time Mrs. White led me back to the Hallbauer residence. Given the state of Mrs. White and Mr. Hallbauer, Monty may well have felt that he'd already had enough excitement — or done enough to diminish it. But I'm concerned about the dear boy. I think he will make a serious miscalculation."

William came downstairs to the kitchen while Hastings was talking. I'm not sure what he made of the talk about Bible-reading; I didn't ask him. But I decided that Hastings and I should have breakfast elsewhere so that we could talk more freely. I thought the Full Moon wouldn't be too crowded on a weekday morning. It is only four blocks from my house, and it's one of our favorite places.

The town is built on the foothills of the mountains. It's common here for a street to be at a very different elevation from a parallel street only a block away, and many of the buildings have an entrance at the front that is on a different floor than another entrance at the rear. Since both of the entrances are at ground level, neither is really the "first floor," so they are usually just referred to as upstairs and downstairs. The Moon is in one of those buildings.

We walked downhill on Larch Street for a block, then along Tamarack where one side of the street is much higher than the other and the sidewalk runs along a cut or terrace, and then we walked uphill for another block on Main. We didn't try to talk much while we walked. As usual, Hastings's eyes were constantly busy. He saw every car that passed, and he assessed every pedestrian. This was the ability that kept him alive.

Unfortunately for us, the Moon was doing a brisk business. There was no table available near the front door, where the counter is and where the coffee drinkers congregate, so we went past the small kitchen into the back room next to the bar. It wasn't crowded there, and Hastings could watch the stairway to the lower level and note comings and goings from the rear entrance. We could talk there.

He was wearing a black wool overcoat with lapels and seven or eight black buttons, a city coat. He looked like a priest or a rabbi, or Dracula. When he took it off, I saw that he was wearing the new keeper's jacket. The tweed is a grey-green with flecks of blue, not an unusual color. What's unusual about it is the weight of the cloth and the simplicity of the jacket. There are no lapels or outside pockets, but it weighs ten pounds. The yarn is a very tight twist, so that every strand has real heft. Hastings and I call it "bullet-proof tweed." The jacket was intended to be worn by a gamekeeper on an estate or by the man who takes care of the hounds used in a foxhunt. It isn't livery.

After we ordered breakfast I said, "Linda is upset."

Hastings carefully lined up the salt and pepper shakers. Then he flicked the salt with his finger, knocked it over, and it toppled the pepper. Only a little salt was spilled on the table. I had seen it before.

He said, "When Linda shot that rifle from the hip and hit her target square on, do you think perhaps she felt a moment of satisfaction? It was a very skillful shot. Might she have felt that it was a job well done? That she was able to handle the situation? Perhaps the regret set in only later. What do you think?"

I considered it. "I don't know. I think I hope not."

"But surely she must have felt a sense of relief, relief that the woman would no longer be shooting at her."

"Relief. Yes, perhaps relief."

"She's human, Joe. She's entitled to react like a human."

"You've never seen her on the tennis court. She doesn't get rattled. She's extremely cool. Nerves of steel."

Hastings felt inside the jacket for his Webley and adjusted it to a more comfortable position.

I said, "We need to find Monty and identify the KGB men when they arrive. Maybe they're already here."

"Yes. Being able to monitor Monty might give us a bit of warning if he becomes aggressive. And we certainly need to be able to recognize the KGB. It's a pity we can't get descriptions from Moscow."

"It is what it is...We need more eyes. Linda is talking to her waitress network, but she's not going to be able to do more looking for us. Rabbit and I decided that she'll go to Canton to get her away from the KGB. There's too much risk at the high school."

"How does Linda feel about leaving town?"

"She's not happy about it. But she knows that, because of her marksmanship, she's become a target, or a potential target, and that makes being at the high school an unacceptable risk. For other people as well as her. She understands the reason."

"What about William?"

"William will go with her. Mac will stay with me. He seldom barks, but he warns me when anyone approaches the house."

"Fearsome."

"No, but helpful. Since Linda will be in Canton, the waitresses will have to report to me if they see a pair of foreign-looking men. That's awkward, but I don't have a way around it. I can't tell them why we're looking for the men—Linda has just told them that I'm trying to protect Air Force secrets about the design of a new airplane."

"The waitresses are a real asset."

"Yeah. Linda worked as a waitress, you know, after her divorce from John, before she met me. She says waitresses talk about being invisible. Some customers don't even see them, don't seem to know they're there. Waitresses make good spies. They hear things. And they have no hesitation about repeating what they've heard. It's all fair game for gossip."

Hastings said, "I'll take the motels. You take the waitresses and the restaurants."

"What about bars?"

"Those go with the motels. Besides, Air Force officers don't lounge in bars."

I laughed.

So did he.

I said, "Monty could be in a small rental camp in the woods."

"Yes. That would be less convenient for us. Inconsiderate." Our breakfast arrived. "What's happening at Camp Drum?"

"Not much, I think. The prosecution of the stolen car ring is proceeding, and the boss has been squeezed for possible connections to the contingency plans, but so far, they can tie him to Alan Cross but no further. Army intel hasn't found contact with Major Bradley or Sergeant Rafferty or anyone else at Drum. So far. They're still working on it."

"Any progress on who killed Cross?"

"No. The coroner has the verdict open. Undetermined. But the papers I found make suicide look more likely. The Pentagon is still going nuts."

"I assume they're throwing a lot of manpower at it."

"Probably. That's what they do. Not much like a lone man scrounging around in an old trunk in a dusty warehouse."

Hastings said, "Ah, the romance of it! Eat your heart out, James Bond."

So, Linda asked her friends to be on the lookout for the two men, but she didn't have much description to give them. Since Rabbit's message described the KGB agents as "experienced," I told Linda the men would probably not be young. She also told her friends that she would be taking a leave from the school and would be away for bedrest because of difficulties with the pregnancy, so they should report any sightings to me. They had to go to our house. My office at the locked campus in Ray Brook was not readily accessible. Our neighbors undoubtedly enjoyed seeing visits from a number of different women while Linda was away.

* * *

It was a Friday night, almost ten o'clock, when I heard a knock on the door. Waitresses couldn't come to the house until after the dinner hour crowd had gone.

Gracie Hefford, a waitress who worked at the restaurant of the Adirondack Hotel in Long Lake, reported that two men who looked like the ones we were worried about had been at the Friday fish fry. Even spies are creatures of habit. Five years earlier, when I was investigating the death of Colonel Kuznetsov, he stayed at that hotel and I went to the fish fry to meet with Bill Reilly, the man who, as it turned out, had killed Kuznetsov. Vasily Rostov, another KGB agent, also stayed there. It is a nice place, with good food, and it appeared to have the KGB's seal of approval.

Gracie said that the men she saw were "fiftyish" with gray skin and gray suits. They didn't have the ruddy complexions of skiers or people who spent much time outdoors. She is a skier. She also said that the men were wearing "ill-fitting," cheap suits. Gracie went to Wellesley. When I asked about their accents, she said, "Not French."

I told Hastings about this. He said, "It's the ultimate insult. They've sent the second team! Not even the young tigers. Maybe they think I'm over the hill, that I've lost my nerve, or my reflexes are gone. Maybe they're right. Well, we will see."

I said, "Experience counts. These men probably know what they're doing."

"I'll take them seriously."

"Gracie didn't know whether they were staying in the hotel. She didn't remember them having overcoats, but they could have hung them in the lobby."

"Did she see a car?"

"No. She wasn't able to watch the parking lot."

"We should go to the hotel and inquire as to whether our friends are in residence."

"I'll go. I'm local. They know me as an Air Force officer. I think they'll cooperate."

"Where else do we look?"

I said, "Beats me. But it's a little easier now after Christmas and before Winter Carnival than it would be in mid-summer. There are fewer places to look."

* * *

I went to the hotel in Long Lake. They had only five guests, and none of them were the two foreign gentlemen.

I had also asked my cousin Vince to be on the lookout for the men. Vince works in the Tupper police, and he fills in at other towns and villages in the area when they need manpower. He knows everyone. I gave him essentially the same description we gave to the waitresses, and I also described Monty. Young Brits are not unknown in the Adirondacks; we get a fair number of them, so I had to try to differentiate Monty. That wasn't easy, but we had the Ibbetson name.

The investment in Vince paid dividends. Monty got hungry. It may be that Alice/Alina had been doing the shoplifting for the two of them and Monty's skills weren't developed. He was caught at Shaheen's store trying to walk away with a package of hotdogs. They called the cops, and the cop on duty was Vince.

A package of hotdogs is not a major offense, but Monty was a foreign national with no permanent address and no money. He was regarded as a vagrant and a flight risk. And Vince knew I was looking for the boy. Monty was locked up overnight pending a hearing in court the next morning. He was entitled to make a telephone call, which he used to contact the KGB men and ask them to bail him out. Since he wasn't calling a lawyer, the police could have recorded the call, but they didn't. Maybe they didn't have the technology. The phone company keeps a record, however, of all numbers called from the police station.

While Monty was making his call, Vince called me. He told me that a young man who had I.D. with the Ibbetson name had been arrested, and he also told me (what I already knew) that Tupper, like other small towns in the Adirondacks, doesn't have a judge or a magistrate on duty at all hours of the night and day. Monty would not be able to go to court until ten a.m. the next morning, which suited me fine. Vince said that the amount of his bail would probably be the same as the fine for the offense, certainly less than fifty dollars. Unless Monty requested a lawyer or a jury trial, which would be foolish and would result in much greater court costs, the hearing would be very brief. He'd be found guilty, there would be a small fine, and that would be the end of it. Vince gave the same information to Monty, who passed it along to his friends. He would be released after the hearing if his fine was paid. He also told them that his car was parked near Shaheen's and arranged for his friends to pick it up and meet him at the hearing.

I called Hastings and we were at the Tupper town hall the next morning in plenty of time. The small hearing room was crowded with police, court clerks, and forlorn men who were locked up to sleep it off and who would be let go with only a lecture unless they had been in a fight. There was an American flag, but no pictures on the walls. The one row of chairs was full, so we stood at the back of the room.

As Monty walked in, Hastings said to him, "Good morning, Son. I'll give you a ride home." Monty didn't speak.

The two KGB men were also there. Gracie had described them well. Gray and gray. What title did Whistler give to his famous portrait of his mother? "Arrangement in Grey and Black"—a description of Whistler's mother and the KGB, except the men were short on the black. We were only about ten or twelve feet away from them but talking was not permitted in the courtroom and they didn't acknowledge our presence.

The hearing went much as Vince said it would, but the

fine was even less than he predicted. It was only twenty dollars. The price of the hotdogs was a little more than two dollars, and the judge apparently felt that a fine almost ten times as much as the price of the dogs was punishment enough. The KGB paid the fine (with cash, not a credit card or company check) and Monty quickly left with the two men.

Hastings and I tried to follow them, but they were better prepared than we were. They had a car waiting by the front door of the building. We were parked a block away. Our mistake. There wasn't much we could do. If there had been a good snowfall overnight, that might have slowed them down, but we hadn't had any new snow for a few days and the roads were clear. We couldn't risk a shootout with them on a public street, out in front of a police lockup. We couldn't even get into an argument with them in a public place—their presence and our work were both supposed to be kept secret. So, we had to watch them drive away, but we got the license number. It didn't do much good. Not surprisingly, the car turned out to be a rental and they abandoned it within twenty-four hours. They left it parked in front of a bar and let the rental agency pick it up—the men had, of course, given the company a phony ID.

But then I got the telephone records with the number Monty had called from the police station, and Hastings and I identified a house in Newcomb that had the number. We talked about how to handle it. We couldn't watch the house around the clock—there were only the two of us. It fronted on a stretch of open highway with no trees and no other houses nearby. For an Adirondack house, it was remarkably out in the open. There was no place for us to park without being fully visible. They could see anyone coming.

It might have been possible to set up a tripod, use a telescopic sight, and pick them off from a distance. But that would have been murder. We couldn't simply disregard state and federal law. Linda's killing of Alice had been self-defense, not a crime. But sniper fire wasn't defensive. Neither Monty nor the KGB men had committed any crime we could prove, apart from shoplifting a small package of hotdogs. They had probably violated immigration rules, but those were irrelevant to self-defense. Someone had shot at (or near) Hastings on the path at Coreys near the Boxall house, but that someone had not been identified. It could have been merely a hunter. And then Monty went to see Hastings at the Sisters camp, but he didn't shoot then. He also disturbed the devotions of a couple at Coreys, but he didn't harm anyone. What aggression could we have been retaliating against or defending ourselves against? We didn't have much justification for shooting them.

Hastings and I went back to my house for a cup of coffee and a private conversation. Linda and William had relocated to Canton for the time being, and I had the whole place to myself. We discussed our options. Hastings put a different spin on it. "Beyond the legalities, if KGB and CIA use snipers to shoot at each other without a very good reason, there'll be no end to it. It'll be counterproductive for all concerned. Covert intelligence isn't open warfare. If there's a face-to-face confrontation and you need to use deadly force in order to survive, then you do it, but using snipers is something else. That being said, I know the KGB would feel justified in using a sniper to kill me. I've been sentenced to death by a kangaroo court in Moscow because they believe I killed Colonel Kuznetsov, Bill Reilly, Vasily Rostov, and the two anonymous agents who perished at Lake Clear. On the first, they are factually incorrect. I didn't kill him. The second was self-defense, the third was done in defense of your life, and numbers four and five had been sent to kill me."

"I thought the two men at Lake Clear died from eating bad mushrooms."

"Oh, come now, Joseph, don't be naive. The fact that their bodies were not discovered for a month or more made the needle marks undetectable, but an injection is much quicker and more certain than dodgy mushrooms. And it's easy to do when they're sedated."

"The kangaroo court may have got that one right."

"The agents would have killed me if I hadn't killed them. It was anticipatory self-defense."

"What about your profession, your career?"

"Assassinations?"

"Yes."

"I've always acted in the service of one government or another. My actions have been backed by people who had the power to make them legal, or at least the power to make them seem legal. I've never been convicted of anything."

"Oh, well then."

"Let's don't quibble about the niceties. Winston Churchill ordered the Special Operations Executive to undertake certain missions that he felt were necessary to secure the defeat of fascism. I believe it was the right thing to do."

"You weren't working for any government when the five deaths that you just mentioned happened."

"No, but I didn't do the first one, and the other four were all done for the preservation of life. In one case, Joseph, your life."

"And I'm grateful. I agree that it was the right thing to do."

"I'm very glad to hear it."

"You have an odd occupation."

"Granted." He finished his coffee and stood. "It would be more honored if my work were done from an airplane at a high altitude."

"Yes. The proximity clearly makes the deaths more controversial."

"I've found that people are unwilling to face realities, to look them square in the face."

21

Then we found that Monty and the KGB men had moved out of the house in Newcomb. Once again, we didn't know where they were. It's pretty easy to be lost in the Adirondacks.

While I went to Canton to retrieve Linda and William for the Winter Carnival, Hastings stayed in the Tri-Lakes area to look for the KGB. He'd survived for many years in similar situations, and I felt sure that he'd continue to escape harm. He was more likely to wreak it.

The start of Winter Carnival was only two days away, and William was scheduled to skate in the pageant and march in the parade. The best part, in his view, was carrying the lighted torch while skating, which is something like chewing gum and crossing the street at the same time. I think he was supposed to be a sort of ice-bound Paul Revere, carrying a message that the British were coming.

To get to Canton, I could have gone north to Paul Smiths and St. Regis Falls, and then across west to Potsdam and Canton, but I decided to go by way of Tupper Lake. From Tupper, you go north and west past the Setting Pole dam to Piercefield and then past Mount Arab to Childwold. This was the same route I took on my trips to Camp Drum. A few miles after Childwold, however, I turned north onto the road to Canton. Near the intersection, there's a small shortcut that permits you to take the hypotenuse instead of the two legs of the triangle.

The road north eventually takes you beyond the Adirondack Park's boundary, which is referred to as the Blue Line for some reason that I don't remember. The size of the mountains gradually diminishes as you go north through the foothills and finally into the wide valley of the St. Lawrence. Your ears feel the change in altitude.

It was a beautiful mid-winter day. The sun was shining, and it is a pretty drive, but the day was warming, and I worried that the Ice Palace might melt. The Palace is built with blocks cut from Lake Flower near downtown Saranac. The sawing of the blocks is done using a sled with a gasoline motor mounted on top, powering a circular blade three feet in diameter. I think this is a homemade tool. They also use one-handled manual ice saws that have blades as long as the men are tall, and then do the finishing work with smaller chainsaws. In temperatures as low as minus fifteen, they cut hundreds of ice blocks in a day, each block weighing as much as four hundred pounds. In the early days of the Ice Palace, before World War I, the cutting was done with a horse-drawn ice plow pulled along a marked line. Instead of a blade, the plow had large teeth that cut into the ice. Now they use tractors, front-loaders, cranes, and excavators with claws. The blocks are pulled to the shore with pikes and stacked following a blueprint kept on site.

The design of the Palace varies from year to year, but there's a crew of contractors and construction men who work on it. Some do it every year.

Linda and William had rented the third floor of a big old Victorian house on Main Street, north of the movie theater and the Grasse River. Linda and I were very glad to see each other, and we greeted each other with affection, even an embrace and a kiss, but we couldn't be too enthusiastic about it because William was there, and we were in close quarters. He was going to school in Canton. It was somewhat out of synch with his classes in Saranac but not a major disruption. Linda said that she had missed her friends, her students, Mac, and maybe me. The three of us went out to dinner at a diner in Canton and the next morning we drove to Saranac. A quick turnaround.

We got back in time for William to take part in the parade, which was fun, and then go to the rehearsal of the pageant. The rehearsal gave him experience in handling the flame. He had to get the torch from the docks near the spillway where the Saranac River flows out of the lake and skate it up to the State docks. The lake is a larger version of a mill pond, created in 1827, and the river flows through it from south to north, continuing on beyond the dam in downtown Saranac. Because of the flowing water, parts of the lake are slow to freeze and the ice near the spillway was thin, so William had to be careful. He also had to avoid the area where the ice was cut to build the palace, but the rehearsal went well. Linda, especially, was worried about the hazards, but she couldn't hover because she was trying to stay out of sight. We didn't know whether the KGB might be watching.

While the Winter Carnival was getting started, I received a telex from Rabbit asking me to give him a call ASAP. I was so busy with William and Linda that I wasn't able to get to my office, and several hours passed before I got back to him. Ordinarily, this would have annoyed him considerably, but when I called, he was in a good mood.

Almost immediately, he said, "You can stop making trips to Camp Drum."

I said, "Good. Why?"

"Angleton and the FBI have plugged the leak of the contingency plans." Angleton was the director of counter-intelligence at the CIA, and the cooperation with the FBI was rare. Rabbit went on. "An executive at one of the private companies employed by the Air Force, Global Peace Incorporated, sold the plans to the Soviets. As the company's name suggests, it is a weapons developer."

"Of course. What else could it be?"

"As you know, Joe, we are fully committed to a strong national defense."

"Fully." I decided that was enough of that. I said, "Who was taking money from the Soviets?"

"A forty-five-year-old lawyer turned entrepreneur, with a wife and three young children. He was providing for their college educations."

"Yes. And no doubt he has a widowed mother who has a wasting disease and needs round-the-clock care."

"No, but he does have a mistress in Prague who appears to need considerable attention. It was his trips there that appealed to Angleton, and it was through her that he and his friends solved the case. With some persuasion, she talked."

"Did he get away?"

"No. He now has his housing and meals courtesy of U. S. taxpayers. But it looks like his kids will be going to college — we haven't yet found the money."

"Or maybe the criminal defense lawyers will get the money."

"That's always a possibility."

I said, "Why do they think they're going to get away with it? Someone is always watching. They've infiltrated us and we've infiltrated them. The enemy is always watching and so are we. Why the hell doesn't an executive know that?"

"Optimism, the source of a great many bad bets. On another subject, what's happening with the KGB and Hastings and his son?"

"Recently, nothing much. I think I told you about the son's arrest for shoplifting, and that it permitted us to track the KGB to a house south of here. But then we lost them again. I've had Linda and our son, William, stowed at a safe distance, but they're back here now, temporarily, for Winter Carnival events."

"Is that a safe thing to do?"

"Not entirely, but it was either that or get a divorce."

"Understood. Where's Hastings while all this is going on?"

"He stayed here and made some efforts to look for his son — rather half-hearted efforts, I think. I'm not sure he wants to find him."

"Yes. I can see that he might well be somewhat conflicted about that."

"In any event, things have been quiet recently. The KGB hasn't made any moves we're aware of."

"Do you think they've given up?"

"I think it would be a dangerous assumption."

"That's right. Stay alert."

"Always."

I followed-up at Camp Drum. The official conclusion of the local police and the Army's CID was that Alan Cross committed suicide. The notebook I found suggested to their psychiatrists, as well as the CIA's, that Cross was "of unsound mind." They saw evidence of severe depression, and his hostility to Major Bradley and Sergeant Rafferty was bizarre. He'd fantasized about killing them, and the conclusion of the authorities was that he acted on those fantasies. I was dissatisfied with the conclusion. It seemed to me unproven. There was no hard evidence for either the murders or the suicide, but I didn't have more to offer, and it wasn't my business. I'm not a law enforcement officer, and I'm not empowered to investigate crimes that don't have implications for national security. The CIA's domestic jurisdiction is severely limited. Unless the conduct has international consequences, we stay out of it. Police departments, whether civilian or military, like to close cases. If you are in the national security business, however, it may be dangerous to close a case too soon.

So I went back to the Winter Carnival, but the unusually warm weather was causing problems. Ice was melting. A decision had to be made about whether the pageant could go ahead as planned. There was a thin layer of water on top of the ice in the lake, but the conclusion was that the ice under the water was thick enough to support the skaters. The pageant proceeded, William transported the flame, and he was happy.

The Ice Palace was another matter. The construction people feared that it would become unstable. In cold weather, spectators can walk around inside and explore the rooms. It is lighted at night, and on a sunny day the views inside are often quite beautiful with the light coming through the ice. The warming, however, made it dangerous. Tests were made and the construction team concluded that there was a risk of collapse. The Palace was immediately closed to public access and a plastic warning tape saying "Danger, Keep Out" was strung thirty feet away from the structure on all sides.

Reluctantly, the committee concluded that the Palace had to be dismantled, which would be a tricky process. Ordinarily, in normal years, it is simply allowed to melt and collapse in on itself after Winter Carnival is over, but the Carnival was still in progress and there were many spectators in the area. The fear, of course, was that a wall of the building might topple. Some of the walls and towers were nearly thirty feet high. So, the committee, using a crane, began removing the highest blocks, working along the walls row-by-row. As the removal of the blocks proceeded, there wasn't enough room for all of them to be spread on the ground next to each other, so some had to be stacked in small piles three or four blocks high, and the lowest parts of the melting walls were left standing because there wasn't a place to put them.

Linda, William, and I were at the park to watch the work. There was a considerable gathering of townspeople as well as tourists because the dismantling of the Palace was at least as interesting as the building of it, maybe more so. Many of the blocks were frozen together. There was an added element of danger.

One of the people in the crowd watching the work on the Palace was Mac Denleigh, shaking hands as a part of his campaign for re-election to the school board. Linda saw him and tried to avoid him, but he caught her eye and greeted her with a big smile.

"Mrs. Boudreau, I'm glad to see you're feeling better. I was told that you were having a difficult pregnancy."

"I've been resting, thank you, but I'm out today to get some fresh air. It's good for the baby."

By that time, Linda's pregnancy was quite visible. She was wearing a full-length overcoat, but it wasn't buttoned in the middle.

She said, "As you can see, Mr. Denleigh, if I were teaching at this point, the students would certainly be able to see that I'm pregnant."

"Well, your pregnancy is a blessing. We will hope that all goes well and that you'll be able to return to teaching in the fall."

"Thank you, I'm looking forward to it."

A lot was happening in the park. William was running around in the whole area. He and his friends were playing capture the flag. Then Hastings appeared. I said, "What're you doing here?"

"Tracking Monty. He was headed in this direction."

"Well, nonetheless, you are able to witness the passing of the Palace."

"We have a great many collapsing castles in Britain, some of them still occupied. Unfortunately, they refuse to melt, and my countrymen appear to believe that they must be maintained, at considerable expense, by the National Trust. Your solution is more sensible."

Then William darted by, chased by another boy. They didn't go inside the area surrounded by the warning tape, but they were having a good time using the discarded blocks as an obstacle course. A few of the piles were big enough for a ten-year-old to hide behind.

Hastings said, "That looks like fun."

Then he caught sight of Monty, and Monty saw him and ran. Hastings pursued him. I think he wanted to catch Monty to lecture him, tell him that he was playing a dangerous game. It would have been a good place to do that because there were many people around and not even Monty would have been foolish enough to use his gun in that situation. He would have had no way to escape.

Mac Denleigh was strolling about in the ice field, commending the laborers on their efforts. William was hiding among the stacks of discarded ice. Monty ran toward both Denleigh and William. Monty tripped. He fell against a pile of four blocks that then leaned toward William. Linda and I saw it in slow motion. The stack of blocks started to topple onto William. But Mac Denleigh saw it too. He acted. He stiff-armed William and knocked him to the side. Most of the ice missed William; he took only a glancing blow. But Denleigh was hit by the full impact of very heavy blocks. He was slammed to the ground and trapped under two of them.

William was on the ground flat on his back and his eyes were closed. He was breathing, and there was a small movement of one arm. Linda was bending over him and calling his name, but he didn't answer. I tried to help, but an elderly gentleman, small, wiry, wearing a suit and a dark overcoat, put a hand on Linda's shoulder.

He said, "Madam, let me help. I'm a doctor."

Linda gave him space, but she stayed next to William.

The doctor approached William carefully. He first felt William's arms and legs and didn't find anything out of line. Then he examined William's head and neck. The doctor didn't use a stethoscope or have any other instrument. He said, "Open your eyes." And William did.

"Very good. Look at me." William did.

"Now look at your mother." William did.

"Now I'm going to hold up one finger and I want you to follow it with your eyes." William did that. The doctor observed him closely.

The doctor said, "Can you talk?"

In a small voice, William said, "Yes."

"Very good. Now I'm going to move your arms and legs. Let me know if anything hurts."

William said, "Okay."

The doctor slowly and gently flexed first one arm, then the other. Then he did the same thing with both legs. All seemed sound.

William said, "I want to get up now."

"No, just rest there a bit." The doctor stood. "I think he

was just shaken up. It knocked the wind out of him. I think he'll be fine. My primary concern at this point is a head injury. We should get him to the ER to have him properly examined."

I said, "Should we call an ambulance?"

"Do you have a car here?"

"Yes."

"An ambulance has already been called. The older man clearly needs one. But your son will get to the ER faster if you drive him there. I think he's stable. Go get your car and bring it as close to here as possible. I'll help you get him into the car, but the boy probably will be able to walk, some. We'll hold onto him."

I said, "Thank you, doctor. I'm Joe Boudreau. Do you practice near here?"

"I'm retired. And I'm Canadian. My name is Gregory Chamness. I live near Peterborough." He turned to Linda. "It was a close call. The boy was fortunate that the man knocked him out of the way."

I said, "Yes." Linda cried.

Hastings helped us half-carry William to the car.

Monty was gone.

22

There was more room for William to spread out on the back seat of Hastings's car, so he drove. Linda went with them and held William. I followed in our car.

We went in through the hospital's front door and William rode in a wheelchair through the lobby to the ER at the back. We were quickly buzzed in by the attendant who had control of the magnetic lock. Phones were ringing. There was a long hallway with examining rooms on one side and doctors' and nurses' stations on the other, and we were shown to a room at the far end of the hall, next to the side door used for patients arriving by ambulance. While a nurse was taking William's vital signs, we heard the flurry of activity when Mac Denleigh was wheeled in on a gurney.

The ER gave William a thorough exam, which reached the same conclusion as Dr. Chamness's quicker appraisal. They found only bruises. Nothing serious.

Mac Denleigh was put in the room next to ours. He was getting more attention than William because he needed it. We heard doctors and nurses talking. Denleigh was bleeding—on the outside and maybe inside too. He had a compound fracture of an arm, broken ribs, and a big gash on his head. Diagnostic work for internal injuries was in progress.

Ellie Castwell was at the hospital. She'd been at the park covering the Winter Carnival for the *Enterprise*, and she followed the ambulance. She stayed in the waiting area but was already drafting a story on the heroic action by Denleigh. Linda and I were not going to argue with that. He had acted quickly, decisively, and at great cost to himself. We had every reason to be grateful, and we were. It was entirely appropriate for the *Enterprise* to celebrate his selfless action.

William was a trouper. Linda held him all the way to the hospital, but once they got there, he wouldn't permit that. He said, impatiently, "I'm okay, Mom." The nurses smiled.

He was released before dinner and Ellie Castwell interviewed William as we were leaving the hospital.

She said, "Were you scared?"

"No. Not at the park. I didn't know what was going on."

"Here at the hospital, did they stick needles in you?"

Linda said, "Ellie!"

William just laughed.

The newspaper reported that William was brave.

By bedtime, he was feeling fine. He wanted to stay up. We had arranged for Linda's mother to come over to our house to babysit with him, so Linda, Hastings, and I could celebrate the rescue by going to the Bide-A-Wee for a ten o'clock drink. Hastings called the Wee and reserved a table. The owner, Beatty Burke, knew Ev and called him "Colonel." Our preferred seating was the gangster table, but Hastings didn't use that term when he called Burke. Instead, he asked to be seated with his back to the framed tartans hung on the rear wall, so that he wouldn't have to look at them. Burke is an Irishman. Distaste for the tartans of the Scottish clans didn't offend him. He is a traditionalist, maybe even a Protestant, but not overtly political. We could tolerate that.

We went in one car. There was a parking place at the end of the row closest to the small building, and we took it. A full moon and no clouds provided bright moonlight.

I said, "You could write your memoirs by the light of that moon."

Hastings said, "It would be very unwise for me to write memoirs."

Hastings always found the Pan-British decor of the Wee amusing. He enjoyed the Irish lyre made of cardboard, the photographs of yeoman warders of the Tower of London (the Beefeaters), tributes to departed royals, and the genuine plaster cast of the statue of Gelert, the heroic and tragic dog who gave his name to a place in the mountains of Wales. He also enjoyed snarling at the swatches of tartans. Some of the ornaments were becoming a bit tired and dusty, but they continued to provide stimulation for stories, sometimes the same stories, a few of them perhaps even true.

We walked past the bar on the way in, greeted Beatty Burke, and ordered two pints of draught Guinness and an orange soda. Because of the baby, Linda wasn't drinking alcohol. Then Hastings gallantly escorted Linda to our table and seated both her and himself solidly against the back wall. That was where he was most comfortable. He left the chairs on the front side of the table empty. The three of us were lined up along the wall where we all had a clear view of the front door. Our Guinness and the orange soda arrived, and Burke congratulated Linda on her pregnancy. We gave him a brief account of William's accident and assured him that William wasn't seriously injured.

Burke said, "You're doubly blessed. Mr. Denleigh has his uses."

We all agreed on that.

When we were alone, I said to Hastings. "Has your assessment of the KGB men changed?"

"The team is the KGB's economy model. Two middle-aged men in cheap gray suits that don't fit, bad haircuts, three-day growth of beard, and my unproven son. I suppose we'll find out whether they can shoot. Maybe they can. Maybe they're great marksmen. Maybe they weren't picked by the fashion department but by the firing range. We'll see. But I know how the story ends."

Linda said, "Oh, for God's sake! Don't say you get slower, your reflexes get less quick, and somebody finishes you."

"No, no."

She said, "Or you lose your nerve."

"No, what happens is that you get dentures and bifocals and hearing aids and you have trouble with incontinence. The same things that happen to everyone else. And then you die when you trip on a loose rug or get hit by a kid on a bicycle. That's how old spies and assassins die. It's poetic justice."

I turned and looked at the tartans right behind Hastings's head. He couldn't see them. I said, "What's that plaid right in the middle of the frame. It's mostly dark blue and dark green and has a red overplaid."

He didn't look. "It's Murray of Atholl. The real name is Macmhuirich."

"What?"

"I'll spell it for you — m-a-c-m-h-u-i-r-i-c-h. Murray."

Linda and I laughed.

He said, "The head of the clan, the Duke of Atholl, has his own private army, you know. It's called the Atholl Highlanders. It's not a large army, but it's sufficient for his needs."

Linda said, "And what are his needs?"

"Why, defense of course. Defense of the clan. Not aggression. We would be better off if all aristocrats and powerful men generally maintained private armies. The armies of nation-states are too large, they do too much harm. Think how much better it would have been if Hitler had commanded only thirty or forty men. And the bombing of Hiroshima and Nagasaki would not have been done by the Atholl Highlanders."

Linda said, "But what would happen if rich men built large armies?"

"That would be illegal. In my regime, large armies would be prohibited by law. That's why we need law."

I said, "But what if rich men violated the law and got together and built a big army? Who would stop it? The procedures of law are slow and cumbersome."

"Ah, that's the genius of distributed power. If there

were a very large number of private armies, they would all compete. The rich men would be jealous of each other, and perhaps fearful, so they would have an incentive to prevent other rich men from amassing a larger army. It would be like private enforcement of what your countrymen call antitrust laws—except, instead of using the cumbersome procedures you mentioned, we would use people like me, private soldiers." He paused. "You see, I have studied this."

I said, "Oh, you're a scholar, no doubt about that. But there would be unending conflict in your system."

"There would be skirmishes, of course, and soldiers would be killed, but the numbers would be trivial. And civilians would be far better off. There would be no carpet bombing of Dresden." He took another drink of Guinness.

I said, "I concede."

Linda said, "I'm glad to hear it."

Hastings carried on. "My occupation, private soldier, would be highly valued. I'd be properly compensated. Perhaps decorated by the Nizam of Hyderabad."

"Yes, your line of work would become more common, I suppose. That's something to contemplate."

"Yes, it is." He paused again. "The Queen, of course, is the commander-in-chief of the British armed forces, but in truth she has little to do with the deployment of troops, on a day-to-day basis, that is." A bit more Guinness. "But she does drill them from time to time."

"So I'm told."

"Good photo opportunities! We would all also be better

off if armies were more about photo opportunities. Mind you, there's quite a bit of that already."

A car pulled in and stopped near the front door. I heard the crunch of the gravel. So did Hastings. He was alert, as always. Two car doors closed, more than one person. The front door of the Wee opened. Monty entered, closely followed by the two gray men in gray suits, all with guns drawn.

They knew where to look. Hastings's preference for a table in the back corner was well-known. We were seated. They were standing. Three of them and three of us. But Linda wasn't armed. Three guns versus two, and one of the two, mine, was not in skillful hands.

They didn't wait. The gray men fired at Hastings and hit him in the shoulder. A woman screamed. Immediately after being wounded, Hastings fired twice. Both of the KGB men were hit square in the middle of their chests. They were knocked back a bit, but both were still standing.

Linda said one word, "Armor." I had my pistol, but I fumbled it trying to get it out of the shoulder holster. Linda tried to grab it, take it from me. I'm sure she thought, with good reason, that she would be more effective, but I held on to it.

Hastings saw what Linda had seen. He fired twice again. One of the KGB men shot at the same time. Hastings took another bullet in the same shoulder, but his second shot hit the forehead of the man who had wounded him.

The other KGB man was a bit slower. He was able to get a shot off, but as he was firing Hastings's second volley struck his open mouth. The KGB shot went wild and beheaded Gelert.

Monty was still standing. He and Hastings were looking at each other, but not for long. Monty shot at his father. The bullet grazed Ev's head, damaged his ear, and hit the Scottish tartans on the wall behind him.

Hastings didn't move. Monty was ready to shoot again. As Linda had warned us, the KGB men were wearing bulletproof vests. I assumed Monty was too. I aimed for his head, and I missed. A head shot is difficult.

Monty saw my shot, and he turned toward me and fired. He also missed.

I was lucky on the second try. My bullet entered Monty's right eye and exited the back of his head.

Hastings still hadn't moved. He was hit, three times, but he hadn't moved. The KGB men got their shots off first, but Ev was more lethal. He didn't miss. When the shooting had stopped, he got up out of his chair, walked over to the three bodies, knelt, and cradled Monty. He whispered something I couldn't hear, stood, and shook his head. Our eyes didn't meet. I'm not sure whether he was avoiding my eyes or I was avoiding his.

I said to Linda, "You okay?"

She said, "Yep."

At first, there was an unnatural silence. The customers were stunned and no doubt frightened. I think people kept quiet because they didn't want to attract the attention of someone with a gun. Men and women were under their tables, which was sensible. Then, suddenly, the silence broke. The air had been sucked out of the room and the quiet was replaced by a tornado. That wasn't surprising. The gunfire had been loud, three bodies were lying on the floor, and there was a lot of blood.

Many people cried and we had one screamer. I kept saying, to anyone who would listen, "It's all over, folks." But everyone was talking at once. People didn't try to go out the front door—that was where the bad guys had come from. Hastings, Linda, and I knew that there weren't any more enemy troops, but the other customers didn't know that.

The bartender had hit the floor and was crawling toward the back door. I thought he'd been hit, but he hadn't. I pulled him up off the floor. I said, "Get to a telephone. Now! Call an ambulance. The three men who came in the door are already dead, or soon will be, but Colonel Hastings is seriously wounded. He needs medical attention. Then call the police. The ambulance first, then the police. Got it?"

"Yes, sir." I think he had served in the Army.

I went over to the front door, turned, faced the room, and used my command voice. The hubbub quieted. "An ambulance and the police are being called. No one should leave here until the police arrive. Three men are dead or apparently dead. Colonel Hastings is seriously wounded. You are all witnesses. The police will certainly want to interview you and ask about what you saw. Just answer their questions and follow their instructions. I don't want to say anything more about it now."

One woman, who apparently recognized me, said, "Are you or your wife hurt, Captain Boudreau?"

I turned toward her. "No. We're both okay. Thank you."

A man said, "Can I call the babysitter to let her know we are going to be late getting home?"

I paused. "I have the same problem, but there's only one telephone. We can't all use it at once. I think we'd better reserve the phone now for the police and the doctors. They may need to communicate with us. When the police get here, they'll tell us how to handle it."

Another man said, "When news of this gets out, there are people who are going to be worried about us."

I said, "Yes, that's true, but the news isn't out yet. This just happened a few minutes ago. We should let the police handle it. Just sit down, try to catch your breath. This was quite a shock for all of us. But just try to be calm. If you are religious, pray. Close your eyes if that will help." I paused again. "Now, I need to attend to Colonel Hastings, who needs a doctor. Is anyone here a doctor or a nurse?" No one spoke up.

Hastings was back at the table, sitting in the same chair. Linda was putting pressure on his shoulder wounds, using a folded napkin, and he was putting pressure on his left ear. There was a lot of blood, but he was conscious.

I said, "Ev, I'm sorry. I'm truly sorry."

He said, "I know. I'm sorry too." There was a catch in his voice. "I just couldn't do it."

I said, "He was going to shoot you again, finish you."

"I know."

"I had to do it."

"Yes. I'm sorry I put you in that position." He drank some Guinness. "This will be therapeutic. Important to take fluids." He paused. "I think he was out of his mind."

I said, "Just try to take it easy. The ambulance should be here soon."

"I'll survive this. I've been through this before. I know which wounds are fatal, and these aren't. I've had worse than this and walked away from it. I may just decide to walk to the ambulance tonight."

"You old fraud."

"We can talk later. We need to keep pressure on the wounds, try to stop the bleeding. I'll slow my heart."

I don't know whether he could really do that or whether it was just another piece of the Hastings legend.

He said, "You hit him in the head. Is that what you were aiming for?"

"The KGB men were wearing body armor. I thought he probably was too."

"Well, he went quickly. He didn't suffer. I think I'm grateful." He drank more Guinness, this time from my glass. "The damage to my ear is courtesy of Monty. Just barely missed taking me out."

"I know."

"It's extremely unlikely that you'll ever be faced, Joseph, with a child of yours shooting at you. That doesn't happen to normal people in good families. But take my word for it, my boy, you would find it difficult. I was frozen."

"Yes. You're human, Ev. You like to pretend that you're not, but you are. Now just rest, old man."

Linda was seven months pregnant and was feeling a bit queasy. Understandably. She went to the Ladies room and threw up. The orange soda didn't agree with her.

Hastings said, "The table protected us from the waist

down. Available targets were reduced. The gut shot was blocked. But they had the advantage of surprise — except that we heard them coming."

Then the ambulance arrived, and the crew stopped his talking. It was our second trip of the day to the ER.

23

One of the appealing things about detective stories is that they suggest it's possible to suffer a catastrophic event and then, with a bit of effort, restore life as it was before. This is the sense in which those stories are fairy tales. In reality, deaths close to us change us, change everything. I don't believe it's possible to engage in a shootout one day, to kill someone, and then go on with your ordinary life the next. It doesn't work that way. I'd never killed anyone before, and I thought about it a lot.

But I needed to report to Rabbit; damage control was necessary. So I called him the next morning, only about eight hours after the shooting. I'd had four hours of sleep. After I'd given him a short description of what happened, he congratulated me on my survival and expressed appropriate concern about Linda's pregnancy, but he was clearly upset. He said, "What are we going to do with you?"

"Good question. There were a lot of witnesses. I think I'm no longer covert."

"We might as well just rent out an office for you downtown and paint CIA on the door. And how am I going to

261

explain Hastings? What in the hell is he supposed to be? Do I characterize him as working for us, our government, or is he supposed to be just sort of a tourist, a traveling adventurer?"

"You'll know how to handle that better than I would."

"Sure. Thanks." Rabbit stopped to light his pipe. I'd seen it often enough to recognize the pattern. He was thinking. He continued. "Somebody in DoD apparently asked him to help. I don't know whether there's any documentation of that, whether he was actually signed up. I suppose I'll have to look, inquire. Could you have done all the shooting?"

"I don't think so. Too many witnesses."

"Does it have to come out that the boy was Hastings's son? If it does, that'll make it a much bigger story, more Hollywood."

"I don't think that needs to come out. Nobody here knows it, except for Hastings, Linda, me, and you. None of us will talk. The boy was using the name Ibbetson."

"What about his family?"

"They're hidden. And inaccessible, even by Hastings."

He said, "Just stay quiet. Let the story die…I suppose we could have you leave the Air Force and become an auditor for the Internal Revenue Service. That should guarantee that people would stay out of your business."

"It would also guarantee that I'd have no friends."

"The ballistics tests that indicate whose guns fired the fatal bullets might be slow coming in. You might be a real sharpshooter."

And that was how it played out.

* * *

An hour later, Rabbit called me back. He said, "Joe, I want Hastings gone. The problem at Camp Drum has been solved. As you know, it turns out that the problem wasn't at Camp Drum. The services of Ev Hastings are no longer required. He's bad news. He brings trouble."

I said, "He saved my life, sir. He did that five years ago and he did it again last night." I only called Rabbit "sir" when I was mad at him. He knew that. "We owe him something. And the debt is not just mine, and Linda's. The CIA also owes him, the institution does, the country. He defended us against enemies. He's wounded now. He needs to heal."

"He's engaged in an immoral occupation, Joe."

"Sir, some people say that about anyone who works for the CIA."

"Yeah, but they're wrong … I don't like professional assassins, Joe."

"Hastings is not a bad man. His problem is that the world he thinks he lives in doesn't exist."

"You respect him."

"I respect his skills."

"Skill in killing people."

"Yes, well, mostly that. But he's also good at gaining people's trust."

"So that he can kill them."

"Only sometimes."

Rabbit made a noise that I couldn't quite interpret. It was either a cough or a choke or a stifled laugh. I'm not sure which.

I said, "He can shoot with either hand. He prefers his right, and I think he's probably better with it. He's been wounded on his left side several times, which I think tells us that he tends to turn his left toward the shooter, and he then shoots from the right, behind the partial cover of the left side of his body. I'm not really sure how he does this, but apparently it works."

"So he's a good assassin."

"Yes, he is. He's very good at what he does."

"And that doesn't bother you?"

"Rabbit, you've been in this business many years. Most of the time the work doesn't require killing. It isn't necessary. But then there are the other times. Sometimes the KGB men walk through the door."

"His work isn't only defensive."

"No, probably not. Neither is yours." I'd had enough. Rabbit wasn't in the room at the Bide-A-Wee. I was. "Field agents who want to live don't screw around in this business. Desk men have to be willing to make tough decisions too, have to be willing to give the orders, or they don't last in this work either. If it gets to the point that it's necessary to kill, when you decide you have to do it, then you kill. I did that yesterday. I didn't plan to do it. But you don't play games. You maximize your odds. The goal is to get it done."

He said, "You're a colder bastard than I would have thought."

"Probably." I decided to say more about Hastings. "Now that you mention it, I've never seen Hastings sweat, winter or summer. The man has some extraordinary temperature-control physiology that keeps him comfortable, or at least it appears to." I paused. "There were three of them and three of us, but I don't think Linda and I counted for much with the KGB. And Hastings is old, and he'd been out of action. They surely knew of his reputation, but they thought he was over the hill. They were right about me, but they were wrong about him. Hastings wasn't slow. The two Russians fired just before Hastings killed them. So Ev got off two shots while the Russians fired one each. He took two rounds in the shoulder. The difference was that Ev hit both Russians in the head. Both collapsed immediately."

I think Rabbit had heard enough about Hastings at that point. He said, "Okay. He's now wounded. He can stay here until he's healed. But I don't want you to be working with him anymore."

"I don't know how we could force him to leave if he didn't want to go."

"How about immigration? What kind of passport did he use? What name was on it?"

"You'd do that even if he was working for DoD? You might have an inter-agency conflict."

"Maybe. What does he do for money?"

"I don't know about money. He apparently has some."

"Probably some stashed somewhere. Like an island."

"That could be." I changed arguments. "But Hastings might still be useful to us. The KGB must be angry about the killing of their agents. They'll be looking for revenge. I think we should expect an attack."

"If I were running the KGB, I'd be cutting my losses. They've lost four agents in the Adirondacks in the last two months. How much are those hemlocks worth to them?

The rule is don't throw good money after bad. It works the same way with agents."

* * *

A week after the shootout at the Bide-A-Wee, Hastings and I went to revisit the scene. He was heavily bandaged but mobile. We tried to apologize to Beatty Burke, but he said, "You've done me a great favor. You've doubled my business, maybe tripled it. This place is now as famous as the OK Corral."

There were a lot of bullet holes, but none by the front door. All of the bullets Hastings and I fired, except one of mine, went into bodies. The table where we were sitting and the wall behind it had holes. A bullet in the wall had been dug out, either by police or by souvenir hunters. It looked like they used a pocketknife. The plaster cast of Gelert had serious damage. A bullet had shattered the dog's neck and knocked the head off the body. The framed Scottish tartans, which were behind Hastings during the gunfight, were hit in the center of the composition, putting a neat round hole in the glass with a web of cracks around it. And it looked like a big moth had eaten the Murray swatch.

I suggested to Burke that, since the shootout had been good for business, he might want to preserve some of the evidence. I told him about the Little Bohemia Lodge in Manitowish Waters, Wisconsin, where my Aunt Mabel lives. The John Dillinger gang had a shootout there with the FBI in 1934. The restaurant is still in business because the customers enjoy seeing the bullet holes.

Burke liked the idea and now there's a copper plaque on the wall with a description of what happened at the Bide-A-Wee. It's hung next to the framed tartans with the bullet hole, but Galert's head has been reattached to his body. Burke enjoys showing customers the repair and telling them that the poor dog's head was shot off. The legend at the top of the plaque reads "Shootout at the Bide-A-Wee."

* * *

Rabbit and his press people handled the media. I don't know how they did it, but I'm sure the words "national security" were used often. Since I was the only person present at the Bide-A-Wee who was more or less authorized to kill people, the CIA apparently decided that I must have killed all three of those KGB agents. I at least had a permit to carry a handgun. Linda was not a CIA operative; she was only married to one. And Hastings, officially, didn't exist. He was already dead and had been for years. I was the only one who could possibly have done it.

As they had five years before, the newspapers said that I was fearsome, a crack shot, and that the public was fortunate I was on the side of law and order, the reincarnation of Wyatt Earp. Since Earp was a phony, that may have been an apt comparison. Rabbit had the true facts, of course, but I don't know what facts found their way into the official records. I think he wanted to preserve the fiction that I was competent. After all, he hired me.

One Congressman tried to cause trouble for us. The

House Committee on Legislative Oversight called Rabbit to testify. Here's an excerpt from the transcript.

Congressman Gleiber: "You have a Colonel Hatter-Hatton working for you, a British national."

Director Maranville: " I don't think so. We have a large number of agents, but the name doesn't ring a bell."

"Perhaps that name is an alias."

"I wouldn't know."

"Perhaps it would help if I told you that the man calling himself Colonel Hatter-Hatton is, in fact, the notorious Ev Hastings."

"That can't be. Hastings is dead. Died of gunshot wounds about five years ago in the Adirondacks. One of my men was involved."

"One of your men killed him, didn't he?"

"Not exactly, no, but he was present, Congressman."

"That sounds like a longer story."

"Unfortunately, yes it is."

The Congressman gave up, or decided that it wasn't worth pursuing, which amounts to the same thing.

* * *

Two days later I met Hastings at the Sisters camp and we took a walk from the settlement to Axton Landing and back. On the way, we talked. There was an eagle soaring overhead, or maybe a hawk. I like to think it was an eagle.

Some of the trash I read describes retired boxers as having "cauliflower ears." I don't know exactly what kind of ear that is, but it suggests an odd shape formed by many years in the ring. Hastings has one now. It spoils his classic Jack Barrymore look, but that doesn't seem to bother him.

He looked up at the hunting bird. He said, "I think, young Joseph, the time has come for me to toddle. The local citizenry is taking too much interest in me. I may have worn out my welcome. Time to move along. I think that bird of prey is eyeing me."

"What if I have more trouble with the KGB?"

"If I leave here, they'll follow me. They won't be back soon."

I said, "Have you told your wife about Monty's death?"

"I've written a message to her, a handwritten message. I'll mail it to Cecil Murphy in the Malagasy Republic and ask him to get it to her. You're mentioned in the letter, not by name." He reached into his inside pocket and pulled out a small sheet of folded stationery. "I'd like you to read it." He handed the paper to me.

We stopped walking. It was good quality rag paper. The letter occupied only the top half of the small page. His writing was small, precise, clearly legible. His hand-eye coordination showed. He executed all of his tasks cleanly. It said, "You may have heard the sad news about Monty through Russian sources. He and his companion both perished in northern New York. I'm truly sorry about Monty. I wanted him to live, but he would not have it end that way. One of my colleagues prevented Monty from killing me. Perhaps it would have been better to let him take me, but I think Monty chose the ending. He must have known what would happen. You and I lost him a few years ago. He was misled."

Hastings watched me while I read it. Then he said, "I intend to add personal words of affection before I sign it. Is it proper?"

I said, "It's fine, Ev, if that's what you want to say. It's not effusive, but nicely put."

When we got back to the Sisters camp, I saw that he was packing to leave. A suitcase was open on the bed and folded clothes were lying beside it. There was also a stack of what looked like a dozen passports issued by, or apparently issued by, a dozen countries.

He saw me looking at them. "One must be prepared." He smiled. "There were a couple of years early in my career when my name was McIntosh. In those days my Christian name was either Robbie or Ian…Ah, what does it matter? I've lost track of them all. McIntosh was the name I had when I was recruited by SOE. I acquired the name owing to some indiscretion under an earlier label." He put the passports in the suitcase. "Sometimes one's name is a good test of one's memory."

The Scottish names early in his career were a clue. I eventually figured out that he's a covert Scot. He claims to hate the Scots, but that's just a part of the cover. In fact, I suspect his real name is Murray and that's why he was so interested in the Duke of Atholl. I wonder if he served in the Atholl Highlanders. But I never had the courage to try this theory out on him. The motto of the Murray clan is "tout pret," always ready. That describes Hastings perfectly.

* * *

Mac Denleigh was still in the hospital for treatment and observation. We went to visit him and took him some chocolates, a Whitman's Sampler. He had a cast on his right leg, a cast on his right arm, and a bandage around his head.

Denleigh said, "I like the Sampler. It has a map showing where to find the ones I like best."

I said, "Those are impressive casts."

"As has been pointed out to me, if you are going to break bones, this is an excellent place to do it. With both a ski jump and a bobsled run in the neighborhood, they have a lot of experience here in putting people back together."

I said, "We hope you're healing."

"They tell me I'm doing well, but it still hurts. It's not the broken bones that are the major concern. It's the softer organs inside."

Linda said, "Mr. Denleigh, we are immensely grateful to you for saving William. He might have died if it weren't for your quick action. It isn't possible for us to thank you enough."

"I was glad I was able to do something, glad to be of some help. I just acted without thinking." He looked at me. "I'm told that later the same day you also acted quickly. I read in the newspaper that you're a national hero. We're all in your debt."

"Oh, hardly a hero. I only did what I needed to do in order to survive—and for Linda and our baby to survive. You didn't have to do what you did, but you did it. That's real courage. That's a real hero."

"It's interesting what we will do when we need to do it." He shifted his position in the bed. He wasn't comfortable.

"I'm told that the men who attacked you were agents of a foreign government."

"I can't really comment on it. The matter is still under investigation, and I've been ordered not to discuss it."

"I understand. But none of our citizens were injured — is that right?"

"Yes, it is."

"Thank God!"

"Yes."

Linda said, "How much longer do you expect to be here?"

"Do you mean here on this earth?" He tried to laugh but it hurt, so he grimaced.

Linda, calmly and quietly, said, "No, in the hospital."

"I expect to be released in a day or two. They tell me I'll be playing golf this summer."

I said, "The school board election is coming up."

He smiled. "I'm still on the ballot. I considered withdrawing, but they tell me I'll be able to serve, if I'm elected."

Linda kept quiet. I said, "We're sure you will be." That seemed a safe enough bet since he had no opposition.

Mac Denleigh still isn't one of our best buddies, but we now think he has merit that we hadn't seen before.

* * *

Two months later, at the end of April, the baby was born. The trip to the hospital was a little exciting — the baby was coming quickly, and I drove Linda in our car. There are only four stop lights in Saranac, and I ran three of them, while laying on the horn. The fourth light was on the other side of town. I didn't feel qualified to deliver the baby.

We got to the hospital just in time. I zipped around the circular drive leading to the front door. It was 11 pm on a weekday, not a busy time. The hospital keeps a wheelchair by the door, and we used it. I pushed Linda through the lobby, fast, and told her not to push.

Then the nurses took over and all went well. A healthy baby with a healthy mother and a happy father. Another boy. We had been expecting a girl. I say "we" but that mostly means Linda. We didn't have a boy's name picked out yet. The birth certificate says something like "baby boy."

William was very pleased. He was almost eleven and was looking forward to supervising the rearing of the child.

Hastings knew the predicted due date, so he called me a few days later and I gave him the good news. He said he wanted to meet the baby, and I advised him to come before the black flies arrived. That pretty much meant before mid-May. The old rule of thumb is that the black fly season is between Mother's Day and Father's Day, but it doesn't last that whole time. We hope.

Hastings showed up on the twelfth of May. His ear looked a bit better, and his wounded shoulder appeared to have good mobility. He claimed that it was fully healed.

I asked him about his travels. He said, "I had a lovely time in Pascagoula, Mississippi. The local cuisine is interesting. Have you ever had hog jowls with black-eyed peas and cornbread? It's heartening, fortifying."

"What wine complements it?"

"In my experience, it is principally accompanied by a spirit made with local ingredients."

I took Hastings to our house and the baby was displayed. Ev made appreciative noises. He had brought a teddy bear as a present. It was the third we had received. Thoughtfully, he had also brought William a present, a pocketknife.

He said to William, "Learn to whittle. You can spend many a pleasant hour whittling. Always keep your knife sharp. That way, you'll be less likely to cut yourself.

Linda said, "Before the baby was born, we decided she was a girl and we were calling her Hephzibah, or Heppy, just to have something to call her. We didn't have pictures made in the womb; we didn't want her being disturbed by sound waves. And then she appeared, and we saw that he was a boy. His name became Oswald, so that we could call him Ozzie."

Hastings said, "But what about Oswald Mosley, the leader of the British fascists?"

Linda and I just looked at him.

* * *

Almost all of the ice had gone out of the Stony Creek Ponds, and I had a canoe strapped to the top of our car. I said, "Is the shoulder good enough for canoeing?"

Hastings said, "Sure."

We used the access point just off the Coreys Road, only about a half mile beyond the intersection with Route 3. Every time I do that drive, I'm impressed by the complete change of scenery. The State route is only two lanes, it isn't ugly, and it has nice views of mountains and the occasional piece of water, but it's a busy road with trucks and traffic noise. The Coreys Road is darker, quieter, peaceful. It's a lane in the woods.

The road dips down toward the ponds. You see the water of First Pond on the left, and the canoe access is from a path along the south shore.

Hastings and I took it easy. The breeze was refreshing, not strong. We went from First Pond into Second, and then paddled through the marsh that connects Second Pond to Third. Those are the names of the ponds if you start from the access on the Coreys Road. If you enter the ponds via the Raquette River and the Stony Creek, however, the one I'm calling Third Pond is called First. I've seen both sets of names on published maps. But Second is always in the middle and always abuts the marsh.

Between the marsh and the entrance to Second Pond, there's a bridge across to provide access to houses on the east side of the ponds. The bridge has posts resting on stone cribs. If the weather is calm, it's no problem to paddle between the posts, but you may need to maneuver. I told Hastings about a bow rudder. If the bow person puts his paddle in the water with the blade vertical, pointing toward the front at an oblique angle, the bow can steer the boat. Basically, the paddle should point in the direction that you want to boat to go. With a bit of luck, we made it through the posts unscathed.

From Third Pond, you can enter either the Ampersand Brook, which flows into the ponds from Ampersand Lake, or you can go into Stony Creek, which flows out of the ponds to the Raquette River, near Axton Landing. We chose the Ampersand. We would be paddling against the current on the way in, but the current would help us on the way back.

A short distance into the Ampersand we came to a fallen tree across the stream, a large white pine. It had leaned out over the water for many years and its roots finally let go. The tree went all the way across the brook and well beyond it, but the trunk, more than two feet across, was about a yard above the water, held there by branches on the underside of the tree. The full weight of the trunk rested on those branches. At some point, the branches would break, and the tree would become a dam. But that hadn't happened yet. We made our way through a gap in the branches and managed to slip under the tree and continue on. We knew we would have to do the same thing on our way back, and we hoped the branches didn't break before we made the return trip.

We went up the Ampersand until we reached a large beaver dam that we couldn't cross without carrying the canoe, and then we floated back downstream to Third Pond. We were the only boat in the water. It was beautiful. We could hear loons, but we didn't see them. They must have just returned from their winter habitat, and it was nesting time. The sun was warm, but we were being careful. We didn't want to tip. There was still a small amount of ice, and the water would be cold.

Hastings was not very experienced in a canoe. He was in the bow, and I was in the stern. The stern has more control over the movements of the boat, but the bow makes a difference too. He was paddling mostly on the left because his shoulder was more comfortable that way.

To get back to the car, all we needed to do was head directly across Second Pond to get to the narrows between Second and First, and then to the access point. Piece of cake. But we drifted too far north in Second Pond, too close to the shore. As we were approaching the narrows, I saw that we were going to have trouble going around the point and into the entrance to First Pond. There are boulders on that point, some the size of a bushel basket and some the size of a Volkswagen, so I started pulling harder. The stern paddler, paddling on the right, moves the bow of the canoe toward the left, which is what we needed.

Hastings, however, because he noticed that I was paddling harder, also started paddling harder. This had the opposite effect. It also made us go faster, faster toward the rocks. I shouted, "Bow rudder, bow rudder." But I think he forgot what a bow rudder was. I shouted, "Stop paddling!" He did. I quickly switched my paddle to the left side and executed a hard rudder. We got by the rocks with about six inches to spare, but at the base of the boulder there was a ledge of rock extending out into the pond, covered by less than a foot of water. The bow of the canoe rode over the rock and for maybe a second I thought we might get by it. Then the boat rolled to the left—rolled surprisingly slowly and gently, or so it seemed at the time, but it very definitely tipped over. There was nothing to be done about it. We were thoroughly wet and our speculation about cold water proved to be correct. Hastings and I were in the water and water was in the canoe.

We were, mercifully, able to find our footing on the rock. There was no real danger except for hypothermia. With some considerable effort, we turned the canoe upside down, lifted it, and flipped it so that it was floating upright with only a little water in it. Our paddles were nearby. We grabbed them. Then all we needed to do was get back into the boat, stay warm enough to be able to move, and return to the car. In a cooperative spirit and with what I thought was remarkably good humor under the circumstances, we coordinated our climb into the canoe, managing to put approximately equal pressure on the port and starboard sides so that we didn't roll the damn thing over again. If the pressures on the two sides are unequal, the canoe will let you know in a hurry. We shipped only a few inches of water, much of which came in on our clothes.

When we got the canoe onto the top of the car, I said, "You may be a swell assassin, but you can't paddle a canoe worth a damn."

Author's Note

The model for one of the characters in this novel, I'm very sad to say, died as the writing was in progress. Mac the dog was a dear friend. The picture Joe Boudreau gives us of him is, I think, about as good as words can do. I'm glad that in Joe's narration Mac is in the present tense. That helps.

Dr. David French advised me on the material concerning the Arctic, especially the science. He did research there in the late 1950s and in 1960. Charles McManus was very helpful in informing an Air Force man about Army matters. Charlie was a helicopter pilot in Vietnam. Kathy Straka generously shared her professional expertise on mental health issues and on the diagnosis of mental illness. My loyal readers, Bill Conger, Meg Randall, and Irv Slate, waded through my drafts and spared me from errors of both style and substance. My wife, Anne, was my constant consultant on matters large and small. The dedication of this book is an inadequate tribute to her contributions. I'm enormously grateful to all of them.

—*J. H., 2022*

About the Author

This is Jack Heinz's third novel. The first two are *Rebellion, Love, Betrayal*, a love story set during the Vietnam war protests in the late 1960s, and *Six Spies in Saranac*, a murder mystery and spy story featuring some of the characters seen here. Heinz taught law at Northwestern University for forty-two years. He also held positions at the American Bar Foundation and Northwestern's Institute for Policy Research. Earlier, he was in the U. S. Air Force. He lives in Evanston, Illinois, and Tupper Lake, New York.